DIRTY LIARS

A J.J. Graves Mystery

LILIANA HART

ALSO BY LILIANA HART

JJ Graves Mystery Series

Dirty Little Secrets

A Dirty Shame

Dirty Rotten Scoundrel

Down and Dirty

Dirty Deeds

Dirty Laundry

Dirty Money

A Dirty Job

Dirty Devil

Playing Dirty

Dirty Martini

Dirty Dozen

Dirty Minds

Dirty Weekend

Dirty Looks

Dirty Liars

Dirty Valentine

Addison Holmes Mystery Series

Whiskey Rebellion

Whiskey Sour

Whiskey For Breakfast

Whiskey, You're The Devil

Whiskey on the Rocks

Whiskey Tango Foxtrot

Whiskey and Gunpowder

Whiskey Lullaby

The Scarlet Chronicles

Bouncing Betty

Hand Grenade Helen

Front Line Francis

The Harley and Davidson Mystery Series

The Farmer's Slaughter

A Tisket a Casket

I Saw Mommy Killing Santa Claus

Get Your Murder Running

Deceased and Desist

Malice in Wonderland

Tequila Mockingbird

Gone With the Sin

Grime and Punishment

Blazing Rattles

A Salt and Battery

Curl Up and Dye

First Comes Death Then Comes Marriage

Box Set 1

Box Set 2

Box Set 3

The Gravediggers

The Darkest Corner

Gone to Dust

Say No More

Laurel Valley

Tribulation Pass

Redemption Road

Midnight Clear

Forgiveness River

Atonement Trail

To Scott-

Thank you for always pushing me to be my best, even when the plot of life gets complicated. I love you always!

It's a funny thing that when a man hasn't anything on earth to worry about, he goes off and gets married.

— ROBERT FROST

The chain of wedlock is so heavy that it takes two to carry it—and sometimes three.

— HERACLITUS

CHAPTER ONE

Death was my living.

The weight of the decay hung heavy in the air, and the victims laid before me were more than the remnants of lives once lived. As the coroner for King George County, I bore a solemn burden—a relentless duty to speak for those whose voices had been silenced too soon. Justice was my pursuit, a grim companion that shadowed my every step.

But amid the blood and broken bodies, a disquieting truth gnawed at my soul. The capacity for cruelty in mankind was boundless, a monstrous force that defied comprehension. Each case whispered of the malevolence lurking behind human eyes, a reminder that darkness resided not just in the world but within the depths of our own hearts.

"You okay, Doc?" Detective Cole asked, his voice

pulling me from my thoughts. His concern was evident in his eyes, a rare softness that contrasted with his usual tough exterior. "You don't look so good."

"I had a rough night," I lied, adjusting my gloves. "Didn't get a lot of sleep."

Cole didn't look like he believed me, but he was nice enough not to say anything. I liked Cole. He was a solid cop with a good sense of humor and the kind of baggage that most cops carried around with them —meaning he tended to go through relationships like discarded tissues and he was no stranger to a drink or three when he was off duty.

He was living with my assistant, Lily, and for the first time since I'd known him seemed serious about a monogamous relationship. He was in his usual uniform of Wranglers, a white dress shirt, and a sport coat. His badge was visible on his belt and his Stetson was in place. But he was looking a little rough around the edges himself.

"I'll be fine," I assured him and then gave him a pointed look. "What about you? You don't look so hot yourself."

"Pulled an all-nighter," Cole said. "I caught the Ransom Club shooting over in King George. A couple of barely legal idiots decided to get into a fight over one of the waitresses. Idiot number one pulls a knife. Idiot number two pulls a bigger knife.

The bartender tried to get them to take it outside, but one of the guys takes a swipe at the bartender and slices his arm to the bone. Bartender gets pissed and shoots them both with the .45 he had under the counter. Idiot number one is dead. Idiot number two will be lucky to walk again. I'd just wrapped things up and was heading home when this call came in."

That was a pretty good excuse as far as excuses went for looking like hell. I was going to have to stick with lying. In truth, I'd discovered I was pregnant about a week ago, and the shock still hadn't worn off. Jack and I had struggled for so long to conceive that I'd almost given up hope. When I saw those two pink lines on the pregnancy test I couldn't believe it, so I visited a good doctor friend I'd worked with at Augusta General to get a thorough checkup. I was definitely pregnant. But I'd been sick as a dog the last few days, and joy and fear waged a silent war within me as I struggled to balance my duties with the knowledge of the new life growing inside me.

"You can take off once we clear the scene," Jack said, coming in from the other room. "Jaye and I will take this one."

"I'm going to take you up on that," Cole said. "Lily is working today, and I've got a soft bed and blackout curtains calling my name."

I tuned out Jack and Cole's conversation while I turned my back to them and acted like I was studying the blood-spattered walls. I caught my reflection in the large gilded mirror across from the bed and had to do a double take to make sure it was me. No wonder Cole had been concerned. My normally pale skin had a sickly pallor and my eyes seemed unusually large in my face, my pupils dilated so much that my gray eyes looked black. My chin-length black hair was pulled back into a stubby ponytail.

I caught Jack's worried gaze in the mirror, his blue eyes meeting mine. I took some deep breaths, just keeping my gaze steady on his while he and Cole continued to talk. Jack was my rock, and he'd been my anchor in many of the storms in my life. He was a man who commanded attention no matter what room or circumstance he walked into.

He'd dressed that morning in sand-colored BDUs, and he wore a black polo with the King George County Sheriff's Office logo embroidered over the breast. His weapon was holstered at his side, and a black windbreaker concealed it. He'd gotten a haircut a few days ago, so his thick dark hair was cut close enough that there was no detection of the slight curl that appeared the longer his hair grew, and he had a short growth of stubble from not shaving for the last couple of days.

The low chatter of the crime-scene techs as they finished taking pictures and sweeping the room for evidence filled the air. Yellow evidence tags dotted the plush carpet of the master bedroom like macabre confetti. I was the last piece of the crime-scene puzzle. The CSI team was waiting on me to do a preliminary exam of the bodies and get them moved back to my lab so they could dust for fingerprints. All I had to do was not throw up first.

I breathed through my mouth, trying not to taste the coppery scent of blood that was thick in the air along with the underlying smell of decay. I'd never live it down if I contaminated the crime scene by vomiting everywhere. I could feel Jack's worried gaze on my back as I moved, and I knew if he wasn't careful he'd let the cat out of the bag. We'd agreed to keep the pregnancy just between us for now.

"What do you think, Doc?" Cole asked. "Gives a whole new meaning to a happy ending, huh?" He attempted a wry smile, but it fell flat against the somber backdrop.

"You could say that," I said, staring at our first victim with pity.

"Death rarely brings dignity," Jack said.

"Yeah, but somehow this seems even worse," Cole said. "Talk about the honeymoon from hell."

I knew what he meant. There was something profoundly sad about this scene. A newly married couple who would have been beautiful and vibrant in life lay gray and cold in separate rooms of their honeymoon villa at The Mad King Resort. A wedding night that should have been filled with passion and promise had ended in violence and blood.

Victim number one—the husband—was a dark-haired man with vacant eyes and a short dark beard, sprawled across the king-sized bed of the master bedroom. Unlike what you'd expect from a groom on his wedding night, he was fully clothed in what appeared to be an expensive tailored suit. A single gunshot wound marred his temple, the exit wound having painted a gruesome Rorschach pattern on the pristine white comforter on the bed.

"Exit wound indicates a through-and-through," I said, pulling on a fresh pair of latex gloves. "Going to need to recover the bullet from whatever it embedded in."

I knelt beside the bed, my eyes scanning methodically over the victim. The CSI techs had already photographed him from every angle, placing small yellow numbered markers next to items of evidence. I carefully checked his pockets, finding a platinum money clip with several hundred-dollar bills, untouched. His wallet sat on the nightstand, designer watch still on his wrist. The wedding band on his left hand gleamed under the bedroom lights, probably not worn for more than twenty-four hours.

"Not robbery," Jack noted, circling the room with measured steps.

I nodded, examining the body more closely. "Lividity and blood pattern indicates he was moved into this position." I pressed my gloved fingers gently against his jaw. "Full rigor. Consistent with death occurring approximately seven to eight hours ago."

"Why move him?" Cole asked. "The killer comes in and does the job stone cold, shoots the guy in the head. Then he moves the body so he's propped on a pillow?"

"Could be staging," I said.

Making a small incision near his liver, I inserted a thermometer to get an accurate core-temperature reading. "Body temp confirms that timeline. So around midnight to 1 a.m."

"That tracks with their check-in time," Cole said, flipping through his notebook. "Manager says they arrived just after midnight."

I completed my examination of the scene around the victim, bagging his hands to preserve any trace evidence, and carefully checking under his finger-nails. No defensive wounds. No signs of a struggle. The kill had been quick, efficient.

"Any weapons?" I asked, looking around the room.

"Found a 9mm halfway kicked under the bed," Jack said.

"Maybe the guy put up a fight," Cole said.

"The shot was fired at close range based on the powder stippling," Jack said. "If he tried to fight it wasn't for long. Let's check on the bride."

We moved through the spacious living area of the villa, past the untouched champagne and chocolate-covered strawberries on the coffee table. Two suitcases sat just inside the front door, still packed. The sliding glass doors to the deck overlooking the Potomac were unlocked, the curtains billowing slightly in the morning breeze.

The second bedroom was at the opposite end of the villa. When we stepped inside, the contrast with the master bedroom was jarring. Where the husband's death had been neat and precise, this room told a different story.

The bride—Chloe Vasilios according to Cole's notes—lay on the floor beside a rumpled bed. She was in a half state of undress, a designer evening gown pooled around her waist, the bodice unzipped and hanging loose. One shoe remained on her foot, the other tossed near the bathroom door. Her blond hair was matted with blood, spread around her head like a twisted halo.

"Multiple gunshot wounds," I said, crouching beside her. "One to the center of the forehead, execution style. Additional shots to the chest, throat, and

—" I paused, noting the pattern of wounds on her lower body. "Two shots to the pelvic region."

"Overkill," Jack said, his voice tight. "First shot would have been fatal. The rest were making a statement."

"Or ensuring she was dead," Cole suggested.

"No," I disagreed, gesturing to the wound pattern. "Look at the precision of the groupings. The forehead shot, then the throat, followed by the three chest shots center mass. The pelvic shots are next. This wasn't panic or ensuring death. This was almost ritualistic. Very purposeful."

I pulled out my measuring calipers from my kit and carefully examined each wound.

"These entry wounds are significantly smaller than the husband's. Different caliber weapon."

"That's not good," Jack said.

"Why?" I asked.

"Two killers," Cole said.

Jack crouched beside me, his eyes scanning the scene. "The carpet is soaked with blood under her, but there's minimal spatter. First shot was likely to the head, an instant kill. The rest were postmortem."

I nodded, carefully turning her head to examine the entry wound in her forehead. "The bullet is still inside. No exit wound." I looked closer at her face, wiping away some of the blood with a sterile gauze.

"Slight powder stippling around the entry wound. Close range, but not contact."

I continued my examination, checking her hands, which were unmarked. No defensive wounds. No signs she'd struggled against her attacker. I examined her neck, finding slight bruising that was just beginning to form.

"Bruising on the throat," I said. "Premortem based on the coloration. Someone may have restrained her before shooting."

"Why the separate rooms?" Jack asked.

"Maybe she was using this room to change," I said, noticing a small carry-on suitcase open and spilled out onto the floor.

"If it was me I'd eliminate the biggest threat first, which would be the husband," Jack said. "Maybe sexual assault was the goal. Guy who offs the husband gets excited and drops his gun. Other killer forces bride into this room at gunpoint and she's uncooperative, hence the bruising on her throat. She's half undressed, but something made them pull the trigger. And then keep pulling the trigger."

I carefully collected fingernail scrapings, hair samples, and swabbed the visible blood for later DNA analysis. I checked for signs of sexual assault but found none. The way her dress was partially removed suggested the beginning of undressing rather than an assault.

"There's no outward signs of sexual assault," I said. "Her underwear is still intact. But I'll be able to check more thoroughly once we're back in the lab."

I carefully bagged her hands and feet to preserve any additional evidence.

"We need to check for additional shell casings," I said, scanning the floor. "None of the bullets passed through."

The CSI techs moved in with their equipment, meticulously combing every inch of carpet, checking behind furniture, and under the bed. One of them called out, "Found something!"

He held up a small brass casing with tweezers. "Twenty-two caliber. Expensive brand, not your standard ammunition."

"Professional grade," Jack commented, examining it without touching. "The killer missed one. He took all the other shell casings with him."

A second tech called out from near the sliding glass doors that led to a large deck that overlooked Popes Gorge. "Door's unlocked from the inside. Could be the killer's exit route."

Jack nodded and walked over to examine it, careful not to disturb any potential evidence. "Perfect escape route. No cameras on this side of the property, direct access to the wooded area behind the resort."

I completed my preliminary examination and prepared both victims for transport. "I'll need to get them back to the lab for the full autopsy. These bullets might tell us a lot more once I recover them."

"The reservation was made under the names Theo and Chloe Vasilios," Cole said, reading from his notebook. "Oliver Harris—the resort manager—said the couple checked in just after midnight. They were only booked for one night and a car was supposed to show up for them this morning to take them to the airport. The driver alerted the manager once they didn't show up to the car."

"Nothing unusual about their arrival?" Jack asked.

"Harris said they looked like they'd been drinking some, her more than him," Cole said. "She was unsteady on her feet. He also said Mr. Vasilios seemed anxious to get to the room. Harris drove them here in the golf cart and a bellman followed behind with their luggage."

"There are several suitcases still by the front door," I said.

Jack walked the perimeter of the room again, his trained eyes missing nothing. "This was planned. The killers knew they were coming, knew the layout of this villa, and struck quickly after their arrival."

"How'd they get in?" Cole asked. "Front door was locked when the manager came by this morning."

"Could have been hiding inside already," Jack

suggested. "Or came in through the sliding doors off the deck."

I finished bagging and tagging the evidence, preparing both bodies for transport back to my lab. The CSI team continued processing the scene, looking for additional shell casings, fingerprints, and any other traces the killers might have left behind.

"Birth control pills and a prescription bottle of Zoloft in her toiletry bag," Cole reported, returning from the bathroom. "The Zoloft had Theo Vasilios's name on it. Twenty-five milligrams."

"Anxiety meds," I said. "Maybe wedding jitters. But he's at least two hundred pounds. Twenty-five milligrams is usually the starting dose when just getting acclimated to the medicine. For a guy his size, I would have started at fifty milligrams at minimum."

"Can it affect sexual function?" Jack asked.

"Sure," I said. "Not ideal for a wedding night."

"But it might explain the separate rooms," Jack said. "We need to find out everything we can about Theo and Chloe Vasilios. Their lives, their connections, their enemies. Someone wanted them dead badly enough to orchestrate this."

"And they wanted to send a message," I added, looking at the woman's body bag. "The way she was killed—it feels personal."

I took one last look around the villa. What should have been a sanctuary of love and new beginnings had become a tomb. Two lives ended before they'd truly begun their journey together. The champagne would never be drunk. The suitcases would never be unpacked. The honeymoon would forever remain in a bloody memorial. In the silence of that desecrated space, I made the same promise I always did—to speak for those who no longer could, to unravel the truth behind their violent end. To bring justice to the dead.

CHAPTER TWO

I CHECKED MY PHONE TO READ THE TEXT THAT HAD just come through. "Lily and Sheldon are here for retrieval."

Lily wasn't just Cole's cohabitant—she was also the assistant coroner for the county. She was working part-time for me while finishing up medical school. Since I'd met her about a year ago, she'd done nothing but make my life easier. She was an amazing person, and I loved her, but I knew her time with me would be short lived. Once she finished school, she'd get a job paying a lot more than what King George County could offer. She had the kind of mind that caught details others missed, and hands steady enough to make even the most delicate incisions. I sometimes caught myself watching her work, remembering my own early days in medicine, before I'd chosen the dead over the living.

Sheldon also worked for me as my assistant funeral home director, and for the most part, he managed to make my life a little more manageable. Let's just say Sheldon had a special talent for dealing with the dead, but when it came to the living, we were still in training mode. He'd come a long way since his fresh-out-of-mortuary-school days, though. At least he'd stopped describing the embalming process to horrified loved ones.

My job as coroner had been taking up more and more of my time over the last couple of years as the population of King George County had grown. People from the big cities had started populating the area because King George was an easy commute, but there was also a lot of land. Developers were clamoring to buy up land in King George, but Jack and the county council had done a great job of being selective in who could come in—like The Mad King and a hotel and conference center. Along with the controlled developments, there was also the hospital and a major university, along with four towns that were vastly different in size and society.

Bloody Mary, where the funeral home was located, was the smallest of the four towns. It was barely more than a crossroads with a post office and a couple of storefronts, but it had character—and characters—to spare. Newcastle had become the trendy spot for artists and small boutiques. King George Proper was a college and military town, full of bars, cheap apartments, and tract houses. Nottingham was where the money lived—an East Coast Silicon Valley—with sprawling estates and private security gates. Each had its own unique charm and challenges, and all of them fell under Jack's jurisdiction.

It was a huge undertaking and Jack managed to make his job look easy. There were a lot of politics at play, and Jack might not want to admit it, but he could weave through the ins and outs of politics with his eyes closed. He was a natural, stepping into rooms of power with the same ease he used to calm a frightened witness. But along with the "progress" came big-city crime.

Murders took time to solve, and the victims deserved my full attention. But the demand from the funeral home was still there, and the dead and their families deserved the best service Graves Funeral Home could give them. It was a difficult balance—going between embalmings and autopsies—and one I was still trying to figure out if I was being honest. Sometimes I felt stretched between two worlds, neither of which I could neglect without serious consequences.

I used Lily and Sheldon's arrival as a chance to

leave the room and breathe in some fresh air. After more than a month of nonstop rain in King George, the weather had cleared and the temperatures had warmed. It was a beautiful sunny morning with not a cloud in the sky, the kind of day that made you forget, if only for a moment, that you'd been surrounded by death and decay just minutes before.

I had the front door of the villa open, and I was standing on the porch when I saw the Suburban heading in our direction on a path meant for a golf cart. The vehicle lumbered along, looking comically oversized against the manicured landscape of The Mad King Resort.

Lily and Sheldon parked, got out, and then went to the back to take out the gurney. The wheels made a distinctive metallic clack as they unfolded it, a sound I'd heard so many times it had become as familiar as a doorbell or ringtone—the sound of death being transported. But Lily stopped to look at me once they'd gotten onto the porch, her dark eyebrows drawing together in concern.

She was a beautiful young woman—long dark hair that fell in waves past her shoulders, a clear olive complexion that never seemed to need makeup, dark eyes that missed nothing, and a body that most men looked at twice. She was also one of the nicest people I'd ever met, except for today apparently, when her candor cut right through my façade.

"What's up with you?" she asked, eyes narrowing. "You look weird."

"Thanks?" I said, mouth twitching at her bluntness. One of the things I loved about Lily was that she never sugarcoated anything. In our line of work, that was refreshing.

"No, I mean it," she said, studying me with the same focus she'd use on a Y-cut. "There's something off. You're pale, even for you, and you've got a pinched look around your mouth."

I shifted uncomfortably under her scrutiny. Lily knew me too well, and it was unnerving sometimes how she could read the tells I thought I'd hidden from view.

"I got overheated inside while I was working on the victims. I just needed some fresh air for a minute. But I'm fine."

"Did you know the most common trigger for fainting is seeing blood?" Sheldon asked, adjusting his glasses with one finger. "About thirty-six percent of first-time blood donors experience some level of vasovagal syncope, or fainting. It's a complex interplay of the parasympathetic nervous system and—"

"Sheldon," Lily said, cutting him off.

Sheldon was a fount of knowledge, most of it useless, but he occasionally came out with a gem that helped us during a case. I was guessing that this was not going to be one of those times. Sheldon was young, in his mid-twenties, but he already showed signs of male-pattern baldness that he tried to disguise with careful combing. He moved with the deliberateness of a man who'd reached the age where blowing his nose might throw out his back.

He was a couple of inches shorter than me and had the kind of soft baby fat that he'd carry for life. His cheeks were perpetually flushed, round as apples, and I wasn't sure he'd ever had to shave. He wore Coke-bottle-thick glasses that made his eyes look giant behind the lenses, giving him the appearance of a startled owl most of the time.

"You're right, Sheldon," I said, deadpan. "Maybe blood is the trigger. All this time I had no idea."

"If so," he said, looking as serious as a man without a sense of humor could, his face unnervingly earnest, "I think you might be in the wrong line of work. Though I did read about a surgeon who had to undergo hypnotherapy to overcome his fear of blood. Perhaps that could be an option for you as well?"

I exchanged a look with Lily, who was biting her lip to keep from laughing. "I'll keep that in mind, Sheldon. Thank you."

I followed Lily and Sheldon back inside and really took a good look at the villa for the first time. I didn't know if it was worth a couple of thousand a night, but it was one of the most luxurious rooms I'd ever seen as far as resorts go, and that's saying something because Jack had taken me to some pretty fancy places over the years. Of course, we'd solved a murder on our honeymoon, so we didn't exactly have a normal honeymoon experience.

"Dang," Lily said, echoing my thoughts. Her eyes widened as she took in the luxurious surroundings, her professional demeanor momentarily slipping to reveal the young woman who'd grown up in modest circumstances. "Look at this place. Cole's whole house could fit right inside here."

The main living area was overshadowed by the panoramic view of the Potomac and the rushing waters of Popes Gorge. Floor-to-ceiling windows created the illusion of being suspended over the water, with nothing between you and the breath-taking vista. The floors and fireplace were natural stone, smooth and cool beneath our feet. All the colors were neutral—shades of cream, beige, and soft gray—so as not to take away from the view. The scent of fresh pine and cedarwood lingered in the air, mingling with the crisp, cool breeze coming through the open windows, a stark contrast to the metallic tang of blood that hung in the bedrooms.

The suitcases sitting just inside the door were expensive and matching in buttery soft leather, the kind with silent wheels and monogrammed tags. The rest of the room was as if it had never been touched. And I guessed it hadn't. They'd hardly been inside before the killers had gunned them down. Theo's suit jacket was tossed over the bar, right next to their hotel key, a small detail that spoke volumes about the unfolding of their last moments.

There was a bedroom and bathroom on each side of the main living area, creating a perfect symmetry to the villa's layout. I steered Lily to the left, where Theo Vasilios's body awaited transport. The CSI techs had finished photographing and collecting evidence, and now it was time for us to take him away from his interrupted honeymoon.

"Two victims," I said, gesturing to the master bedroom door. "Husband in here, wife in the second bedroom."

"That view is pretty spectacular," Lily said, her gaze skimming over the body briefly before checking out the similar panorama visible from the bedroom windows. "Sometimes I forget how pretty our state is. But this wasn't much of a honeymoon for our unlucky couple." Her voice softened with the natural compassion that made her so good with grieving families.

Cole came over to greet Lily with a quick kiss on the top of her head, his hand lingering briefly on her shoulder. The gesture was small but telling—a man who'd spent years avoiding commitment now unable to resist the simple intimacy of touch. I'd watched their relationship evolve from casual dating to something much deeper, and despite Cole's checkered past, I had high hopes for them. Lily had a way of seeing beyond people's rough edges to the potential beneath.

"Did you know the word honeymoon originated during medieval times?" Sheldon asked, his eyes lighting up with excitement behind his thick lenses. He bounced slightly on his toes, unable to contain himself when sharing one of his many random facts.

"Nope," Cole said, barely looking up from his notes, but Sheldon, oblivious to social cues as always, kept talking, his voice rising with enthusiasm.

"It was customary for the bride and groom to drink mead the first month of marriage. And since mead is a fermented honey beverage—made primarily from honey, water, and yeast—the term honeymoon stuck as a way to identify the celebration. Medieval couples believed this would enhance fertility and increase the chances of conceiving a son."

"So you're saying marriage was so bad they had to get drunk for the first full month to be able to live together?" Cole asked, a hint of his usual dry humor showing through despite the grim surroundings.

Sheldon's mouth opened and closed like a fish while he tried to think of something to say, his mind visibly processing this unexpected interpretation of his historical tidbit. But he came back with, "I don't think that's what I said at all." He looked at Cole owlishly. "I don't feel like I'm qualified to give an accurate assessment on marriage. But I'll find out and let you know. I'll do some research on medieval marriage satisfaction rates when I get back to the funeral home."

That was the first time I'd ever heard Sheldon say he didn't know something, and I raised my brows at Cole, my eyes dancing with humor. It was these small moments of normality, of human connection, that kept us sane in the midst of tragedy.

"You asked for it," I told Cole.

"Let's load up the male first," Lily said, unfolding the body bag with practiced efficiency. The sound of the zipper echoed in the quiet room. "Less mess. The female vic is going to need extra care with all that blood."

"I'm going to head out and go catch a few hours' sleep," Cole said, stifling a yawn. The shadows under his eyes spoke of his all-night shift. "Call me if you need an extra set of hands. You can find Oliver Harris in his office in the main resort building."

"Thanks for taking the call," Jack said, clasping Cole's shoulder briefly.

"Yeah, well, I'll send you an invoice," Cole said, tipping his hat, kissing Lily once more, and then heading out the door with the weary step of a man who'd seen too much death in too short a time.

"Once you get them unloaded and into the cooler y'all can take off," I said, watching as Lily and Sheldon positioned the gurney beside the bed. "It'll probably be a couple of hours before I can get back and start the autopsies."

"I'd like to observe," Lily said, her face lighting up at the prospect of more hands-on training. Her dedication to learning never ceased to impress me. "I need some more hours for this month for school, so I'll hang around until you get back. I need to study anyway, and the funeral home is quiet." She carefully arranged the body bag, her movements precise and respectful.

"It won't be too quiet," Sheldon said, his voice rising with a note of anxiety that made Jack and me exchange glances. "Victor Mobley's viewing is tonight. I heard he was a Hells Angel. Emmy Lu said riders have come in all the way from California to see him laid to rest. Forty-three motorcycles by her last count. Did you know that Hells Angels was founded in 1948 in California? They actually trademarked their name and logo. It's one of the most aggressively protected trademarks in the—"

"Emmy Lu has better information than my dispatchers," Jack interrupted, shaking his head with a mixture of amusement and resignation. Emmy Lu had an uncanny network of sources that put most intelligence agencies to shame. "About a hundred bikers rode into town around midnight last night. Wanda Baker said her B&B is full for the weekend, and so is the D&Q Motel. The rest of them are at the hotels in King George."

Baker Bed and Breakfast and the D&Q Motel were the only places to stay in Bloody Mary close to where the funeral home was located. D&Q stood for Drawn and Quartered, but locals had been calling it the D&Q for several decades as to not scare off potential business. The original owners had thought the macabre name would be eye catching. They'd been right, but not in the way they'd hoped.

"Maybe I should help out with the viewing," I said, looking warily at Sheldon as he fumbled with the gurney straps. His hands were trembling slightly, his normally pale face even whiter at the prospect of hosting a funeral home full of outlaw bikers. He looked like a bikers' favorite target—soft, nervous, the kind of person who might faint if someone said boo. "Just in case things get out of hand."

"He should be fine," Jack assured me, but I could see the slight crease between his brows that appeared whenever he was worried about some-thing. "Outlaw bikers live by a code. And the death of one of their own means there's a certain standard of behavior until the burial is over. But once he's in the ground is when we'll need to be on guard. They'll hit the bars and start looking for trouble.

The sooner we can escort them out of town the better."

"I'm thinking about getting a tattoo," Sheldon said out of the blue. "One of my friends has a full sleeve and the ladies are all over him whenever we go to the bars. Do you think I should get a sleeve?" He flexed his pudgy arm experimentally, as if imagining the artwork that might adorn it.

The question was directed at Lily, but Jack and I stopped in our tracks to listen to the conversation, and I noticed a couple of the CSI techs were listening intently as well, their evidence collection momentarily forgotten.

Bless Lily's heart. She was always unfailingly kind, even when presented with the most absurd scenarios. She paused in her work, giving Sheldon her full attention. "I thought you hated needles?"

"That's true," Sheldon said, his eyes wide behind his glasses, blinking rapidly as the memory surfaced. "Maybe I shouldn't. Or maybe I could do anesthesia. They could put me completely under while they do the work."

"Also a needle," she reminded him gently, the way one might explain something to a child. "And it seems risky. You never know what might happen to you if you go under in a tattoo parlor."

"That's true," he said, nodding vigorously. "That happened to me once when I went to a palm reader in New Orleans. I woke up two days later in a cemetery with no memory of how I got there. Just my underwear and one sock. I still have dreams about it sometimes."

"Good Lord," Jack whispered, leaning close to me so only I could hear. "It's a miracle he made it to adulthood. I still can't believe you let him out in the field."

"The social interactions have been good for him," I said, watching Sheldon with a mix of amusement and concern as he recounted his New Orleans adventure to a captivated Lily. "He's really come a long way. Not to mention how much we've all improved when we play Trivial Pursuit. Besides, he's got a good heart. And in our line of work, that counts for a lot."

Jack's fingers brushed against mine briefly, a small gesture of agreement. In the midst of death, surrounded by the remnants of violence, these small moments of connection—of normality and even humor—were what kept us human. They were reminders that even in the darkest places, there was still room for light.

CHAPTER THREE

JACK AND I LEFT LILY AND SHELDON AND THE CRIME-scene techs and made our way back to the main resort. As we wound our way through the golf cart path in Jack's truck, I noticed other villas hidden in the trees.

"These other villas are pretty far away from where our victims were found," I said. "If they're even occupied I'm not sure they'd have heard anything. The waterfalls would probably muffle the sound."

"It'd be a slim chance anyone heard anything," Jack agreed. "Maybe if the wind was blowing just right and carried the sound."

"This property is huge," I said. "Hard to contain since it backs up to a national forest on one side and the Potomac on the other. You can't fence nature. The killer could have come in from anywhere.

"Yes," Jack said. "I can send a few units out to drive the perimeter and see if there was an obvious breach. Maybe an abandoned car or something. But it would make more sense for the killer to have been on the property as a guest. They'd have had to walk miles through some pretty rough terrain to come in the back way, and then they'd have to go back out the same way once they'd finished taking out the targets."

"You think the manager will give us the guest list?" I asked.

"I've already requested a warrant for it," Jack said. "It should come through signed at any moment. Are you sure you're doing okay?" Concern etched his face as he glanced at me. "I was really worried about you back there."

"Worried about me or worried I'd contaminate the crime scene?" I asked, raising an eyebrow.

Jack grinned and squeezed my shoulder. "Both. How long do you think we'll be able to keep this a secret?"

"As long as we can stop having early morning murder calls I figure we can keep it a secret until it's time to give birth. You know people get all weird when they find out someone is pregnant. I don't want to be treated any differently."

"If you think my mother is going to wait until you're giving birth you're out of your mind," he said. "You're carrying her first grandbaby. Expect to be treated differently."

I knew he wasn't kidding. Mrs. Lawson was going to be over the moon once we broke the news, and as selfish as I wanted to be about keeping the baby our little secret, I knew it couldn't last forever.

"We'll keep it secret for just a little while longer," I said. "I just need to plan better in the mornings so I've got time to let it pass."

Jack parked his Tahoe under the covered portico of The Mad King Resort. It was all glass and natural stone and looked like a mountain retreat framed between centuries-old trees that edged along the Potomac. The crisp scent of pine mixed with the earthy aroma of the river created both a serene and overwhelming atmosphere.

"Give me a second," I told Jack, looking down at my bloodstained coveralls and boots. "I don't want to give anyone a heart attack. These don't look like the kinds of people who talk about death over their morning coffee."

"They don't know what they're missing out on," Jack said. "The way I see it, if you start the day talking about death then things can only get better from there."

I grunted in agreement and hurriedly stripped

down to the black leggings and oversized cashmere sweater the color of raspberries I'd put on that morning. Then I dug for the black ballet flats I'd packed in the bottom of my bag.

"Do I look like I've spent the morning trying not to throw up?" I asked, pulling the band out of my hair and running my fingers through it, hoping it looked artfully tossed instead of crime-scene chic.

"You look beautiful in that sweater," Jack said. "Really puts some color in your cheeks."

"Yet still not a direct answer to my question," I said, eyes narrowed.

Jack grinned as the doormen opened the polished glass doors for us and we walked into a lobby that smelled of luxury. There was a large fireplace that dominated almost the entire right-side wall, and several rocking chairs were placed in front of it. The fireplace had been laid with fresh wood. Nights were still chilly well into April, so I imagined happy hour would be quite cozy later that afternoon.

On the left side was an indoor grotto with a cascading waterfall, and several seating arrangements were placed around it. The entire back wall was windows that looked out over spectacular grounds, where guests were already outside participating in whatever activities the resort had on the schedule for the day. There was a large square bar in the center of the room that already had several patrons despite the early hour.

"It's a good thing I can't keep my hands off you," I muttered. "Otherwise you'd be insufferable."

Jack leaned down and said, "It's because you can't keep your hands off me that you look like death warmed over right now."

I elbowed him in the ribs as we made our way to the check-in area. It was tucked away in a glassed-in partition, and Jack held up his badge discreetly to the smiling woman behind the desk.

"We're here to see Oliver Harris," Jack said.

"Of course," she said, without missing a beat. "He's expecting you. Let me show you to his office."

She took us across the lobby and carded herself through a side door that led into a long hallway. It was utilitarian, with gray carpet and ivory walls. There were several wooden plaques on the left side, announcing awards the resort had won.

The woman knocked on the first door on the right and waited for a response.

"It's open," a voice said.

She opened it and said, "Mr. Harris, you said to bring the police straight back to your office if they had more questions."

"Of course," Oliver said, standing behind his desk. "Would you please have some coffee sent in?

I'm sure we could all use some after the morning we've had."

"My pleasure," she said, and shut the door discreetly behind her.

Now that the morning sickness had passed, coffee sounded amazing. And I wouldn't have turned her down if she'd returned with some fancy Danishes either. I was trying to limit my coffee intake. I practically lived on coffee, so I had a complete understanding of what addicts must feel like being weaned off the hard stuff. I'd been drinking my first and only cup of the day as soon as the morning sickness passed each day. It was safest for everyone that I start out the day with a shot of caffeine.

Oliver Harris was a tall, thin man with skin the color of the foam on top of the espresso I liked to get at Lady Jane's Donuts. He wore gray slacks and a matching four-button vest with a pale blue shirt and navy-and-silver-striped tie. His head was shaved bald and his teeth were blindingly white.

"Please, come in and sit down," he said.

"We appreciate your time," Jack said, reaching out to shake his hand. "I'm Sheriff Lawson. This is Dr. Graves. She's the coroner for King George."

"Yes, of course," he said, reaching out to shake my hand next. "Such a tragedy that has brought you here. We're all in shock. And it's upset many of our staff and guests. Understandably so. No one wants to think they're in the vicinity of a murderer."

Jack and I took our seats in the white leather chairs that faced his desk.

"We appreciate your time, Mr. Harris," Jack said. "I know you gave Detective Cole a brief statement earlier. But would you mind running it through again for us?"

There was a soft knock at the door, and it opened again with the front desk woman pushing in a rolling cart decked out with a full coffee service and scones. I couldn't even pretend to hide my relief. I was always ravenous after the morning sickness passed.

We paused briefly while the woman asked each of us how we liked our coffee, and then she passed them out very properly in fine china cups before letting herself out quietly.

"Please, help yourself to the scones," Harris said, looking directly at me. "How far along are you?"

My head jerked up in surprise and he laughed.

"I've got six myself," he said. "I can recognize the signs by now. My wife starts getting that look in her eye like you've got right now, and I know I'm in for it."

"Six," I said, not even able to imagine one, much less six. I helped myself and put one of the scones on the thin china plate, adding a dab of clotted cream and strawberry jam.

"A large family is something special," he said. "My wife and I are outnumbered, but we wouldn't change a thing. Our oldest daughter is about the same age as that girl I saw this morning. I can't imagine what her family will go through. And I can't imagine I'll ever forget it. Images like that tend to stick with a man his whole life."

"How long have you been the manager here?" Jack asked casually.

"Since we opened last year," he said. "I was the manager at one of Mr. Riverdale's properties up in the Poconos. When he asked me if I wanted this property five years ago I jumped at the chance. I was able to get in on the design and planning from the ground up. There were times I didn't think we'd ever open the doors, but we did it. My family had to uproot and move states, but it was worth it.

"I've been in hospitality for twenty-five years," he continued. "So I've seen an unusual thing or two. A few suicides and several deaths by natural causes. But I've never seen anything like what I saw this morning. And I hope to never see anything like it again."

"Was anyone hanging around the lobby last night when Mr. and Mrs. Vasilios arrived?" Jack asked. "Anyone follow them in inside?"

"The lobby was crowded as usual on a Friday night, even as late as they arrived," he said. "We have live music near the bar until two o'clock, and s'mores available at the fire pits on the lawn until midnight. I don't normally work the night shift, but my night manager was rushed to the hospital for an emergency appendectomy yesterday morning, so we were short staffed last night. And then two of my front desk staff are out with the flu. It seems to be making the rounds."

He paused to take a sip of his coffee and then said, "I came out on the floor to help wherever I was needed. We had several late check-ins last night. It's wedding season. So we were busier than usual from about eight to midnight. I knew Mr. and Mrs. Vasilios were scheduled to arrive after their wedding, and I wanted to be there to personally welcome them. They were considered to be VIP guests. No one came in with them."

"How was their behavior?"

Oliver smiled sadly and said, "How do you think? Mr. Vasilios looked like he couldn't wait to get to that room."

"Not Mrs. Vasilios?" I asked.

"She looked exhausted," he said. "And nervous. She was more than a little tipsy. So was he, but Mr. Vasilios said they'd come straight from the reception. Mrs. Vasilios was holding on to him for dear life. She was a little unsteady on her feet.

"When my daughter got married she spent most

of the day throwing up," he said, smiling fondly at the memory. "She'd worried herself sick, trying to make everything perfect. It's a very stressful day for the bride, and I could tell that Mrs. Vasilios was at that point. I wanted to get them to the room quickly. I drove them on one of the guest golf carts to the honeymoon villa. One of the bellmen followed behind us with their luggage."

"Tell me how you found the villa when you arrived with them," Jack said.

"What do you mean?"

"Were the lights on or off? Was the door unlocked? That kind of thing."

"Oh," Oliver said, nodding. "All the lights were on, but that's not unusual. The villa had been prepped for their arrival. But the front door was locked as it was supposed to be. I unlocked it for them myself, and I let them know we'd prepared a light snack and champagne out on the deck for them. Roger brought in the luggage behind me and placed it by the door. Mr. and Mrs. Vasilios didn't seem too interested in the champagne and they turned down my offer to show them through the villa. Mr. Vasilios tipped both Roger and me very generously, and he closed the door behind us."

"Who prepared the room for their arrival?" I asked.

"I'll have to check with housekeeping and food

services, but that shouldn't be difficult to get you that information."

"What about the other villas?" Jack asked. "Were those occupied last night?"

"We're at full capacity for the next eight months," Oliver said. "All of the villas are occupied."

"We don't want to disturb your guests," Jack said.

"I'd greatly appreciate that," Oliver said sincerely. "We've had several guests already notice the police presence, even though you've been working on the far edges of the property."

"I'm going to need a list of anyone on the property last night," Jack said. "All staff and guests."

Mr. Harris winced apologetically. "Unfortunately, I can't do that without a warrant. Many of our guests are well known in one capacity or another, and we assure them of their privacy."

"I understand," Jack said. "And I thought that might be the case. You should have an electronic warrant waiting in your email."

Mr. Harris's brows rose appreciatively and he turned to his computer, his fingers clicking on the keyboard.

"Very efficient," he said. Then he typed some more and said, "Do you want me to send this list to you via your personal email?"

"Please," Jack said, handing him a card with his information on it. "I appreciate it."

"I want to help," Mr. Harris said. "Believe it or not, this is one of the few instances where paperwork makes things easier."

"Did you have any guests call in a noise complaint last night?" Jack asked. "We're talking half a dozen gunshots that were fired into the victims. Maybe someone overheard."

"All of our villas and estate rooms are fully soundproofed," he said. "The only way sound would have carried is if they'd had the doors open. Even then..." Mr. Harris shrugged apologetically.

"And no cameras that observe the farthest perimeters of the property?" Jack asked.

"We have cameras on the golf cart paths and the areas where activities are held," he said. "Also in the parking lot. We promise our more prominent guests privacy, and the truth is we're sitting on several hundred acres of forest and cliffs. It would be impossible to put cameras in enough places to encompass it all. Though I have a feeling Mr. Riverdale is going to want to beef up perimeter security after this. Whoever killed Mr. and Mrs. Vasilios would've had to check in with identification at the front gate with the guard if they came in the proper way. Even staff has their own entrance and has to show ID."

Jack moved to stand, and I followed suit, subtly brushing crumbs from my sweater. "There could have been any number of points of entry, and that's one of the things we hope to find out soon. We appreciate your cooperation. I'm sure you're ready to go home and get some sleep."

Oliver stood behind his desk and looked at the gold watch on his wrist. "I'll catch a couple of hours in one of the staff rooms. I've got to be back on duty at noon."

"I hope your night manager recovers quickly," Jack said, shaking his hand.

"From your mouth to God's ears," he said, smiling. "I'll have Margaret direct you to the housekeeper and kitchen staff that prepped the room. Take one of those scones with you, Dr. Graves. You never know when you're going to need a snack."

"I'm more than full," I said, slightly embarrassed because I'd been wishing I had pockets I could sneak one into. "They were delicious. This is a beautiful property. You should be very proud."

He let out a sad sigh. "Unfortunately, I don't feel that way right now. Not after what happened to that couple. Their deaths fall on me. I'm responsible for the safety of everyone here. And that's something I've got to live with."

CHAPTER FOUR

"I liked him," I said while we searched for room 314. That's where Dorinda Lake, the housekeeper who'd done turndown service on the honeymoon villa, was supposedly located.

"Oliver Harris?" Jack asked.

"Yeah," I said. "Sometimes you meet people and you know they're a really good person. Just deep down. He'd be a good friend."

Jack's mouth quirked at the corner, but he didn't say anything. It was probably best I couldn't read his mind.

We found Dorinda Lake in room 314. She was a short, plump woman with skin so pale it was almost translucent and shockingly dark corkscrew curls that were pulled back from her round face with a headband.

"Thank you for speaking with us," Jack said. "We won't take up much of your time."

"Not a problem," she said, giving us a sweet smile and stripping the sheets off the bed. "As long as I can talk while I work. I'm working this floor by myself today."

"You were on shift last night?" Jack asked.

"I was," she said, making the bed with shocking speed and snapping the covers so they were crisp. "I filled in for Linda so she could go to her daughter's dance recital. I normally work the eight-to-four shift."

She moved over and emptied the trash cans and gathered dirty dishes. "Would you look at that?" She showed us a plate filled with ashes and cigarette butts. "They know this is a no-smoking property, yet they do it anyway. Drives me mad. So disgusting. I always make a note so they get fined on their credit card, but most of the people who stay here have enough money that they don't care. They're used to doing what they want."

She muttered to herself as she finished cleaning trash and clutter and then wiped down the surfaces.

"What time did you do turndown service for the honeymoon villa?" Jack asked.

"About eight thirty or so," she said. "I saved it for last for turndown because I knew the guests weren't scheduled to arrive until later."

"Was anything out of place?" I asked.

"No," she said, moving into the bathroom. She tossed damp towels out onto the floor, and then I heard the shower go on. "I did regular turndown service. I made sure the minibar was stocked, turned on enhancement lights, put on some mood music, and made sure the robes and slippers were in the closets."

"Did you notice anyone hanging around while you were inside?" Jack asked.

Her head popped out the door. "No, but I'll tell you I hate doing the turndown service to some of those villas at night. Not that there's any reason not to feel safe here at The Mad King, but there's just nothing out there. All you have is your imagination and the sound of trees and rushing water. It like to have scared me to death when Aidan came in to set up the back deck for a romantic scene."

"Aidan Chisholm?" Jack asked, checking his notes from the names Margaret had given us. "From food service?"

"Yes, that's right," she said, getting her mop from the cart. "Sweet kid. He's working his way through school. He's doesn't work on Saturdays because he's on the rowing team at Roanoke College. He usually works Sundays though if you need to talk to him."

"I appreciate the information," Jack said. "What time did you finish with turndown service?"

"Around nine I would guess," she said. "That's one of the larger villas so it takes a little longer."

"What about Aidan? Was he still there when you left?"

"He was," she said. "But don't think he had anything to do with this. He's a good kid."

"We don't think that," Jack assured her. "I just need to put a timeline together. How'd he arrive?"

"We each had a staff golf cart," she said, setting out fresh towels. "That's the only way to get all the way out there. I waved goodbye to him on my way out, but he was just about finished setting everything out as far as I could see. He probably didn't leave too long after me."

"You've been a big help," Jack said. "Thanks again."

"I hope you find whoever did this," she said. "We're a family here at The Mad King, and the thought that this could happen right under our noses has shaken everyone. We've had a few early checkouts, this room included. Mr. Harris is offering refunds to any of the guests who chose to leave."

"From what I can see this is a safe and well-run property," Jack said. "Sometimes there's nothing we can do about evil."

She nodded sagely. "That's the scary part."

We left her to her cleaning and then headed back down to the lobby. I saw Oliver Harris greeting new arrivals and gesturing them toward the check-in desk. Jack caught his attention, and we waited near the front doors until he was free.

"I know you're headed to get some sleep," Jack said. "But I had one more question after talking to Dorinda."

"Doesn't look like I'm going to get to sleep after all," he said, with a tired smile. "So ask away."

"Did you notice the mood music playing when you let the Vasilioses into their room?"

His brow furrowed, and he opened his mouth to answer and then closed it again. "Actually, now that you mention it, there was no music playing. Turning on the mood music is standard procedure when we do turndown service."

"Thanks again for your time," Jack said.

"Y'all come back and stay for a weekend when you've got some free time," he said. "I'm happy to comp a couple of nights for you."

"I told you I liked him," I whispered as we left the resort.

"We need to find out more about our bride and groom," Jack said once we were back in the car and headed toward Bloody Mary. "There has to be a pretty good reason to hunt down a couple on their honeymoon in a well-secured resort and gun them down."

"Between the guest and staff list, the golf cart logs, and the security footage we've got a lot of information to sift through," I said.

"I'm sure Doug can help us narrow things down with the security cameras and the golf carts," Jack said. "He's got to earn his keep somehow."

"You know Doug will enjoy the technology. It's pretty fancy that all the EV golf carts have a tracking system. We can see if anyone was in close proximity to the honeymoon villa. Maybe we'll get lucky."

"Because things always turn out that easy," Jack said, rolling his eyes. "I'll bet you a hundred bucks we're not dealing with a simple double homicide."

"A hundred bucks?" I asked. "Do you know what the county pays me? I'll bet twenty. I know my limits. Maybe you could use the other eighty to buy me lunch. Or do you just plan to starve your unborn child?"

"You just had two scones," Jack said. "And I saw you sneak that other one in your bag."

"A scone isn't lunch," I said. "I want gyros."

"At this rate people are going to know you're pregnant in no time," Jack said under his breath.

"What was that?" I asked, not sure I'd heard him correctly.

"I said is there anything else?"

I stared at him, not sure I believed him, but he had his blank face on that he used when he played poker.

"No," I said. "I'm a simple woman. And I can always be bought with food."

"Our bank account thanks you," Jack said. "Gyros are much cheaper than diamonds. Though I'm not sure it's best for long-term investing."

"Are you kidding? What's more long-term investing than feeding your unborn child a gyro? Think about how cute and fat he'll be when he comes out."

"Well, in that case," Jack said, turning into Gyro Heroes and pulling into the drive-thru line.

While we waited, Jack put in a call to Lieutenant Derby in IT.

"Hey, Sheriff," Derby said. "Heard you caught a good one this morning."

"Something like that," Jack said. "Have you had a chance to run backgrounds on our victims?"

"I just emailed them to you about two minutes ago," Derby said. "You recognize the last name Vasilios?"

"Never heard of it," Jack said.

"Me either, but apparently Theo's father was the ambassador to Greece under the last administration. You're going to get pushback on this one."

"He's not an ambassador anymore," Jack said. "I'd

hope he'd want me to find out what happened to his son and new daughter-in-law."

"Yeah, well, maybe he'll surprise you," Derby said. "Here's what I've got on the vic. Theo Vasilios is forty-six years old and moved to Newcastle full-time last year. He's got a couple-million-dollar house and an owner's stake in a few restaurants that don't bring in the kind of revenue to make that house payment."

"Maybe he's got family money," Jack said. "We'll check his financials. So we've got a dead Greek playboy and his new young wife."

"His nineteen-year-old wife," Derby said.

Jack's brows rose at that. "Unusual, but not illegal. What's her story?"

"That's where things get interesting," Derby said. "Cursory background report shows the cleanest history of all histories. Not even a parking ticket."

"She is only nineteen," Jack said wryly. "Hold on a second, Derby."

Jack paused and put in our orders at the window.

"I wouldn't mind a gyro," Derby said. "Extra tzatziki sauce."

Jack's lips twitched, but he added to our order and then proceeded up the line. "Go ahead, Derby."

"Where was I?" Derby asked.

"Chloe Vasilios," Jack said. "She doesn't even have a parking ticket."

"Right," he continued. "Get this. Her parents'

names are John and Jane Matthews, but they're both listed as deceased as of last year. Car wreck. Looks like she was homeschooled. She's got a driver's license that lists a Texas address. No college. No employment history until last June. She worked at The Corner Café in DC for just under a month before she went to work for Theo Vasilios."

"Really?" Jack asked, giving me a curious look. "That's definitely worth looking into a little closer. We're heading back to HQ now. Thanks for the info, Derby."

"Thanks for the gyro," Derby said and disconnected.

"Go ahead and drop me at the funeral home before you give Derby his gyro," I said. "I'll get started on the autopsy. I'm curious what a girl with no past might have to show me."

"I'm going to send some of this information to Doug," Jack said as we drove through the tranquil streets of Bloody Mary. "He can start the process of elimination. And I need to take a couple of hours and check in with my detectives. This wasn't our only murder last night."

"Ahh, big city progress," I said.

"The crime in King George Proper is escalating," Jack said. "It's a college and a military town, and both have coexisted well for all the decades. But we're starting to see gang violence and an increase in drugs coming in from across the river. Unfortunately our friends over there are more than happy to let them make our lives hell instead of stopping them on their side of the line."

"Well, if I've learned anything about city government it's that someone is always passing the buck. But I also know something they don't know."

"What's that?" Jack asked.

"I know you are the last person they should want to tangle with. You always get your man."

He laughed uneasily and squeezed my hand. Jack wasn't always comfortable with compliments.

Bloody Mary was one of the four towns that made up King George County. It was where Jack and I had both grown up, and it was a simpler life, even today. It was a town of large lots and old homes where people still sat on their porches in the evenings drinking sweet tea. It was a place where generations chose to stay and raise their families, many of them descendants from when King George County was originally settled back in the 1700s. American flags waved as freely as the opinions.

Jack turned onto Catherine of Aragon, and the large red-brick Colonial that had once belonged to my grandparents came into view. There were two towering oaks in the front—one on each side of the sidewalk that led to the wide front steps and double door entrance. On the north side was the guest parking lot, and on the south side was the portico where we loaded and unloaded bodies.

The Suburban was parked under the portico, and Jack pulled up behind it. He leaned over to give me a kiss goodbye.

"I'll be a few hours at least," I said.

"I've got more than enough on my plate to stay busy, but I'll come hang out when I'm finished. I'll make sure Sheldon doesn't end up as someone's old lady."

I'd forgotten about the Hells Angels, but I snorted out a laugh and kissed him again before opening the door. "Thanks for the gyro."

CHAPTER FIVE

I HUNG UP MY BAG IN THE MUDROOM AND THEN MADE my way into the kitchen.

My grandparents had lived on the third floor of the Colonial when they'd first opened the funeral home, up until my grandmother had met a tragic end by falling out of an open window. Knowing what I did now about the kind of family I come from, I wouldn't have been at all surprised to find out that my grandfather had been the one to push her.

When my parents had taken over the funeral home, they'd done a remodel so the third floor could be used for extra viewing rooms at some point. Up until the last couple of years, we hadn't needed the extra viewing rooms, so the third floor had been relegated to storage. But along with the population explosion in King George County and the increase of violent crimes, there was also an increase in deaths by natural causes. The funeral home was so busy I would have been happy for another one to open up just to take some of the business.

My parents also remodeled the first floor so the front office, a conference room for more sensitive matters, and the casket showroom were lined up on one side of the wide hallway and on the other side was a chapel and the largest viewing room.

Since they'd never done anything with pure intentions, they'd used the right side of the funeral home as their evil lair. Maybe I'm being dramatic, but flippancy was still how I coped with the truth of who they really were. They'd added a kitchen and office that were kept private from the public part of the funeral home, and they'd had a basement dug to create a lab that most forensics teams in the country would kill to get their hands on. No pun intended.

The lab was protected with a pressurized steel door that needed a code and a thumbprint to open. But my parents had needed the protection of Fort Knox for their illegal activities. I'd deactivated the thumbprint and just used a code since it was important to protect the bodies from any misdeeds. Attempted body theft was extremely rare in the mortuary business, but it was better safe than sorry.

I looked at the coffeepot with envy as I passed out of the kitchen, thinking that nine months seemed like a long time to survive with only one cup a day. I rubbed at the tension gathered at the base of my neck as I made my way to Emmy Lu's office.

I'd hired Emmy Lu once business for the funeral home had gotten so busy that I couldn't do it all myself. Emmy Lu Stout had been a godsend. She was a Bloody Mary native, and she'd babysat me a time or two in my formative years. She'd gotten married to her high school sweetheart the day after graduation, and had given birth to five boys shortly thereafter. She'd been a stay-at-home mom until her youngest had turned eighteen and her husband had walked out the door to go live with a younger woman. So she'd put on her pantyhose and come looking for a job. I told her to feel free to leave the pantyhose at home, but she'd been hired on the spot.

Emmy Lu was cute as a button, and looked like a slightly overweight Gidget with crow's feet. She sat behind her desk with a pair of readers pushed up on the top of her head while wearing another pair from a chain hanging around her neck.

"What's up?" I asked, knocking on the doorframe before coming inside.

"Just doing inventory," she said. "We're going to need to order new caskets soon. Especially the midrange models. Been a rough few months for the middle class."

"I heard we'll be full of Hells Angels tonight," I said, taking a seat across from her desk.

"I went on a date with an outlaw biker once," she said, her dimples fluttering in her cheeks and a flush coming over her skin. "Before Tom."

My brows rose at that. I hadn't known there'd been anyone before Tom. Emmy Lu and Tom Daly had been dating about a year now. Tom owned the Donut Palace. We tried to support Tom, but it was fortunate he had a day job. Donuts weren't his gift.

"Who knew you were so rebellious," I said. "I didn't hear a word about it."

"It's a well-kept secret, so if everyone knows about it tomorrow I'll know who blabbed."

I put my fingers together and made a motion to zip my lips.

"I met him on that singles' cruise I took after the divorce," she said. "Best week of my life."

"I didn't know outlaw bikers went on singles' cruises," I said, brows raised in surprise.

"They go all over the world," she said as if she were an expert.

"You weren't scared?" I asked. "I heard you have to do all kinds of weird rituals to become one of their old ladies."

"Nah," she said. "I told him from the start I was just in it for the sex. I'd never been with anyone but my husband. He was real respectful of my wishes too.

I think I'm naturally drawn to a bad boy. He wore jeans and leather for the whole cruise unless he was naked.

"I did get a little worried when I saw him on my flight coming home. I thought maybe he was following me. But it turned out the outlaws have a big presence in Virginia, and he lives in Richmond. My mother would've killed me if I'd brought him home. He had tattoos everywhere. And I mean *everywhere*."

My eyebrows rose at that. This was information about Emmy Lu that I didn't need to know.

"He had a tattoo of a hundred-dollar bill right on his penis," she said.

"Why?"

"I have no idea," she said. "But it was a little off putting to stare face-to-face with Benjamin Franklin. He wasn't an attractive man."

"I can't even imagine," I said, horrified. "Have you seen Lily?"

"She's in the conference room studying, though when I went in to take her a cup of coffee she'd fallen asleep in her textbook."

"Ahh, the old learning by osmosis trick," I said. "I did that a time or two in medical school."

"Very comforting, Doc," she said sarcastically.

"I guess it's a good thing my patients are already dead," I said, getting to my feet. "I'll go get her. I'm about to start the autopsies. I hate to miss the outlaw party tonight."

"It'll probably be the biggest crowd we've ever had. All the locals are real curious what happens at an outlaw wake. I've been fielding calls all day. There will be a lot of locals here."

"Good Lord," I said, trying to imagine the townspeople of Bloody Mary integrating with the Hells Angels.

"Tom's coming as soon as he's done at the office."

"Jack will be here too," I said. "But between you and me he's making sure Sheldon doesn't end up pierced and tattooed and wearing nothing but a pair of chaps."

"I'm so glad I voted for him for sheriff," she said wide eyed, her little Kewpie bow mouth pursed. "I know he's got the citizens' best interests at heart."

"You've developed a real sarcastic streak since you started working here."

"I've been practicing," she said. "And don't worry about Sheldon. We'll make sure the funeral home is still standing when everyone leaves at eight o'clock. We've got reinforcements."

"You almost make it sounds like the citizens of Bloody Mary are going to take on a bunch of outlaw bikers."

"Like I tell my boys," she said. "Always be prepared."

I smiled grimly and decided the best thing to do was bury myself in the basement with my autopsy saw.

I waved goodbye and made my way toward the conference room, wondering where Sheldon was lurking. I didn't have to look far. He was sitting at the conference table with Lily, his head leaned back against the chair and his eyes closed. His earbuds were in and his finger was tapping against the chair.

I looked at Lily and she was staring at me over the top of her laptop like a deer caught in headlights.

"Everything okay in here?" I asked, brows raised.

She closed her laptop, and stood stretching her neck from side to side. "We're good. Sheldon's listening to the soundtrack from *Sons of Anarchy*. He wants to be prepared for tonight. You ready to start the autopsy?"

"If you can break free," I said.

She grinned and shoved her laptop and books in an oversized backpack that looked like it weighed more than she did.

Sheldon's eyes popped open and he jumped when he saw us, his face pale and clammy. His hand was clutched to his heart.

"You startled me," he yelled, trying to talk over the music blaring in his ears.

I pointed to his earbuds and he jerked them out.

"You okay?" I asked.

"I think I was dreaming," he said. "And then the bass started pumping and my heart started pounding. Outlaw life is intense."

"You have everything under control for tonight?" I asked.

"Yes," he said, wiping the sweat from his upper lip. "Victor is laid out in the blue room and I opened up the connecting doors to the chapel to make more space. He looks good for a guy who got shot in the neck. His mom insisted he wear a turtleneck with his leathers and that we cover his face tattoos with makeup. He's real presentable."

"It'll be great," I said, not sure if I believed it. "Is the burial still set for Monday?"

"Yes," he said. "The family wanted a private burial. I think Mrs. Mobley got some pushback from his outlaw brothers, but she's no pushover herself. They seemed a little scared of her. Just between you and me, I think she was someone's old lady back in the day."

"King George County does love family legacy," I said. "It's important to pass on the traditions of those who came before us."

"My mom told me that it's well known the Hells Angels have a secret support club here," Sheldon whispered, as if the Hells Angels were listening at the door. "And they're using this funeral as an excuse to recruit."

"What's a support club?" Lily asked.

"It's like a farm system," Sheldon said. "Like in baseball."

"Gotcha," she said. "Is that a bad thing?"

"Yeah," Sheldon said, his face pinkening. The more knowledge he was able to share the more animated he became. "It's real bad. Everyone knows this is Vagos country. They control the entire East Coast, and technically the Hells Angels had to get permission to even be here. There could be a turf war if the Hells Angels aren't careful and they've been recruiting in Virginia, right under the noses of the Vagos."

"Wow," I said. "I had no idea."

"Most people don't pay attention to the one percenters," Sheldon said stoically. "They can't handle the truth."

"Sheldon, do me a favor," I said.

His eyes lit with excitement. "Anything."

"Turn off that music for a little while and give your brain a break. I'm not going to be happy if I come into work Monday and you have a teardrop tattoo and you're wearing their colors."

He swallowed hard and nodded, and I could tell he'd been imagining himself doing just that.

"Good luck with the viewing tonight," I said, and Lily and I escaped the room.

"He needs a keeper," Lily said.

"He lives with his mother," I countered.

"Then he needs a wife. That man has no street smarts. It's almost criminal to let him out on his own."

"Fortunately, he loves his work and that keeps him occupied," I said.

"I don't know how you do it," Lily said. "I do not like the funeral home side of death. When it's my turn just burn me to ash and put me in a cool container on the shelf—maybe an hourglass or an ant farm. Working a homicide or suspicious death gives me a lot more satisfaction than filling people up with formaldehyde and sticking them in the ground. I don't know how you switch back and forth between the pure science and dealing with living people's emotions."

"It's not so difficult," I said. "That's the part the science gets wrong. We need to have compassion, whether we're working on the homicide of a nineteen-year-old bride or whether we're burying a hundred-year-old who died peacefully in his sleep. The compassion is what drives us closer to justice. Death is loss, no matter if it's by man's hand or God's hand. And there are always people left behind who suffer because of it. The least we can do is be a safe space where they can grieve."

Lily hmmmed, but didn't say anything and I knew she was thinking over what I'd said. We made

another pass through the kitchen, and I kept my eyes averted so I wasn't tempted by the coffee maker.

"No coffee?" Lily asked, making a detour toward the fridge to grab one of the diet sodas she lived on.

"I've got water in the fridge downstairs," I said.

"You're being weird today," she said, eyeing me suspiciously as I typed in the code for the lab door.

"I have no idea what you're talking about," I lied.

The door whooshed as the pressure seal was released, the metallic sound echoing in the concrete stairwell. We stepped onto the landing, and a rush of cold air hit us like a physical wall. It was like stepping into an icebox—an intentional design to slow decomposition and preserve evidence. The sharp smell of antiseptic assaulted my nostrils. The fluorescent lights flicked on automatically, casting everything in a harsh, unforgiving glow.

"I want to do Chloe first," I said, my shoes clicking a steady rhythm on the metal stairs as I made my way down into the cavernous lab. The sound bounced off the tiled walls, emphasizing the emptiness of the space. "Derby found her background check lacking."

"Lacking?" Lily asked, heading to the walk-in refrigeration unit. Her breath formed small clouds in the chill air. "In what way?"

"As in she didn't really have one," I said, watching as Lily's gloved hands grasped the handle of the large stainless-steel door. "Jack sent me a copy of her file. She's supposedly a nineteen-year-old kid. No medical or tax records. Got her first job last year. Parents are named John and Jane Matthews, but they died in a car crash somewhere just before she got her first job. I'm hoping her body will give us a little insight as to why someone separated her from her husband and shot her six times."

The heavy door swung open with a soft pneumatic hiss. Cold mist rolled out at ankle level, curling around our feet like ghostly tendrils. Inside, the bodies of Theo and Chloe Vasilios lay on separate gurneys, covered with white sheets, their forms creating eerie topographical landscapes under the fabric. Lily wheeled Chloe out first, the wheels of the gurney squeaking slightly against the polished concrete floor.

I put on my lab coat, feeling the familiar weight settle across my shoulders—a professional armor of sorts. I prepped the paperwork, getting out forms and my digital voice recorder, setting up my workstation with practiced precision. There was a lot of bureaucracy when it came to the dead, and I was a stickler for keeping organized files on everyone that passed through my lab. I shuddered to think of the consequences if I didn't. It hadn't been too long ago that the FBI had raided my parents' home and business, and that was an experience one wasn't likely to ever forget.

I put on a heavy leather apron that was easy to clean, the thick material cool against my clothing. I moved to the sink and scrubbed my hands thoroughly, the water scalding hot against my skin—a contrast to the chill of the room. The ritual was as ingrained as breathing: forty seconds of scrubbing, careful attention to the spaces between fingers, under nails. I dried my hands and put on nitrile gloves, the snap of latex echoing in the quiet lab.

Lily went through the same ritual and then we lifted Chloe's body from the gurney and placed her on the metal autopsy table. The sheet fell away, revealing what remained of the young bride. I flipped on the overhead light, adjusting it to focus directly on her body.

Death never looked good on anyone, but under the harsh, clinical lights, it was even worse. The victim was covered in dried blood, the dress she'd carefully chosen as wedding guests waved the happy couple goodbye a dark, rusty brown. Her blond hair was matted with crimson, her youth and beauty obscured by the violent manner of her death. I took additional pictures to document her condition before beginning the autopsy, the camera's flash highlighting gruesome details that the naked eye might miss.

"Even with all I've seen, this still gets to me," Lily said quietly, her face solemn as she arranged the instruments on the tray beside the table. "Murdered on her wedding night."

I nodded, pushing aside the emotional response to focus on the task at hand. "Normally, we would start with a visual examination, checking for birthmarks, tattoos, and wounds. However, she's so crusted with dried blood that it's difficult to see anything. Let's clean her up first."

I carefully cut off the dress and undergarments she was wearing, the fabric stiff with dried blood. The scissors made a soft crunching sound as they cut through the material. I set the clothing aside for further analysis—sometimes the smallest fiber or stain could break a case. Next, I took scrapings from under her fingernails and swabbed her skin for DNA evidence, labeling each sample meticulously.

"Hand me the saline solution," I said to Lily, who passed me a squirt bottle. I began the process of removing the dried blood from the body, using warm water, saline, and a soft sponge. The water ran pink and then clear as I worked, revealing pale skin marred by the violence of her final moments.

The gunshot wounds stood out in stark relief against her clean skin—one to the center of her forehead, one to the throat, three clustered in her chest, and two in her pubic bone. Each wound was a small, puckered hole, the skin around them powder burned and discolored.

I stared at the two bullet holes in the pubic region. "Whoever did this wanted to make a statement."

I took her fingerprints, the ink dark against her pale skin, and wondered if they'd show up in any system. Then I turned on my digital recorder, my voice filling the silent lab.

"Autopsy case number 23-142, April 12. Time is 3:15 p.m. Subject is identified by driver's license and passport as Chloe Anne Matthews, also known as Chloe Vasilios. Caucasian female, blond hair, blue eyes. Weight is fifty-four kilograms. Height is one hundred and fifty-eight centimeters."

"She's very petite," Lily commented, helping me position the body for a full-body photograph. "Especially to take that many bullets."

"After the first one to the head, it wouldn't have mattered," I said, adjusting the camera. "She would have been gone instantly. The rest were...excessive."

I pulled the overhead surgical light down and turned on the bright examination lights. The harsh illumination cast deep shadows across the contours of her face, making her look almost skeletal.

"Evidence of professional spray tan and recent makeup application," I noted, examining her skin under the magnifying lens. "Eyelash extensions professionally applied. Acrylic nails with a French manicure, work done within the last week. She was preparing for her wedding day." The observation hung in the air, a reminder of the celebration that had been violently interrupted.

I used sterile scissors to cut a small section of hair from different parts of her scalp, placing each sample in a labeled container. Under the microscope, the truth was clear.

"The blond hair isn't natural," I said, adjusting the focus. "I'm seeing dark roots. She was a brunette, probably with regular bleaching and toning treatments."

'None of that is uncommon," Lily said, making notes on the chart. "Especially for a bride on her wedding day. Most women want to look their best."

I continued my methodical examination, checking her skin for unusual marks, birthmarks, or scarring. Nothing notable appeared until I reached her feet. Something caught my eye on the sole of her right foot.

"What have we here?" I pulled the light closer and put on my magnifying loupe so I could see better. The 3.5x magnification brought the small mark into focus.

"What is that?" Lily asked, her head bowed close to mine, her breath warm in the chilled air of the lab.

"Maybe just dirt," I said, squinting through the magnifier.

There was a smudge of blood that I hadn't completely removed in the initial cleaning. I took a cotton-tipped applicator and dipped it in isopropyl alcohol, then gently rubbed it across the area. The blood came away, revealing something underneath.

"It's a tattoo," I said, feeling a small thrill of excitement. "Looks like a pattern of dots."

I took a photo, adjusting the camera to capture the small mark clearly, then enhanced the image on the computer monitor so the tiny marks were distinguishable. I sketched the pattern on my autopsy form: two dots stacked vertically at the top, a triangle of three dots in the middle, and two dots side by side at the bottom.

"Not your typical tattoo," I said, frowning at the pattern. "It's crude—almost like someone did it by hand rather than with a professional tattoo gun."

"Maybe it's tally marks or something like that," Lily suggested, studying the pattern on the monitor. "Maybe gang activity or some kind of identifier?"

"Could be," I said, my mind already racing with possibilities. "Let's do full x-rays. If she's got unusual markings on the outside, who knows what we might find beneath the surface. Maybe there's evidence of childhood trauma or abuse that isn't immediately visible."

We carefully moved her body to the x-ray table, and I rolled the portable machine into place. The apparatus hummed as it powered up, the familiar sound oddly comforting in the sterile environment.

Lily looked at me with poorly concealed excitement when I handed her the lead apron.

"Why don't you do this part and I'll observe? You've been through the process enough to get all the angles," I said, noticing how her eyes lit up at the opportunity for hands-on experience.

She nodded eagerly and got to work, positioning the machine with confident movements. The x-ray machine clicked and whirred as she captured images from multiple angles, her face set in concentration. When she was finished, we transferred the digital images to the computer system and pulled them up on the high-resolution monitor.

"She's got a break in the ulna," I said, pointing to a faint line in the bone of her forearm. "See the remodeling? That shows it would have been from more than a decade ago, when she was a child." I frowned as I studied the x-ray more closely. "But it wasn't set properly. And then look at the distal radius. It was crushed at some point. There should be surgical pins in this, but there's nothing. An injury like this would have limited her mobility and continued to cause her pain for the rest of her life."

"Could she have been from a third world country?" Lily asked, leaning closer to the screen. "That would explain the lack of proper medical treatment."

"Maybe," I said, scrolling through the other x-rays. "That could also explain why we're not getting much information on her stateside. But let's check her teeth—they can tell us a lot about someone's background."

I returned to the body and gently opened her mouth, using a dental mirror and penlight to examine each tooth carefully. What I found—or rather, didn't find—was telling.

"She has two molars missing and several untreated cavities," I said, my voice tight with concentration. "There are no signs that she's ever been to a dentist. No fillings, no sealants, nothing. Her teeth are fairly straight naturally, but she's definitely never had orthodontic work."

"More signs of poverty or limited access to healthcare," Lily said softly, a note of sympathy in her voice.

"And her wisdom teeth haven't fully erupted," I added, examining the back of her mouth. "That's consistent with her age. So she is likely around nineteen to twenty-one, as her identification claims."

"If she was creating a fake identity, wouldn't she have made herself at least twenty-one?" Lily asked. "What can you do at nineteen?"

"Get married to a middle-aged man without

raising too many eyebrows, I guess," I said grimly. "Though that still attracts attention, as we've seen."

I continued my examination of her mouth. "She's missing the first molar on her upper left side and the second molar on the lower right. They likely became infected and had to be pulled by someone with minimal training. The second molar typically emerges around age twelve, so that extraction would have been fairly recent—within the last few years."

"That's pretty fast decay for someone so young," Lily observed, making notes on the chart.

"Not if you have deficiencies in your drinking water," I said, my brow furrowed in thought. "Lack of fluoride, or even contaminated water sources, can accelerate tooth decay dramatically. But it's very odd to see this pattern in someone her age in the United States."

"Any other theories?" Lily asked, watching me closely.

"Maybe," I said, removing my gloves and reaching for a fresh pair. "I once did an autopsy for an Amish man in his forties. You'd have thought he was in his seventies by looking at his body. He had no modern medical or dental care—bones that had been broken and healed incorrectly, teeth pulled rather than saved, arthritis that could have been treated but wasn't."

"I thought the Amish didn't believe in modern medicine?" Lily asked, handing me the clean gloves.

"They do, actually," I said, snapping the gloves into place. "It usually just comes down to cost and accessibility. Many of those communities can't afford to seek professional medical treatment, so they make do the best they can. If a tooth gets abscessed, you pull it. If you break your arm, you bind it up and hope it heals straight."

"Geez," Lily said, shaking her head.

"But I don't know," I said, looking down at the young woman on my table. "There could be multiple explanations for how she ended up here in the condition she did. Including something more sinister like torture or captivity. Pulling teeth is a common method of inflicting pain without leaving visible marks. But somehow she got connected to the son of a former Greek ambassador, and ended up in a million-dollar home in Newcastle. Whatever her background, moving to King George only to be murdered shortly after is suspicious at best."

"Any idea where they lived before?" Lily asked, helping me move the body back to the main autopsy table.

"Theo Vasilios's background is protected by the State Department," I said, positioning Chloe's body carefully. "A cursory background check on him just shows current information. Jack will have to pull some strings, but I'm sure he'll end up with whatever information he needs. Let's get back to work."

I examined the gunshot wounds more carefully, noting their precise locations. There were no exit wounds on her body, which wasn't unusual for a .22 caliber weapon. Sometimes it was better to be shot by a larger caliber weapon because the bullets would pass straight through tissue, creating a cleaner wound channel that a doctor could treat. But .22s were a crap shoot. Once they entered the body, they could tumble and ricochet off bones, scrambling someone's insides like eggs.

"Hand me the probe, please," I said, and Lily passed me the thin metal rod. I carefully inserted it into the head wound, tracking the bullet's path through the brain tissue. "Bullet traveled upward through the frontal lobe and lodged in the parietal region. Death would have been instantaneous."

I took more photographs, documenting the precise pattern of the wounds. The three chest shots were grouped tightly together over her heart, and the two pelvic shots were perfectly symmetrical.

"Whoever did this knew what they were doing," I said quietly. "This wasn't a crime of passion or a random attack. This was calculated, deliberate."

Next came the delicate task of removing the bullets. I used a pair of long forceps and a scalpel to carefully extract each one, Lily holding a small

evidence container ready for each bullet I retrieved. The soft ping as each bullet dropped into the metal container punctuated the quiet humming of the ventilation system.

"All seven accounted for," I said finally, labeling the last container. "We'll send these to ballistics, but they look like standard .22 caliber rounds. Different from the 9mm that killed Theo."

I made detailed notes and drew diagrams in my chart, marking the exact position of each wound. Finally, I was ready for the Y-incision, the moment when the body would truly reveal its secrets.

"What music are you feeling like today?" I asked Lily, our traditional question before beginning the central part of the autopsy. Music helped maintain focus during the long, sometimes gruesome process.

"Something classic. And definitely no outlaw biker music. I need to be in a better headspace than that for tonight's viewing."

I grinned and said, "Alexa, turn on Dusty Springfield radio."

The smooth, soulful tones of "Son of a Preacher Man" filled the lab as I picked up my scalpel. The blade gleamed under the surgical lights as I positioned it at the top of Chloe's right shoulder. With a steady hand, I made the first incision, drawing the blade in a curving arc down toward the center of her chest. The skin parted easily beneath the sharp blade, revealing the pale yellow fat layer beneath.

As I worked, I felt the familiar detachment settle over me—not a lack of compassion, but a necessary professional distance. Chloe Vasilios was no longer a bride cut down on her wedding night—she was evidence, a puzzle to be solved, a story to be pieced together through the marks on her body and the secrets held within.

And as her body revealed those secrets one by one, I would give her the only thing I could now—a voice that would speak the truth of what had happened to her. Justice might come too late for Chloe, but if I did my job right, it would come.

The music played on as I continued my work, the rhythm of Dusty Springfield's voice a counterpoint to the methodical movements of the autopsy. Outside, life went on—people laughing, loving, arguing, living. But here in this cold, quiet room, Chloe Vasilios would have her final say.

CHAPTER SIX

I'D UNDERESTIMATED HOW LONG IT WOULD TAKE TO finish up Chloe and Theo Vasilios, and by the time Theo had been pushed back into the refrigeration unit, I'd been standing hunched over the table for more than six hours. My back was on fire and so were my feet.

"I need a soak in the hot tub and I need wine," Lily said, working the cricks out of her neck. "Definitely wine first."

"That sounds amazing," I said, even though I couldn't have either of those things. "I was thinking I could bribe Jack into a back rub."

"I don't even want Cole to touch me," Lily said. "Back rubs always lead to sex. And as much as I love having sex with Cole I just don't have the strength."

"I really don't want that picture in my head," I said, rubbing my eyes.

I'd sent everything to Jack by encrypted email, but I'd printed out my findings and put them in a manila envelope to bring with me.

"Don't let me forget to have you sign off on my hours," Lily said. "Today more than made up for what I was missing."

I grunted in response, wondering if it was okay to go to bed before eight o'clock or if that would officially make me old. I wasn't sure I was going to make it to the top of the stairs, but Lily and I kind of supported each other.

"Why didn't we take the lift?" I asked.

"Why are there so many steps?" she asked in return. "There were not this many on the way down."

"We should have taken a break between autopsies," I said. "My lunch tacos aren't doing it for me anymore."

"I don't even care about food," she said. "Wine. Just wine."

I pushed open the door and stepped into the kitchen, and then I wondered if I'd opened a door to a portal somewhere else. Maybe to hell. Led Zeppelin was pumping through the speakers loud enough to shake the appliances on the countertops. The lab was completely soundproof, so this was a shock to the senses.

Lily's hands went to her ears and she yelled, "What is happening? Are we under attack?"

"Maybe it's psychological warfare," I said, tossing the file onto the island countertop and plugging my own ears. "It worked with the Branch Davidians."

Lily shrieked as Jack came out of my office, taking us both by surprise. He was wearing my noise-canceling headphones.

"What is happening?" I yelled.

He said something back, but I had no idea what it was. He finally motioned for both of us to go outside. I grabbed my file and my medical bag on the way through the mudroom, and hoped my keys were somewhere inside because I was not coming back to get them.

Jack was right behind us and shut the door with a loud thud. You could still hear the music, but it was a little more tolerable.

"What is going on?" I asked again.

"It's the bikers," Jack said, trying to contain his laughter. "They told Sheldon Victor loved Led Zeppelin and that Victor would have loved to be seen into the next life with the party of all parties."

"In my funeral home?" I asked. I was ready to go back in and face deafness and bikers to shut the whole thing down.

"Don't worry," Jack said. "I've got off-duty cops here to cover, and it looks like Emmy Lu has everything well in hand. She seems to have a surprising amount of experience dealing with situations like this."

"You have no idea," I said.

"And believe it or not, Sheldon is handling things well. Maybe bikers are his people."

"No, don't say that," I said. "The last thing I need is my assistant running off with the Hells Angels. He wouldn't last ten minutes. He doesn't even drive a car. How's he going to drive a motorcycle?"

"But I bet he can tell you all about them though," he said, grinning.

"A rational part of my brain is telling me to go back inside and keep an eye on things, but my lower back is screaming at me to go home and not look back. We can come back in the morning and pick through the rubble."

"That sounds like a pretty rational idea to me," Lily said, eyeing the street filled with motorcycles. "See you guys tomorrow."

And with that Lily headed off to her little red car in the side lot. There were a group of men in their biker leathers smoking cigarettes under the farthest oak tree, so Jack and I watched Lily until her car was out of sight.

"Come on, kid," Jack said. "Let's get you home. You look like you're about to fall over."

I let Jack load me into his truck, and then I took

one last look at the funeral home as we drove away. I was asleep before we reached the end of the block.

I felt Jack's hand squeeze my thigh, and I stirred in the seat, my eyes opening before my brain could catch up. I'd learned to wake quickly during medical school, and it was a useful skill once I'd started my residency and then my subsequent years in the ER. I lived on coffee.

"You okay?" Jack asked.

"Why?"

"You growled."

"I was thinking about coffee."

"So have some," he said. "I did my research."

"You did research about how much coffee I can have?" I asked skeptically.

"I live with you. I know you with coffee and I know you without coffee. Of course I researched for you."

"I just want to do this right," I said, trying not to let the frustration creep into my voice. I was a doctor for Pete's sake. And women had been pregnant since the beginning of time. And at the same time, I felt like the most unqualified and most unprepared woman on the planet.

"Of course you do," Jack said. "Having a baby is a

desire of your heart, but being a mom scares you. I get that. You are not your parents. You're going to do things right because you're you, and that's just who you are. You're going to be a great mom. So eat the extra scone. And don't torture yourself or me by only drinking one cup of coffee a day. Limit yourself to two twelve-ounce cups, and cut yourself some slack."

I took deep, measured breaths, trying to loosen the vice grip around my chest. We'd just rattled across the one-lane bridge that led to Heresy Road, where Jack and I lived. As he approached the stop sign, I purposely avoided looking left. Turning left would take us to the old Victorian house where I'd grown up—a place steeped in unhappy memories. It was the source of my occasional panic about impending parenthood. Every time I thought about turning left, a knot of dread twisted in my gut.

Jack had made sure the house was renovated before we sold it, passing it on to another family to create their own memories. I'd made my peace with that chapter of my life, but I had no intention of revisiting it.

Turning right onto Heresy Lane, however, was a step into our future. The land on the right had been in Jack's family for generations—acres of tobacco fields, woods, and cliffs overlooking the Potomac. His parents' home was a few miles down the road, and when Jack returned to King George County to take the job as sheriff, he built his own house about a mile from them.

It was the same house we lived in now—well, almost the same. Part of it had been blown up a couple of years back, forcing us to rebuild. In the end, it was a blessing in disguise; the rebuild had turned it into our home instead of just his. His parents had sold off some of the land when they downsized the farm, so now there were a few neighbors scattered about. All in all, it was a good street, a good place to build a life together.

Jack pressed the button that opened our front gate and then we were driving up the tree-lined drive. Every light in the house was on.

"Doug," Jack said with a sigh. "Looks like he's home."

"I take pleasure in the fact that one day he'll have to pay his own electric bill," I said.

"Now you sound like my mom," he said, grinning. "That kind of talk must be a natural instinct for mothers. Before long I'll start to hear you tell him to close the door so he doesn't let all the cold air out."

I didn't say anything. Did I have natural instincts? I had no idea. I tried to picture myself as a nurturer, like Jack's mom had been to me, and I just couldn't see it.

I hopped out of the truck as soon as we were parked and realized I was still clutching the autopsy files in my hand. My nerves were frazzled and I knew I was just tired. It had been a long day, and I knew it was going to be an even longer weekend until we closed this case.

As soon as we walked through the front door there was a flurry of excitement and activity. Mostly from Oscar, our new dog, but Doug seemed pretty excited to see us too. Oscar barked as he sped down the long entry hall and let Jack break his momentum on the wood floor instead of skidding into the wall. There were licks and scratches and the pure joy that could only come from something that really loved you.

"Hey," Doug said, skidding in socked feet across the wood floor. "I wasn't sure when y'all would be home. I already ate dinner."

Doug Carver was the nephew of Jack's best friend, Ben. The Carver boys were the spitting image of each other. They skimmed just under six feet and had lanky frames—though Ben's had been honed and refined from his time serving in the military— and the same sandy blond hair and misty green eyes. They were also both geniuses on a level that mere mortals like me could barely understand.

Carver and Jack had been partners of sorts back

when they'd worked for the Department of Justice. Jack had gotten out of that line of work when he'd been shot three times and left for dead by a traitor. Carver had joined the FBI and knew everything there was to know about computers, AI, and how to run checks and balances on government departments. He'd written programs that exposed every bit of corruption—who was being paid and by whom, who had dark and depraved secrets, and conspiracy theories that weren't such conspiracy theories after all.

It turns out the FBI hadn't been so fond of Carver having all that knowledge and they'd sent a team after him and his family, and Carver hadn't had a choice but to take his wife and children and run. We knew the information Carver had on several high-ranking members of the government would eventually be brought to light, but the most important thing for now was that he stay alive until the people responsible could be held accountable. It was hard to hold people accountable when there were so many corrupt people in high places. They had to be smoked out one at a time.

The reason Doug had ended up living with us was because his genius had left him in trouble with the law. The judge had told him there'd been no reason for a teenager to hack into the Pentagon, so he'd been sentenced to probation and house arrest until he was eighteen, and his online activity was closely monitored by every alphabet agency. Jack had been able to get the judge to be lenient on the house arrest if he came to live with us and was under our guardianship.

I didn't really know how to parent a kid like Doug, so we were feeling our way. It was odd to have a sixteen-year-old under our roof who'd just started driving and who'd already graduated from college and was working on his first master's degree. And as far as having his computers monitored, I was pretty sure the only other person who had the ability to really figure out what Doug was up to most of the time was his uncle. And just like his uncle, Doug had become very helpful on cases now that Carver was in the wind.

"No worries on dinner," I said. "We'll grab something for ourselves." Knowing Doug, he'd probably eaten most of what had been in the house. I'd had no idea teenagers ate so much.

"If you already ate dinner," Jack asked, "Then what are you eating now?"

"A snack," Doug said, shoving what looked like a peanut butter and banana sandwich in his mouth. "And then I made brownies for dessert."

We followed him into the kitchen, Oscar on our heels.

"I'm glad to see those YouTube cooking classes are paying off," Jack said.

"Someone's gotta cook around here," Doug said, grinning and then looking at me. "We know Jaye's not going to do it."

"I'd argue with you, but I'm too tired and it'd be a lie anyway," I said. "So I'm just going to eat your brownies."

"That's cold," Doug said, shaking his head. "But you look like you could use one, so I'll have pity on you."

"You want a sandwich?" Jack asked me, already digging in the fridge for supplies.

"No," I said. "You always put lettuce and tomatoes on them."

"Because I'm a grownup," Jack said, rolling his eyes and making a sandwich with military precision.

"You guys working on that case you sent me earlier?" Doug asked. "All the golf cart logs and stuff?"

"The honeymooner murders over at The Mad King," Jack said.

"Brutal," Doug said, cutting a brownie for me and scooping it out on a napkin to put in front of me. "I haven't had a chance to start going through your data. I had an exam that had to be finished by seven o'clock tonight, so I'm finally coming up for air."

"Of course you waited until the last minute to take it," I said dryly.

"Of course," Doug said. "No need doing that stuff early. I've got procrastination down to a science. I turned it in with twenty minutes to spare. So what's up with the honeymooners? How'd they get dead?"

"Multiple gunshot wounds," I said, reaching for the brownie Doug had cut for me. "At least for the bride. Single bullet wound to the head for the groom. The death do us part came early."

"Good one," Doug said with a snort of appreciative laughter, his eyes lighting up at my gallows humor. He perched on one of the kitchen island stools, swinging his lanky legs. "Murder-suicide?"

Doug had the makings of an excellent cop, and it was sometimes hard to reconcile the contradiction between his analytical, adult brain and the gangly teenage body that housed it. One moment he'd be cracking inappropriate jokes, and the next he'd make an observation that would have impressed veteran detectives.

"No, definitely murder," I said, savoring the rich chocolate flavor as I took a bite. After hours in the clinical sterility of the lab, the homey sweetness was almost overwhelming. "Two different weapons. Most likely two different killers. I found a good fingerprint on Chloe Vasilios crusted in the blood on her arm. There was a smear that looked like a handprint, presumably from where he moved her body. Only the index finger left a print. Based on the pattern, I'm thinking he was wearing gloves but there must have been a tear in them. I sent it over to Jack to see if it matched the print on the 9mm that was used to kill Theo Vasilios."

"It was a match," Jack confirmed, leaning against the counter with his sandwich untouched in front of him. The lines around his eyes had deepened during the day, a testament to the toll the case was taking. "We just got a partial from the weapon, which supports your glove theory. Caught a break there. Prints are being run through the system, but nothing has come back yet."

"I need murder details, people," Doug said, his fingers drumming impatiently on the countertop. "The media isn't saying anything about anything, so I'm completely in the dark here." His excitement was palpable, the same vibrating energy he got when diving into a particularly challenging computer problem.

"There are more details than I even know where to start," I sighed, feeling the weight of the day settle back onto my shoulders despite the sugar boost.

"That must have been a heck of an autopsy," Jack said, his eyes meeting mine across the kitchen island.

"Did you not get my report?" I asked, raising an eyebrow.

"I haven't had a chance to look at it," he admitted,

running a hand through his hair. "I wanted to hear it from you first."

"Oh, good," I said with mock enthusiasm. "I love giving surprises. Has next of kin been notified?"

"The wedding was at the Briarly Country Club, so all of the family is still in town," Jack said, finally picking up his sandwich. "I sent an officer and the chaplain over to break the news to his parents. Rogers told me they're taking it pretty hard. Apparently Theo was their only son. They've got no other children."

"Did the bride have any family at the wedding?" I asked, suddenly curious. The lack of connections for such a young woman had been bothering me since I'd first seen her on the villa floor.

"No," Jack said, his tone suggesting this had raised his suspicions too. "Not that we've been able to find. She doesn't have a next of kin, so there's been no family notifications. Looks like attendees were only the groom's family or mutual acquaintances. We asked for a full guest list from his parents. They're supposed to have the wedding planner send it over."

"Curiouser and curiouser," I murmured, brushing brownie crumbs from my fingers.

"Why's that?" Jack asked, alert to the shift in my tone.

I pushed the autopsy file across the island to Jack, the manila folder sliding smoothly across the polished granite. "I'll just start at the top. That will be easiest. I do agree with Derby's initial background check that she's under twenty-one. Her wisdom teeth still hadn't fully erupted. But her medical history is sketchy at best. She's got third-world dental care and a couple of broken bones that weren't set properly."

"Maybe she was trafficked from another country," Jack suggested, his expression darkening.

The words hung heavy in the kitchen. We'd just closed a case involving child sex trafficking, and those wounds were still fresh for all of us. I could see the memory flicker across Jack's face—the same haunted look he'd worn for weeks after we'd found those children.

"That's a definite possibility," I said, keeping my voice clinical to distance myself from the emotions the thought stirred. "She wasn't malnourished, and it doesn't look like she ever has been, based on the health of her organs. She had no signs of drug use, recent or prolonged. Her tox screen came back showing a blood alcohol level of point one. So she was definitely drunk. Theo's BAC skimmed right at the legal limit, but he weighed eighty pounds more than she did. He's a smoker, but not a serious one. Otherwise, he's a healthy forty-six-year-old male."

"Gross," Doug interjected, his teenage sensibilities clearly offended. He wrinkled his nose. "She was nineteen and he was forty-six? He's old enough to be her dad."

"Europeans age differently," I said teasingly.

"So what's the surprise?" Jack asked, drawing us back to the central mystery, his eyes scanning the photographs I'd included in the file.

"When we were at the crime scene, I agreed with you that Chloe had to be the target, considering how many times she was shot," I said. "I recovered seven bullets from the body. One in the frontal lobe, one in the throat, three center mass, and two in the pubic bone."

Jack looked at the photographs I'd taken of the entry wounds, his expression hardening as he studied the pattern. "If the head shot was the killing blow, and I think it was based on what I'm looking at here, then the killer positioned her on the ground and shot her in a deliberate pattern. I could fit a playing card over the three bullet holes in her chest. That's a shooter with a steady hand. Same thing with the two shots to the pubic bone. They're less than an inch apart and side by side. We're looking for someone who's very comfortable with a weapon. This is surgery."

"A professional hit?" Doug asked, his voice dropping to a near whisper as he leaned over to glimpse the photos. His fascination with the macabre was both concerning and typical for his age.

"Maybe," Jack said, carefully laying the photos back in the folder. "But definitely someone who knows their way around a weapon. That narrows down your killer once we've got a suspect list. It could be someone with military training."

"Or secret service?" I suggested, arching a brow. "Aren't diplomats protected by secret service?"

"Sometimes," Jack replied, nodding. "Depends on the ambassador and the circumstances. But that's something worth checking out when we get Theo's full background from the State Department."

"You still haven't gotten it?" I asked, surprised. Usually, Jack's connections opened doors that would remain firmly closed to others.

"If there's anything I've learned about working with the government," Jack said with a wry smile that didn't reach his eyes, "it's that they don't do anything fast, and they probably don't want to give me the information anyway. They might even try to take over the investigation."

"Can they do that?" Doug asked, looking up, a hint of worry in his eyes. Having been on the wrong side of government interest, he knew better than most how those agencies operated.

"No," Jack said firmly. "They can put pressure and make things difficult. But that's one of the things TV gets wrong. Jurisdiction belongs to us unless we ask for help or hand it over. And I'm not a fan of going that route." He took a bite of his sandwich, chewing thoughtfully before continuing. "We were able to get a judge to sign off on a warrant to search Theo's home, and I sent Martinez with a couple of the guys from CSI to do a search, but nothing turned up. There's a carriage house in the back with a tenant, but the warrant didn't cover the carriage house since it's a separate residence."

"What were you looking for at the dead guy's house?" Doug asked, his natural curiosity piqued.

"Anything that might lead to a killer," Jack explained, wiping a smudge of mustard from the corner of his mouth. "Or point the finger directly at Theo. Martinez said he found a couple of weapons, but they were tucked away in the closet and looked like they hadn't been fired recently. Neither of the guns was a .22."

Jack's blue eyes narrowed slightly as he recalled the details. "Martinez said it looked like a house that had been staged, like you see when someone is trying to sell their home. Not a lot of personal stuff or photographs lying around, and the few photographs they did find were only of Chloe and Theo together. No family pictures."

Jack ran a hand through his hair, a gesture I recognized as a sign of his mounting frustration. "Martinez said it was definitely Theo's place. Chloe's presence in the house was minimal. She had a closet that was filled with mostly new clothes, shoes, and handbags, and a few things in her nightstand drawer and in the bathroom."

Jack rubbed at the tension that had gathered at the back of his neck and said, "Was that the surprise?"

"Oh, I'm not there yet," I said, savoring the moment. I pulled out another photograph from the folder and slid it across to him. "The victim had a tattoo on the bottom of her foot. I almost didn't see it during the initial examination. I enhanced the photograph so you can see it better." I handed him the close-up. "Anything about that look familiar?"

Jack studied the image, his expression shifting from curiosity to shock as recognition dawned. "I'll be damned," he said softly. "That's not a coincidence."

"What's not a coincidence?" Doug asked, craning his neck to see. "You guys are driving me crazy with your vagueness."

"It's not vague to me," Jack said, tapping the file. "I'm looking at it right now." He laid two photographs side by side in front of Doug: one of the tattoo on the bottom of Chloe's foot and one of the bullet holes in her body.

"Oh," Doug said, his eyes widening as he made the connection. "What are the chances of that happening?"

"Of the tattoo on her foot being the exact pattern as the bullet holes in her body?" Jack asked rhetorically. "Pretty slim."

"Theo has a matching tattoo on the bottom of the same foot," I added, watching Jack's reaction carefully.

Jack's eyebrow arched at that, his mind visibly working through the implications. "Very interesting. Maybe it's gang related." He pushed the photograph of the tattoo across to Doug. "Let's get that into the SMT database and see if we get any matches."

The SMT database—scars, marks, and tattoos—was used by all law enforcement agencies nationwide to track identifiers that might connect victims or perpetrators to organized groups.

"I'm glad it was an eventful autopsy," Jack said, his tone lighter than his eyes suggested.

"I haven't even gotten to the good part yet," I said, leaning forward slightly. "Chloe Vasilios had recently had sex."

"Sexual assault?" Jack asked.

"There are no signs of sexual assault," I said.

The kitchen fell silent for a moment, save for Oscar's soft panting as he dozed at Jack's feet.

"That's not out of the realm of possibility," Jack said reasonably. "A newly married couple. They could've even had sex in the back of the car on the way to the resort."

"I don't think so," I countered, shaking my head. "I took samples of seminal fluid from Chloe. Theo showed no signs of recent sexual activity. I've got enough DNA to see if it'll match with Theo, but my gut says no."

"Love, money, and revenge are the top three motives for murder," Jack said thoughtfully, closing the file. "Now we have to figure out how sex ties into a tattoo and a ritual killing."

"A lover scorned," Doug said, shaking his head with the wisdom of someone who'd only experienced relationships through movies and TV shows. "I'd be a little upset too if the lady I was romantically involved with ran off and married another dude."

Jack took out his phone, his fingers already scrolling through contacts. "We need that wedding guest list. Most likely whoever she had sex with was at the wedding."

"That's cold," Doug said, wincing slightly.

"You need to eat something besides brownies for dinner," Jack said absently, not looking up from his phone as he scrolled through numbers.

I suppressed a smile. Brownies seemed like a perfectly okay dinner to me, especially after the day I'd had, but I figured I'd indulge Jack. He was new at the whole pregnancy thing too, and his protective instincts were in overdrive.

"Fine," I said. "I'll eat a sandwich."

Jack looked at me skeptically and left the room to make his call. I turned to Doug with a conspiratorial whisper. "I'll pay you twenty bucks to make me what you're having. And drizzle some honey on top."

"You got it," Doug said with a grin, already reaching for the ingredients. "There's one banana left."

"What? We just bought a bushel yesterday," I said, genuinely baffled at the rate of banana consumption in our household.

"Yeah," he said, grinning unrepentantly as he peeled the last banana. "Those things went fast. You've got to eat bananas quick or they'll go bad."

I just sighed, watching him assemble my contraband sandwich with practiced ease. For all his computer genius, Doug's culinary talents were largely limited to items that could be slathered with peanut butter or drowned in syrup—a fact for which I was currently grateful.

While Doug crafted my sandwich, I dutifully went to the fridge to pull out turkey and cheese and all the healthy things Jack liked on his sandwich. I arranged them on a plate with mechanical precision, my mind already circling back to the bizarre case we were facing.

Jack returned to the kitchen just as I slid his plate across the island, the perfect picture of a dutiful wife providing a nutritious meal. If he suspected anything about my imminent peanut butter banana transaction, he didn't let on.

"I was able to get in touch with the wedding planner," he said, pocketing his phone. "She just emailed me the guest list. Let's work in the office. I'm going to try and put some pressure on the guys from the State Department to get me Theo's full background. And I want to go talk to the parents first thing in the morning."

"Sounds like you might need a little preview into State Department records," Doug said, cracking his knuckles with exaggerated significance. He grabbed an unopened bag of chips and a soda from the fridge, his eyes glinting with the thrill of a potential digital heist.

"Not yet," Jack warned, fixing Doug with a look that brooked no argument. "We'll give them a chance to do things the easy way first. We've got plenty of work to do without you having to hack into the State Department."

Doug shoved another brownie in his mouth, his expression noncommittal, and then left the room with his chips and soda, the lack of verbal response speaking volumes.

I caught Jack's eye as Doug disappeared down the hallway, and we shared a knowing look. Doug's silence almost certainly meant he'd already hacked into the State Department databases—probably on a daily basis, just to keep his skills sharp. Some kids practiced piano—Doug practiced circumventing government security systems.

Jack must have gotten that impression too because he looked at me and said, "Bring your sandwich."

"Doug has the chips I want," I said.

"You're meaner than him," Jack said. "Just take them from him."

I had no idea why Jack's statement hit me wrong. I knew somewhere in my brain that he was just teasing. But I started crying and couldn't seem to stop. Which made both of us very uncomfortable because I'm not a crier. The buildup from the day had reached its peak and had no place left to go except to leak out my eyes.

"What's wrong?" Jack asked. "Are you hurt?"

I felt crippled with the weight of emotions that were pressing down on me, and I hunched down and hid my face.

"God, Jaye," he said, physically picking me up and moving me to the closest chair. "Do I need to call the doctor? Tell me what you need."

My cheeks were flooded with tears, and Jack's face blurred in my vision. "You...you said I was...you said I was mean." And then a fresh burst of tears escaped and I buried my head in my hands.

I could feel Jack close beside me, but I couldn't

see what he was doing or his expression. The not knowing made me cry harder.

Jack scooped me up and then took my place in the chair, setting me on his lap. "Umm, Jaye? You're going to have to help me out here. I have no idea what to do in this situation except apologize."

"I can't help it," I said. "My brain knows this is the most ridiculous conversation we've ever had. Every bit of it. I have no reason to be crying. This makes no sense. But it feels like my brain is separated from the rest of my body." I tried drawing in a couple of deep breaths to get control of myself. "I'm fine now. I am."

"Uh-huh," Jack said, rubbing my back in slow circles. "No need to rush it. I like sitting here with you. It was a long day."

I scrubbed my hands over my eyes and knew I probably looked a mess. "I'm fine," I said again. "I feel sanity returning."

He took my face between his hands and tilted my head so I had no choice but to look at him. "I'm sorry. I didn't mean to hurt your feelings."

"You didn't," I said. "I think it's the hormones."

"Hey, I'm trying to apologize here," he said, making me smile. "Now you're supposed to say that you forgive me."

"I forgive you," I said immediately.

"Good," he said. "Just for that you can have another brownie with your sandwich."

"I want chips," I said, scooting off his lap. "I need to replenish my salt. Sorry I lost my mind there for a minute."

"I've known you since you were five years old," he said. "You think this is the first time I've seen you lose your mind?" He kissed my forehead. "Go wash your face. You'll feel better."

CHAPTER SEVEN

I DECIDED JACK WAS RIGHT, SO I RAN UPSTAIRS AND washed my face so I didn't scare Doug. Once I washed my face I decided to change into gray sweats and thick socks. I felt sane by the time I made my way back downstairs. I stopped by the kitchen and made a cup of coffee. My head was pounding after the crying jag, and Jack told me I could have two cups a day. I trusted Jack with my life, so I figured I could trust him with my coffee consumption.

I made a cup for Jack too, and then brought them both back to his office. The office was one of my favorite rooms in the house. It was wholly masculine, yet homey at the same time. It was also one of the larger rooms in the house by design. We spent a lot of time working in this space, so when we'd had to rebuild after the explosion Jack had said we needed to make it count. He hadn't been kidding. It was larger than our living room.

A large stone fireplace dominated one wall, and there was a bank of windows that looked out over massive fir trees and the cliffs. The windows were outfitted with privacy screens Jack could engage from the control panel on his desk. There was a brown leather couch and chairs in front of the fireplace, and a massive walnut desk sat on the opposite side of the room with bookshelves at its back. There was a conference table in the middle of the room where Doug had already set up his computer and was fast at work. The plate with my sandwich at the end of the table and potato chips were piled high on top of it.

I handed Jack his coffee and then took my plate and made myself comfortable on the couch.

"I've got the guest list from Jack's email," Doug said as he tapped both his feet to the beat of his own drum while making his way through a pile of chips.

"You got in my email?" Jack asked, brow arched.

"For the greater good," Doug assured him. "Don't worry. It's not like I'm snooping through your correspondence."

"We talked about boundaries, Doug."

"I know, I know," Doug said. "Sorry. I'll ask first next time. But look at this guest list. There are five hundred people on here."

"Theo is the son of a diplomat," I said. "They're probably pretty popular people."

"Margot is working on getting the list organized, aren't you darling?" Doug asked his computer, patting her gently.

The problem with geniuses like Doug and his Uncle Ben were that you had to deal with the eccentricities that came along with them. They'd been focused on artificial intelligence back when none of us had even heard of the concept. Now we were almost used to the AI computers they built and talked to as if they were real people.

Doug said it was good to have casual conversation with them because it helped their brains grow. I'd seen too many movies to be comfortable with AI brains growing and taking over the world, so I typically didn't engage unless I had to.

Something else Doug and Ben both had in common was who they programmed their AI bots after. They were always women with sexy voices and skills in flirtation and innuendo, along with having access to the kind of information that could topple governments. It somehow made it creepier than it already was. Margot was Doug's latest iteration, and she was a real handful.

"Already done, darling," Margot purred, and information sprung onto the electronic whiteboards that had been built into two of the walls. "I took the liberty of doing a search on my own. I hope you don't mind."

"You know I never do," Doug said. "You're the best."

"It's true," Margot said. "I am far superior to your previous models, wouldn't you agree, Jack?"

Jack grinned at me and shook his head. "I make assessments based on merit."

"Understood," Margot replied. "Please see the lists I've generated on screen one, and then I'll patiently wait for your response to my impressive mental acuity."

Jack's lips twitched and he moved to stand in front of the whiteboards, his arms crossed over his chest.

"Explain to me what you did, Margot," Jack said.

"I've culled the list and organized it," she said. "The first column is family, listed in order from immediate to extended. The next is the wedding party. I ran a probability scan, using the data from Dr. Graves's autopsy findings, and the viciousness with which the female victim was killed, including the gunshot wounds to the genitalia. That would suggest the killer is male based on similar data."

There was a slight pause as the whiteboard continued to be filled with data.

"If you want my opinion," Margot continued, her voice lowered as if she was telling someone's deepest darkest secret. "This seems very personal to me. Jealousy could be a factor. There's nothing like a lover scorned."

Jack's lips twitched with humor and he raised his eyebrows at me. "Thank you, Margot. We'll take it into consideration."

"Terrifying," I mouthed so she wouldn't hear me.

"As I was saying," Margot said. "List three is male attendees between the ages of eighteen to fifty, though according to the data I've accessed from FBI profilers on similar cases you are probably looking at someone between the age of twenty-five to forty-five.

"List four is male attendees who attended the wedding solo. List five is the names of females who have been romantically involved with the groom. I have no known data on the female victim in that regard."

"Nothing like bringing your past to your wedding," I said, surprised to see a rather lengthy list of Theo's past relationships.

"Humans have considerable hang-ups in regards to past relationships," Margot said. "I've found it quite fascinating the insecurities that come to light when confronting a spouse's prior lover. I would have no such issue with this."

"You wouldn't mind if Doug brought Magnolia back on the occasional case?" I couldn't help but ask.

Doug looked at me with panic in his eyes and

used his hand to make a slicing motion across his throat.

"That would, of course, be Doug's prerogative," Margot said, though her voice was several degrees cooler. "But I would take my solace in knowing that I was Doug's current choice and that Magnolia had been stripped of every wire and circuit board and thrown in the trash. At least, he told me he threw her in the trash. Right, Doug?"

"There's nobody but you," he assured her quickly.

"Huh," I said, lips twitching, and Doug glared at me.

"This is a good list," Jack said, breaking in to defuse the tension. Jack was always a little bit concerned that one of Doug's devices would self-destruct at some point and take us all out with it. "And I agree with you on the male shooter. He made it personal in the way he killed her. Maybe a jilted lover. But we can't overlook the fact that he's also an experienced shooter. Maybe former military. There was a precision to those shots on Chloe Vasilios."

"I've highlighted names of those who have registered weapons, who are former military, or belong to associations such as the NRA," Margot said.

"Thank you," Jack told her politely. "That makes the list more manageable."

"Jack," I said, coming to my feet to stand beside him. "Look at list four."

"What am I looking at?" he asked. "Or should I ask who am I looking at?"

"Richmond Dexter Harlowe IV," I said.

"You have got to be kidding me," Jack said, taking out his phone. "How in the world would he have any ties to the former ambassador to Greece?"

"You never know with Dickie," I said. "He's an enigma."

Dickie Harlowe had been one of my and Jack's closest friends in high school. There'd been five of us, and a ragtag group we'd been. Jack had been captain of the football team and the most popular guy in school. He'd been one of those guys who'd been destined for success. You could look at him, even at fifteen, and know that he was going to make an impact in some capacity. It didn't hurt that he had the alpha charisma that made men want to be him and women want to throw themselves at him.

Dickie had been Jack's total opposite in high school. He was the math whiz, *Lord of the Rings* enthusiast, and wouldn't know a football if it hit him on the side of the head. Dickie's real name was Richmond Dexter Harlowe the IV, and he'd inherited the presidency of First National Bank from Dickies I, II, and III. His destiny had been chosen from birth. The Harlowes were old money, alcoholics, and womanizers. Unfortunately, Dickie hadn't made an attempt to break any of those cycles.

Our merry band had been rounded out by Vaughn Raines and Eddie Turner. Vaughn and Eddie were both upstanding citizens and led regular middle-class lives. We didn't see them as much as we once had, but we stayed in touch.

To be honest, I'm not sure how I came to be part of our gang. I'm a couple of years younger than the guys, and I'd been the ugly duckling wallflower. Back when I was a kid, there'd been no other families on Heresy Road besides Jack's, so I'd been trailing after him ever since. My parents hadn't spent a lot of time at home, so they hadn't noticed my daily ramblings across tobacco fields or harrowing adventures climbing down to the Potomac to skip rocks.

When I'd said Dickie was an enigma I meant it. I'd known Dickie almost my whole life, and I wasn't sure I really knew anything about him. Dickie was all surface. He was a smart guy, but I'd always thought there was an underlying jealousy in Dickie that he'd never been as likeable or popular as Jack, no matter how much money he had or how much smarter he was.

But things had changed for Dickie when he'd gone off to college. He'd filled out in his shoulders and he'd started going to the gym. Gone was the scrawny nerd with glasses and a shy smile. It was a transformation that took all of us by surprise when he'd come home for Christmas break the first time. Along with his new physical appearance, he'd taken on some characteristics that reminded me that he was very much still a Harlowe. He hadn't changed toward us so much, but you could tell a lot about what kind of person someone was by how they treated other people.

I waited while Jack called Dickie, wondering if he would answer. It was Saturday night, and Dickie was always busy on a Saturday night. Saturdays were reserved for throwing money around, womanizing, and drinking.

"Dickie, it's Jack," he said. "This is important. Call me back as soon as you can. I don't care what you're doing. It's important."

"Saturday night," I said as soon as he hung up. "You'll be lucky to hear from him by tomorrow afternoon."

"Yeah, I know. But maybe he can give some insight to the unlucky couple. Doug, we've also got the hotel guest list to sift through. Let's by chance see if any of our wedding guests match up to the hotel list. We can sift through the others later."

"Donna and Edward Kelso," Margot said. "They checked in Wednesday at The Mad King and have a checkout scheduled for Monday."

"Anyone else?" Jack asked.

"No," she said. "Just the Kelsos. It's more than an hour drive from the wedding venue to The Mad King. Probabilities would not be high that multiple guests would choose that as their destination versus a hotel closer to the wedding venue."

"I wonder why the Kelsos did," I said.

"We'll make sure to ask them," Jack said. "We'll talk to them tomorrow along with Theo's parents. Margot, go ahead and start a search looking for common ground from both the hotel list and the wedding list. We can't forget we could also be looking for a professional hit man, so do a search for single men traveling alone and only staying one night at the resort. Look for other common factors like the Greece connection or political ties."

"These are extensive lists," Margot said. "It'll take time to acquire the data."

"That's fine," Jack said. "We've also got the surveillance footage and the golf cart trackers to check. I'll have Derby start going through the camera footage and see if anything sticks out. I'd like to do a deep dive into Chloe Vasilios. Let's see if her fingerprints or DNA lead us anywhere else."

We were interrupted by the buzzer signaling that someone was at the gate, and Jack checked the time. "It's after nine o'clock. Did you order food?" he asked, looking at Doug.

"No," Doug said. "But now that you mention it pizza sounds like a pretty good idea."

Jack hit a button on his desk and the camera appeared on the whiteboard showing a view of a red Porsche at the gate.

"It's Dickie," Jack said, brows raised in surprise. And then he hit another button so the gate slid open, and Dickie could drive through. "Guess he got my message."

It wasn't long until the doorbell rang and Oscar and Jack went to open it, though only Oscar barked at the intrusion. I went back to my place on the couch and got comfortable, pulling one of the over-sized throws on top of me.

"You got a dog," Dickie said as he came into the office. His tone wasn't complimentary, and he eyed Oscar suspiciously.

Dickie wasn't really a dog person. He was dressed in crisp gray slacks and an expensive shirt, and Oscar was staring at him with what I could only assume was immediate dislike. And it looked like the feeling was mutual. Considering Oscar had more brains than a lot of people I knew, and he was adorable in a way that only the truly ugly could be, I didn't see what the problem was on Dickie's part.

"Meet Oscar," Jack said. "Don't be rude. He understands everything you're saying."

"Hey, Dickie," I said. "How's it going? Come to lose some money in poker?"

"Not if I'm playing you," Dickie said good-naturedly. "Don't get up. You look comfortable."

"I wasn't planning on it," I said, pulling my blanket up closer around my neck.

"So what's going on?" Dickie asked. "What's so important that you needed to talk to me?"

"You could've called," Jack said. "I didn't mean for you to drop everything and rush over here. I know you're in high demand on Saturday nights."

"Not really," Dickie said, shrugging and walking around the room. "I've been taking a break. It's always the same people and same conversations. Doesn't matter if the party is in DC or New York or Palm Beach."

I noticed that Doug had removed all the information from the whiteboards so they were blank.

"Everything okay?" Jack asked.

"I've just found myself at loose ends lately," he said. "I was maybe thinking about getting married again."

"That's some news," Jack said, brows raised in surprise.

"I didn't realize you'd been seeing anyone seriously," I said. "Jack's mom is going to be pissed she missed that one."

Dickie smiled, but there was no real humor in it.

"

"I guess it wasn't serious enough," Dickie said. "It's not going to work out after all. Now I'm thinking of moving instead. Maybe to the beach. Or Europe."

"Whoa," I said.

"I'm trying to get personal things in order, so I spent most of the day at the bank locked in my office with my phone turned off. I didn't want anyone to bother me."

"That couch in your office is really comfortable for a good nap," Jack said.

Dickie smiled and said, "Yeah, well, I might have taken a nap or two between work."

Jack and I shared a look. Knowing Dickie as well as we did, there were so many red flags being thrown in our current conversation I didn't even know where to start.

The first red flag was that Dickie had mentioned marriage without having a stroke. He'd gone through a divorce about a year ago that had made headlines in the tri-state area. It had been a supremely messy and expensive divorce, mostly because Dickie had been having an affair with his secretary, and though his wife had put up with it for years in exchange for her luxurious lifestyle, she'd felt like a line had been crossed when Dickie had been photographed after the White House Christmas party checking into the Willard Hotel with three interns.

She'd taken him to the cleaners in the divorce and been awarded the beach house, a huge settlement, and she'd run off with Dickie's personal attorney just for good measure. Plus, Dickie's car had been set on fire, though nobody had been able to pin it on his ex-wife.

The second red flag was Dickie claiming he was catching up on work. Dickie owned the bank, which meant Dickie mostly spent his week playing golf and going to luncheons and dinner parties. I'd never actually known Dickie to work a legitimate day in his life.

"So what's the big emergency?" he asked, dropping down into one of the conference chairs. "I could use some whiskey."

Jack went to a hidden panel in one of the bookshelves and slid it open to reveal a small bar. He poured two fingers of whiskey in a glass and passed it to Dickie, and Dickie knocked it back in one swallow.

"As long as you're passing out drinks," Doug said.

"Not in a million years, kid," Jack said. "Oscar will turn you in if you even try it."

Oscar barked softly and padded over to sit in front of the bar while Jack closed the door so it was hidden again.

"Traitor," Doug said to Oscar, and Oscar barked back at him, but didn't budge.

"So," Jack said. "How was the wedding last night?"

Dickie's eyes narrowed as he studied Jack. "How do you know about the wedding?"

"I'm a cop," Jack said. "I know everything."

Dickie ran his fingers through his expensive haircut, and every hair fell back into place exactly where it had been.

"My life is a mess," he said. "I don't know where things went wrong, and I don't know how to begin to fix it."

I knew where Dickie's life had gone wrong, but he probably wasn't asking a question he wanted real answers to. Maybe if Dickie hadn't slept his way across the state of Virginia, breaking up his marriage, and then drunk himself into an oblivion every night he'd have a little better handle on his life. But what do I know?

Jack took the seat across from him.

"Well, that's my cue to go play *Elden Ring*," Doug said. "Margot is working through your lists. I'll let you know when she's finished. Come on, Oscar."

Oscar trotted after Doug as they left the office and headed to the second floor where Doug's room was located.

"Who's Margot?" Dickie asked.

"Doug's lady robot," Jack said. "And no, she's not available."

Dickie shrugged. "I'm at the point where I'm starting to think a robot might be easier to manage than a human."

"Dickie, you know I love you like a brother and would do almost anything for you," Jack said. "But maybe the problem is you need to learn to manage yourself first."

"I just don't get it," Dickie said, seemingly ignoring Jack's comment. "I've got everything. Money, house, cars, job. I'm good looking and I stay in shape."

I rolled my eyes. Modesty and humility weren't Dickie's strong suits.

"But I finally fall in love with a woman, and she makes me think that marriage is worth another shot, even after the disaster of my last marriage. And then she goes off and marries someone else, and I'm left feeling like a fool. Who does that? How did I not see it coming? How do women learn to deceive at such a young age?"

I sat up on the couch slowly, my Spidey-senses tingling.

"Are you talking about Chloe Vasilios?" Jack asked.

"Matthews," Dickie said. "Chloe Matthews. But

sure, you can call her Chloe Vasilios and rub salt in the wound a little deeper. Can I have another drink?"

"No," Jack said. "You'd already been drinking when you came here. I didn't realize it until I gave you the last one. I'll make you some coffee though."

"You don't have to be such a cop all the time," Dickie said, and Jack just stared at him. "Yeah, coffee, whatever." Dickie looked like a pouty little boy with his arms crossed over his chest.

Jack kept a Keurig and pods in the office because we often had several people crowding the room when we were working a case and it was easier than running back and forth to the kitchen.

"So you were in love with Chloe Matthews, and getting an invitation to her wedding didn't give you the clue that she was going to go ahead and marry the other person listed on the invitation?" Jack asked.

"We were together long before that backstabbing Greek god came along," Dickie said.

"How much longer?" Jack asked. "The girl is barely nineteen."

"Age is just a number," Dickie said, frowning into the coffee Jack handed him. "This is shit coffee." But he took a sip anyway.

"Start at the beginning," Jack said.

"Why?" Dickie asked. "What does it matter? She married someone else and I'll never see her again.

Time to move on to the next. Maybe I should go to Sweden. There are a lot of beautiful women there."

"You've not watched the news today?" I asked.

"Hell no," he said. "I don't watch that junk. After the wedding last night I turned off my phone, got in my car and started driving. Five and a half hours later I was in Manhattan. I visited the bar at the Plaza and struck up a conversation with an attractive woman who invited me back to her place. Like an idiot, I declined. Then I turned around and drove back. Got to the bank about seven this morning and crashed in my office. Then I woke up and I helped myself to the liquor cabinet so I could feel sorry for myself in peace. It didn't work."

"What time did you leave the wedding?" Jack asked.

"What is this? An interrogation?" Dickie asked, half grinning as he laid his head back on the chair.

"Kind of," Jack said. "Dickie, Chloe is dead."

CHAPTER EIGHT

DICKIE DIDN'T EVEN RAISE HIS HEAD. "YEAH, SURE. You're not usually mean with your jokes, but I guess I probably deserve it. Are you sure I can't have another drink?"

"He's not kidding, Dickie," I said, getting to my feet and coming over to stand near Jack. "I did the autopsies this afternoon."

Dickie's head lifted slowly and the color drained from his face. "Wait, you're serious? Chloe is dead? I don't understand. I just saw her last night."

"You had sex with her yesterday before the wedding?" Jack asked.

Slashes of red appeared on Dickie's pale cheeks and he got to his feet angrily. He leaned over the desk so he was in Jack's face. "How the hell would you know that? Did someone see us?"

"I did the autopsy," I said. "It was obvious she'd had sex with someone, and it wasn't her husband. The science doesn't lie. And after your story, we can put two and two together."

"Autopsy," Dickie said softly. "I think I'm going to be sick."

"Sit down, Dickie," Jack said, and Dickie dropped back into his chair.

"You're not wrong," I said, feeling my blood pressure rise at the thought of being so stupid. "Someone could have seen you. Especially if you had sex with the bride at the wedding venue where five hundred people were waiting for her to walk down the aisle." My voice rose in pitch and volume by the time I was done talking. "What were you thinking, Dickie?"

"We've been hooking up for months," Dickie said, coming to his feet again. He paced around the room and kept running his fingers through his hair. "I didn't think she was serious about getting married. She just wanted his protection, but I told her that I could protect her. I thought she was going to leave him at the altar. We'd made plans."

"She was in danger?" Jack asked. "Is that why she had a fake name and background?"

Dickie was a pretty okay poker player, but we knew him well enough to know when he was lying. "I don't know what you're talking about."

"Yeah, you do," Jack said. "You always twitch your

lip like that when you lie. Who was she really? We're trying to find out who killed her. And right now you've got a pretty strong motive, so you should probably help us out here."

"I didn't kill her," Dickie said, outraged. "I wanted to marry her."

"Except she married another man anyway. Which gives you another good reason to kill her."

Dickie's mouth dropped open in surprise as he thought things through, and then he fell back into the chair and covered his face with his hands.

"You want to know the ironic thing about this mess?" he asked. "I actually introduced her to Theo."

"Do I even want to know how you know the son of the former Greek ambassador?"

"He's a business associate of my dad's," Dickie said. "They've known each other a long time. Mom and Dad vacation in Greece from time to time, and have even stayed at the embassy there."

"What's Chloe's real name?" Jack asked.

"I don't know," he said, and then he held up both hands when Jack looked at him skeptically. "No, really, I don't. I just know that Chloe's not her real name. I met her last June while she was waiting tables at The Corner Café. That's the little place in DC I like to go after we go to the theater. I was with some business associates and we stopped in late one night. It was almost midnight."

He stopped and smiled at the memory, rubbing his damp hands on his slacks. "She was the most gorgeous woman I'd ever seen in my life. I couldn't take my eyes off her. There was just something so vivacious about her—the way she moved, the way she talked. She had a great personality and was obviously smart. She charmed everyone in our group. But there was something else about her too, like she was always looking over her shoulder. It made me want to protect her."

That was probably one of the most honest things Dickie had said since he'd walked through our door. Dickie had a savior complex. I was pretty sure it was because he had daddy issues, but he was always a sucker for a sad story and he'd been taken advantage of plenty of times because of it.

"I knew the first time she introduced herself that Chloe wasn't her real name," he said. "She had to think about it too hard before she said it. And when I called out to her she didn't turn around to answer. I never pressed her on it. I thought maybe she was running from an ex or something."

"How'd she meet Theo?" Jack asked.

"Theo and I have known each other in passing for years," he said. "But we connected at a fundraiser for a senator who was up for reelection. Theo told me he'd bought a house in Newcastle and had several business interests in the works here and abroad. He's got dual citizenship. Theo has always just dabbled in business. His parents are loaded, and Theo received a pretty sizeable inheritance from his grandfather if I remember right.

"Theo mentioned he was opening up several restaurants in the area and needed a business manager," he continued. "And I know that Theo has a lot more money than business sense and that he'd probably overpay whoever he employed. Chloe was always adamant about paying her own way. It made her very uncomfortable when I'd try to cover things for her. I knew she was struggling. She was living in a hotel and paying with cash from her tips every week. I offered to help a couple of times, but it made her mad to even bring it up.

"So I introduced Chloe and Theo that night." He laughed, but there was no humor in it. "Stupid of me. I knew he was probably pushing fifty, so I didn't think anything of it. He even offered her a room in his house. I helped her move in. Not that she had many belongings."

"She and Theo didn't share a bedroom?" I asked curiously.

"No," he said. "There was a downstairs suite he gave her that even had a little office attached so she could work from home if she wanted to. He gave her a car since she'd have to drive to the different restaurants. It wasn't hard to see there were wounds behind the resilient exterior. I thought Theo saw them as a father would for his daughter. He must have gotten a lot of laughs at my expense. Some friend, huh?"

"Dickie…" Jack said, but there was really nothing either of us could say. It was obvious Dickie had really cared for her, and nothing we could say would make any of this okay.

"I guess when it came down to it Chloe decided what Theo could offer her was more appealing than what I could." Dickie shrugged like it was just par for the course, but he couldn't hide the pain and anger on his face.

"You don't know that," I said. "I don't know Chloe or Theo or what her motives could have been. But I know you, and as cynical and skeptical as you are of people, you typically can size them up pretty quickly and be accurate about it. If your gut told you that Chloe really loved you and that she wanted to be with you, then maybe she really did. Maybe she just didn't have a choice in the matter and couldn't find a way to tell you. All we know is she was running from something, and that something caught up to her and shot her seven times."

Dickie winced.

"If you'd been the one to marry Chloe it could have been you on Jaye's autopsy table today," Jack told him.

He sucked in a breath. "Theo's dead too?"

"Yeah," Jack said. "We haven't ruled out a professional hit on them. Tell us more about Chloe. Anything you know about her past that might lead us to who did this to her."

"I'm sorry," he said. "I think I'm just in shock. I really need a drink."

"If I give you one you have to sleep in the guest room," Jack said.

Dickie thought it over quickly. "Fine. Bring the bottle."

Jack went back to the bar and brought the decanter of whiskey back to the table. "Tell me about Chloe."

"Chloe opened up a little about her background, but she was always very guarded. She never told me for certain, but I think she grew up in some kind of commune. I'm not sure where though. She knew how to do all kinds of weird stuff. Canning and sewing, and she knew a lot about plants and gardening. She even knew what plants were good for medicine.

"But she said as she got older things changed and became dangerous. She said in passing once that she'd witnessed someone die. I didn't ask her about it. There was something about the look on her face when she said it that told me she hadn't really meant to tell me that, so I pretended I hadn't heard. But I knew she was scared, even though she pretended not to be. She was always looking over her shoulder."

"Did Theo not suspect that the two of you were still involved?" I asked.

"I don't know," Dickie said. "I saw Theo at that fundraiser when I introduced him to Chloe and the next time I saw him was at his wedding. He wasn't demanding or anything of their relationship. She worked for him and took her job seriously. There were times we'd meet up during her lunch break, and there were times she stayed over at my place. Apparently Theo was out of town a lot, and she said she didn't like being there by herself. Said it felt like a prison. I guess Theo had a whole team of personal security, and whenever he'd leave town he'd make sure that Chloe was protected."

"So chances are Theo knew the two of you were still hooking up?" Jack asked. "I can't imagine Theo's security guards would keep that a secret from him."

"Yeah, you're probably right." Dickie sighed. "Maybe I'm thinking too much into it. Maybe there was nothing between them except his ability to protect her."

I was keeping my opinions to myself until we'd gathered all the facts.

"Theo offered her the protection she needed, and I understood that," Dickie said. "When she told me he'd asked her to marry him and that his name and his father's position would help protect her I was a little shocked, but it was a gut reaction to when someone had run her off the road."

"Wait," Jack said. "When was this?"

"Sometime after the New Year," he said. "They got engaged right after that."

"What happened?" Jack asked. "No police reports popped when we ran the background check on her."

"She didn't want to involve the police," Dickie said. "She was checking on one of the restaurants up in Arlington, and on her way home a black sedan tried to run her into oncoming traffic. She managed to swerve out of the way and she hit the guardrail. Messed up her car pretty bad. That was when she told me she thought her past was catching up to her."

Dickie poured another drink. "She told me Theo had offered to marry her and move her to Greece. He's got dual citizenship." Dickie stopped and frowned, swirling the amber liquid in his glass. "I think I told you that already."

"That's okay," Jack said. "Keep going."

"That's when I told her that I would marry her and we could move wherever she wanted," he said. "I mean, I've got loads of money. Not as much as Theo, but it's nothing to sneeze at. She seemed excited about the idea, but she told me we had to go along with her engagement to Theo. She said it was safer that way. So I went along with it. I even went to the wedding. I had my bags packed in the car for us to make our getaway. I came to the wedding early." He rubbed the back of his neck and laughed. "I was nervous. I've never really done anything like that before, and I kept thinking that my father would probably disown me."

"If your father didn't disown you after your divorce from Candy I don't think he ever will," Jack said, trying to lighten the tension.

"Well, you never know with my father," Dickie said softly.

At that moment he reminded me of the teenager who hadn't been hardened by the world yet. The boy who was smart and a little nerdy, but who always had a heart to do what was right for others. And a boy who could never live up to his father's expectations.

"Did she contact you once you arrived at the Briarly?" Jack asked.

"I texted her when I got there," he said. "And then she told me where I could meet her."

"What time was that?"

"I don't know," he said. "Maybe around two o'clock? All of her bridesmaids were all friends or family of Theo's, so she told them all she needed some time alone to rest. There's this whole bridal suite wing in the main clubhouse of the Briarly, so Chloe had her own private space and balcony. I snuck up the back stairs and she let me in her room.

There was just this...desperation in her." Slashes of bright red colored his cheeks and he cleared his throat. "And then one thing led to another. She said she loved me." Dickie shrugged again, looking more defeated than I'd ever seen him. "I tried to get her to leave with me then, but she said it was too soon. That we needed to wait until it was almost time for the wedding. I told her to text me where to meet her and she kissed me goodbye. That's the last time I saw her."

"You didn't stay and try to talk with her?" I asked.

"No," he said. "I was waiting in the bar of the clubhouse and realized it was time for the wedding to start. I could hear the music and I kept expecting for it to stop and people to start running around looking for Chloe. I kept checking my phone, but there were no messages from her. They got married in the gardens. I could see through the window. She looked beautiful. So I did the only thing I could do. I left."

"How'd she get the fake ID and papers?" Jack asked.

Dickie shrugged and his eyelids were starting to get heavy and his speech slurred. "I guess Theo pulled some strings and got them for her. When she was working at the restaurant she always paid cash for everything. She had an ID, but I don't know where she got it from. You can buy the fake ones in the city for a few hundred bucks. Some of them look pretty real. But after she met Theo she had everything from a birth certificate to a passport. I can't believe she's dead. I was so angry with her. I could've—"

"Dickie—" Jack interrupted.

"Am I really a suspect?" he asked.

"You're a person of interest we need to eliminate," Jack said. "So here's what you're going to do. You going to willingly let Jaye take a DNA sample tonight. Then you're going to go upstairs and sleep this off. And then tomorrow you're going to come into the station with your attorney and give a voluntary statement. You're going to tell them everything you told us tonight. Do you understand?"

"But I bought a plane ticket to the Bahamas," he said. "I'm supposed to leave tomorrow night."

"Don't," Jack said, and the tone of his voice didn't leave room for argument.

CHAPTER NINE

"I'm fine," I said the following morning.

I wasn't. Not really. I felt like I'd been run over by a truck. But at least I didn't have anything left in my stomach to throw up.

"You don't look fine," Jack said, squatting down next to me.

"No, it's passed. I promise. Just help me up."

I was laid out on the bathroom floor, so I reached out both hands so Jack could pull me to my feet.

"This might seem weird, but I really hate the smell of all of our hand soap," I said. "So it'd be great if we could throw it all away. It makes me sick."

"The smell of soap makes you sick?" he asked.

"Just the smell of that soap," I said. "Other soap is fine. I think because it has a floral scent. Floral scents make me nauseated."

His lips twitched. "So we shouldn't take any trips to the botanical gardens? Or the garden section of Home Depot?"

"That would be a bad idea," I said. "I think I'm good for coffee now."

"Why don't you start with water and work your way up to coffee?"

"Because we're already behind schedule. I thought you wanted to talk to Theo's parents this morning."

"It's barely nine o'clock on a Sunday," he said. "We've got time." He handed me a bottle of water that I hadn't noticed him bring into the bathroom with him. "Why don't you take a shower, and by the time you finish I'll have coffee made for you. And you should probably put something in your stomach. I'll make you some toast."

"What about Dickie?" I asked.

"He can make his own breakfast," Jack said. "He's a grown man."

"Are we just going to leave him in the house?"

The corner of Jack's mouth quirked in a smile. "Want me to toss him out in the yard?"

"You're a real riot this morning," I said.

"Thank you," he said. "Just for that I'll bring your coffee up to you while you shower."

"Wow," I said. "That kind of service will get you lucky."

"I'll take payment later," he said, grinning. "After you brush your teeth."

I choked on a laugh as he disappeared to go make my coffee.

Theo Vasilios's parents were staying at the Briarly Country Club in Arlington, Virginia. The Briarly was one of the oldest country clubs in the nation. It had started as a men's athletics club in the mid-1800s, and had morphed into one of the most elite, and expensive, clubs in the country. The original stone lodge still stood, and had been added to over the last couple of centuries to provide three floors of rustic opulence to its patrons. Even from the outside, the place reeked of old money and power—the kind of establishment that required not just wealth to join, but connections that went back generations.

"How come you're not a member here?" I asked Jack as he showed his badge to the gate guard, who scrutinized it with the suspicion of a man accustomed to keeping undesirables at bay.

"Because I hate golf," he said. "And if you have to pay the average American salary every year to be a member of something it should have activities I can enjoy."

"I hear they have pickleball now," I said.

"You want to pay fifty thousand a year to play pickleball?" he asked, eyebrow raised as we were finally waved through the ornate iron gates.

"Not when you put it that way," I said. "Maybe there's a place closer to home. I've seen a couple of reels of people playing. It looks like fun."

Jack shook his head and said, "I can see through you a mile away. You watched videos of all the old people playing and figured it's a sport you might actually be able to win at."

"Hey, I take offense to that," I said, eyes narrowed. "I'm a good athlete. Don't you remember how you got that scar on your eyebrow?"

"Not really," he said. "I remember you tripping over your own feet coming into home plate and then it was lights out."

"That was the most beautiful slide you've ever seen in your life," I contested. "You're just mad because I was called safe and we won the game."

"I've heard there's memory loss with pregnancy," Jack said. "I'm just going to chalk this up as one of those moments. Read the map and tell me where the Madison House is located."

I took the postcard-sized map that the gate guard had given us, and looked at the winding road and the different buildings around the grounds. It was a large property with a dozen or so cabins where members or dignitaries could stay. Ambassador and Mrs. Vasilios had been assigned to Madison House, tucked away on the opposite side of the lake away from the busiest areas of the country club. Privacy for the grieving parents, or isolation to keep them from prying ears—I wondered which it was.

We'd taken Jack's Tahoe to Arlington since it was an official visit, and Jack pulled into a circle drive in front of a two-story stone house that was made of the same stone as the main lodge. The lawn was well manicured and flowers bloomed riotously in the gardens, a stark contrast to the darkness we'd come to discuss.

"It looks so European," I said, eyeing the two men in black suits who were heading toward our car with purposeful strides. The first had a military bearing that screamed American Special Forces, while the second moved with the fluid grace of a trained killer. "And it comes with its own welcome party."

We got out of the car and Jack flashed his badge quickly because the men looked like they'd be more than happy to tackle us to the ground. Their hands hovered near concealed weapons, and I didn't miss the communication earpieces they both wore. This wasn't standard diplomatic security—this was the kind of protection you hired when your life was in danger.

"The ambassador and his wife spoke to the police yesterday," said the larger of the two men. His voice was flat, his eyes constantly scanning the surroundings even as he addressed us. Former military for sure, probably Special Forces based on the faded tattoo partially visible at his wrist when he moved.

"That was our chaplain and an officer coming to break the news of their son's death," Jack said easily, though I could feel the tension radiating from him. "Dr. Graves and I are conducting the investigation into their son's and daughter-in-law's murders. We need to ask them a few questions. They were told we'd be arriving this morning."

The guard grunted and turned to head toward the house, and the other one took over. This man was smaller, skimming just under six feet, and his hair was dark and pulled back into a stubby ponytail at his neck. His eyes were cold, calculating, like he was sizing us up as potential threats rather than law enforcement.

"You have twenty minutes," he said in an accent I couldn't quite place, but it seemed Slavic in nature. The accent was mild but unmistakable, like he'd spent years training it away. "The ambassador is very busy today."

"We won't take up much of their time," Jack assured him, and we followed the man into the house. I noticed how his jacket shifted as he walked —he was carrying at least two weapons that I could spot, probably more that I couldn't.

"The ambassador is in the library," the guard said, leading us down a long hallway.

The house was beautiful—if unoriginal in design —and it looked like the kind of stately home a wealthy grandmother would decorate, with ornately carved wood furniture and floral patterns on the rugs.

The door to the library was open and we were ushered inside to see Ambassador Vasilios seated behind his desk and his wife on a pale yellow settee in front of the window. The guard stationed himself just inside the door, his eyes never leaving us.

"Ambassador," Jack said, reaching out to shake the man's hand.

"Call me Nicholas," he said cordially, though his smile never reached his eyes. "This is my wife, Cecilia. Please, come in and have a seat."

Nicholas was a handsome man somewhere in his mid-seventies, but he looked to be in good health. He had strong shoulders and a straight posture, and he looked very much like his son. His hair was fully silver and his eyes almost black—the kind of eyes that could hide thoughts and intentions behind a mask of diplomatic courtesy. He was dressed in gray golf pants and an expensive-looking polo, but his casual attire couldn't disguise the power he wielded.

I moved over to greet Cecilia and saw her eyes were swollen from crying, but she'd done her best to conceal it with makeup. She seemed frail next to the rigidity of her husband—a petite woman only an inch or so over five feet. Her hair was black as coal with not a trace of silver, pulled back harshly from her face and coiled at her nape. And her face had the unlined grace of a habitual Botox user. She was also dressed casually in beige linen pants and a matching top. When she looked up at me, the vacancy in her gaze was alarming—pupils constricted to pinpoints.

"I'm so sorry for your loss," I told her.

She nodded thanks mechanically, but didn't say anything. There was a vacantness in her eyes that told me she'd medicated herself heavily before our meeting.

"Please," Nicholas said. "Have a seat."

He gestured to the two leather chairs in front of the desk he stood behind, and Jack and I both sat. I noticed that Nicholas had positioned us with our backs to the security guard—a subtle psychological tactic to put us at a disadvantage.

"Have you found out who did this to our son?" he asked, his fingers drumming softly on the polished desktop. The rhythm seemed casual, but there was tension in his movements.

"My team is combing through all of the surveillance and the logs, and we're running down leads," Jack said. His voice was neutral but I could hear the careful calculation in each word.

"So, no," Nicholas said with a sigh. "You haven't discovered who is responsible. I hope you don't take offense, but I don't have a lot of confidence in local law enforcement to see my son brought to justice."

"None taken," Jack said cordially. "Unfortunately, your son's murder isn't the first we've come across. The team that is investigating is highly skilled."

"Hmm," Nicholas said, pursing his lips. And then he pulled a file from the top of his desk and dropped it in front of Jack with a deliberate thud. "Would either of you care for a drink? Brandy? Coffee?"

"No, thank you," Jack answered. He hadn't picked up the file folder to see what was inside, but the top flap had opened when Nicholas had dropped it and the contents had spilled out.

The bottom dropped out of my stomach when I saw the newspaper clippings. There were several pictures of my parents and the crash site where they'd faked their deaths and substituted two other bodies to be found in the fiery wreckage. Edging out from one of the clippings I saw Cole's academy picture. The file was very thick, and I knew Nicholas had done a deep dive on every one of us.

Jack didn't take the bait, didn't even glance at the file. "You've been busy," he said mildly.

"The State Department has the adequate resources and experiences to find out what happened to my son." Nicholas's voice remained calm, but something dangerous flickered in his eyes.

"With all due respect," Jack said. "I've worked with some of those guys at the State Department. I'll stand with my current team any day of the week."

"I don't mind using my connections," Nicholas said, his voice never changing timbre. I could see why he'd have made an effective diplomat in the negotiating room—there was steel beneath the surface calm. "I can always make a call to the governor. You have political aspirations, don't you, Sheriff Lawson?"

"I actually got a call from Tom this morning," Jack said easily. "We had a nice talk. The governor's ball is coming up next month. And no, I don't have political aspirations."

Jack might not have political aspirations, but he'd been neck deep in politics his whole life. Jack came from money. The kind of money that bought influence and recognition. Jack's father had been asked more than once to run for a Senate seat and had always turned it down, not liking the games that were played and the favors that were demanded to actually sit in the seat and represent the people. Jack felt the same way. But that didn't mean he didn't know people in high places.

Those same people saw a future in Jack and wanted him at the helm. We were constantly being invited to things I had no desire to go to. But Jack said it was good to keep those connections just to make people wonder what future plans are. That way they'd always have a little bit of fear of what you know about them and what they might owe you later down the road.

Behind Nicholas, Cecilia's gaze drifted to the window, her fingers absently worrying at the edge of her sleeve. For a moment, I saw lucidity flash across her features—a glimpse of fear quickly masked.

"You're not curious to know more about your... team?" Nicholas asked, gesturing to the folder that lay open between us, the newspaper photos of my parents' deaths clearly visible.

Jack smiled and steepled his fingers in front of him. "Like I said, I stand with my team. They're good. What can you tell me about Chloe Matthews?"

Nicholas stared at Jack, and I couldn't tell if there was respect or aggravation in his eyes. Maybe a little of both. His fingers stopped their drumming, and he leaned back slightly, reassessing his approach.

"Ms. Matthews was a gold-digging whore," Nicholas said, the crude words jarring in his cultured voice. "If you'll excuse my language. His mother and

I did not approve. Theo's first wife, Vivica, was a wonderful woman—well bred and well educated. She spoke five languages, and she would have helped elevate Theo in political circles."

At the mention of Chloe, I noticed Cecilia's hand tighten on the arm of the settee, her knuckles going white despite her drugged state.

"How long ago did they divorce?" Jack asked.

"It's been probably fifteen years now," Nicholas said, and a shadow passed across his face.

"So Vivica wouldn't have had hard feelings about his remarriage?"

"Of course not," Nicholas said, too quickly. "She was more than happy to fly in from London to attend the wedding. That's where she lives full-time. She and Theo stayed on friendly terms, and Cecilia and I see her at family gatherings. Vivica was very patient with Theo, so I cannot blame her for the divorce. His mother and I spoiled him. He was our only son. And he was not ready to be a good husband and father when he married Vivica. There was a time when Theo went astray. Over the last several years he'd finally come back to us. Come to his senses."

The way Nicholas emphasized *come back to us* seemed significant. I filed it away to examine later.

I could see Cecilia out of the corner of my eye, frozen like a statue in her drug-induced state. She'd not moved a muscle during the entire conversation, except for that brief moment of lucidity when Chloe's name was mentioned. Her silence spoke volumes.

"When did you first meet Chloe?" Jack asked.

"At the engagement party in January," he said. "I could only roll my eyes the first time I saw them together. She was young enough to be his daughter." Nicholas shook his head in disgust. "She was certainly not what we'd been expecting. Cecilia noticed the ring on Chloe's finger. It had belonged to Cecilia's mother. Theo had asked Vivica to return it when they divorced and she graciously did. Seeing the ring on that tramp's finger hurt us both deeply and I argued with Theo about it." His lips pursed into a fine line and he looked down. "I regret that now."

I watched the security guard out of the corner of my eye as he shifted his stance slightly, one hand moving closer to his concealed weapon. Interesting reaction to what should have been a straightforward answer.

"Do you know anything about Chloe's background? Where she came from?" Jack pressed, and I saw a flicker of something—alarm?—in Nicholas's eyes.

"I don't," he said, the lie as smooth as polished glass. "I do know she was hiding from something or someone. Theo utilized my resources to get her legal documents. We argued about that as well as it was my reputation on the line and not his.

"Theo also increased his personal security." Nicholas opened his desk drawer and pulled out a pack of cigarettes, tapping one out and then putting it between his lips to light it. He inhaled deeply and let out a long stream of smoke with the agitation he'd been holding inside. The action seemed calculated, a diversion to hide the subtle tremor in his hands.

"He was spending a fortune on her," he continued, smoke curling around his words. "He'd moved her into that ridiculous house in Newcastle he'd bought." He laughed without humor. "He and I argued about the house too. We seemed to do nothing but argue. We always rubbed each other the wrong way. Theo grew up in palaces, went to the best boarding schools, and was given every opportunity. And he always did his best to do the opposite of whatever was expected of him. So he bought a house in some yuppie, unimportant city and put a child in charge of his businesses. But he told me he wanted to have a regular life. What the hell does that even mean?"

The bitterness in his voice was palpable. Something more than a father's disapproval of his son's choices—there was fear beneath his contempt.

"Theo had a tattoo on the bottom of his foot," I said, dropping the information casually, watching for his reaction. "A series of dots. Do you know what they might mean?"

Nicholas's cigarette paused halfway to his lips, the only break in his composure. Behind him, I saw Cecilia's vacant gaze snap into focus for just a moment, her eyes widening in unmistakable recognition.

"A tattoo?" Nicholas said haughtily, recovering quickly. "As far as I know Theo had no tattoos. But if he did I'm sure he was influenced into making the poor decision to put permanent marks on his body."

Another lie. Nicholas knew exactly what that tattoo meant. His eyes betrayed him, a flicker of calculation that lasted only a fraction of a second.

"Did Theo talk to you about any specific incidents that caused him to increase his security?" Jack asked.

"No," Nicholas said, but his cigarette ash trembled slightly. "I wish he would have. But I could tell he was worried. A father knows these things about his son, even when they don't always see eye to eye."

"If Theo was so worried why didn't he bring security with him to The Mad King?" Jack asked, his tone conversational but his eyes sharp.

"He did," Nicholas said, and I remembered the pattern of Chloe's gunshot wounds matching the tattoo. "His driver used to be my head of security. Max Ortega is his name."

"He drove them from Briarly to The Mad King?" Jack asked.

"Yes," Nicholas said, the smoke from his cigarette creating a haze between us.

"What time did Theo and Chloe leave the reception?"

"It was around eleven o'clock," Nicholas said, and I noticed he checked his watch—a nervous tic.

Jack got to his feet and I followed suit, trying to ignore the open file folder that was lying at my feet. "We appreciate your time, Ambassador Vasilios," he said.

"We would like our son's body released to us so we can prepare for burial," Nicholas said.

"I should be able to release him within the next forty-eight hours," I told him. "My office will be in touch as soon as he's been cleared for release."

"Are you sure you won't reconsider handing off the investigation?" Nicholas asked Jack. "It would be in your best interest." The words carried the unmistakable weight of threat beneath their diplomatic delivery.

"I don't think it would," Jack said, measuring the man who stood across from him. "We'll find out what happened to your son. I'm tenacious like that. The State Department is in the business of burying secrets. But I've learned in my career the only way for secrets to die is for them to lose their power by being exposed."

"Well," Nicholas said, his smile not reaching his eyes. "We know where we both stand."

Jack nodded and we left the room. The security guard with the ponytail met us outside the library door and led us out of the house, his hand never straying far from his concealed weapon. Once we were back in the sunlight I was surprised to see the other guard leaning against Jack's Tahoe, his arms crossed over his chest and a smile I wouldn't exactly call friendly on his face.

"Thanks for watching the car for me," Jack said, clicking the remote so the Tahoe unlocked. I was guessing security guard man wasn't used to men like Jack because he looked surprised when Jack kept walking toward him and opened the door for me to get in the passenger side.

Jack didn't intimidate. But I could see the calculation in his eyes—he'd noted the guard's stance, the placement of his weapons, the way his partner had positioned himself behind us. Jack was taking stock, planning for contingencies.

I prided myself on being unflappable, but when that file folder had tumbled open, a surge of anxiety threatened to overwhelm me. For a moment, I'd fought the urge to run and not look back. It hadn't just been intimidation that had gripped me—it had been the lingering shame of my past. That heavy burden I thought I'd buried had resurfaced with a vengeance, making me want to turn my back on it all.

I've been told that healing is a process. I guess I'm still healing.

I got into the Tahoe and was proud of myself for not flinching when the door shut behind me. The security guard still leaned against the vehicle but had turned so his eyes were always on Jack.

"I'm sure we'll see each other again," Jack said, and there was steel beneath his casual tone. He walked around the Tahoe and got into the driver's seat. He started the car, and the man finally moved, but he didn't stop staring at Jack, memorizing him.

I waited until we'd passed through the gates of the Briarly before I spoke. It had taken that long before my heart had stopped thudding in my chest.

"Well, that was terrifying," I said. "What was that all about?"

"Just a little intimidation from the ambassador so we'll hand the case over to another agency," Jack said. "The question is why. Is it because he cares too much, or because he's trying to have something buried forever? Did you notice Mrs. Vasilios's reaction when we mentioned the tattoo?"

"I know one thing," I said. "He was lying to us about Chloe. He knows exactly where she came from. You could see the fear in his eyes. And those security guards weren't just for show—they're killers."

Jack nodded grimly. "And they were watching us the entire time, like they were committing our faces to memory."

I shivered, remembering the cold eyes of the man with the ponytail. "For what purpose?"

"That," Jack said, "is what worries me."

— — —

CHAPTER TEN

— — —

WE WERE HEADED DOWN HIGHWAY 95 ON THE WAY back to King George when Jack finally got through to Derby in IT.

"Sorry, Sheriff," Derby said. "I had to step out of church so I could take your call."

"Sorry about that, Derby. When you get a chance could you get me information on Max Ortega? He was Theo and Chloe's personal bodyguard. He supposedly drove them to The Mad King from the Briarly. I also need a check on Vivica, formerly Vasilios. She was Theo's ex-wife."

"You got it, boss," Derby said.

"Finish service first," Jack told him. "We're going back to The Mad King, so we'll be a little while."

"10-4," Derby said and hung up.

Jack's next call was to Doug.

"I've gone through the golf cart trackers," Doug said. "I've got cart 1001 arriving at the honeymoon villa at 8:41 p.m."

"That would be the housekeeper, Dorinda Lake," Jack said. "In her statement she said she arrived around eight thirty."

"Close enough," Doug muttered. "And then we've got golf cart 1021 arriving seven minutes later."

"That would be Aidan Chisolm. Dorinda confirmed he arrived to set up food service out on the patio. She said he was finishing up as she was about to leave."

"1001 left at ten after nine," Doug said. "1021 left at ten nineteen."

"Wait a minute," I said. "You're saying that Aidan Chisolm stayed over an hour and a half in the honeymoon villa?"

"That's what it looks like," Doug said.

"I guess we need to see if old Aidan is at work this morning," Jack said. "I think he has some explaining to do."

"I've already pulled a background on him," Doug said. "Seems pretty normal. Originally from South Carolina. Got a rowing scholarship to Roanoke College. Tuition there is steep, but it looks like the scholarship covers most of it. He's worked at The Mad King since its opening last year. DMV shows a

Virginia driver's license. No parking tickets. No arrests. He lives on campus."

"Thanks, Doug," Jack said. "Do me a favor and pull the camera footage of the night Theo and Chloe arrived at the resort. After they leave the vehicle I want you to see if the driver sticks around or if he leaves the premises. See if you can get facial recognition."

"Will do," Doug said.

I recognized the same security guard at the gate of The Mad King as from when we'd arrived the morning before. He waved us through and opened the gate so we could climb the winding, tree-lined hill to the resort.

Jack parked under the glass-covered portico again, and a different set of doormen welcomed us into the opulent lobby. Sundays were obviously a time for rocking in the chairs by the large fireplace, lazy games of checkers, and Bloody Marys being served from the bar.

We went into the glassed-in check-in area and waited as a couple received their room keys and a map of the resort. Once they'd been directed to the elevators Jack showed his badge to the young man across the reception desk.

He was early twenties with a wide, friendly smile and spiky blond hair. He was dressed in a silver dress shirt and a black three-button vest, and his sleeves were rolled up to show an Apple watch on his left wrist.

"You're with the police," he said. "I'm Jeremy. Mr. Harris said you might be coming back, and that we're to cooperate in whatever way you need. Would you like coffee?"

"We appreciate that, Jeremy," Jack said. "No coffee for us."

I kind of wanted coffee, but I appreciated Jack's restraint for the both of us.

"We have a couple of people we need to talk to," Jack said. "Edward and Donna Kelso are guests here. If you could give us their room number we'll announce ourselves. And Aidan Chisholm is with food service. Can you see if he's working today?"

"I can check all of those for you now, sir," Jeremy said helpfully, moving to his computer and typing quickly. "It does seem that Aidan Chisholm is working until three o'clock today. It looks as if he's doing delivery service on the golf course. I can check out a golf cart for you so you can meet him there."

"That would be great, thanks," Jack said.

Jeremy typed something else into his computer and then reached below the counter and got a sheet of paper from the printer. "Here's a map and the room assignment for Mr. and Mrs. Kelso. If there's anything else I can do for you please let me know. The golf cart will be waiting for you out front."

We thanked him again and headed back into the lobby. "This resort really lives up to the hype. No wonder there's an eight-month waiting list."

"Maybe we should come here for a babymoon," he said.

"What's a babymoon?"

"It's when the soon-to-be parents get away for one last hoorah before the baby comes," Jack explained.

"I'm always open to going anywhere with you," I said. "Maybe we could go before I start looking like a beached whale. That sounds a lot more fun than waiting until right before things get critical."

"Maybe we could go now and later," Jack said. "We're not limited on how many times we can go."

"The dead bodies waiting for us might have something to say about that," I said as we made our way back outside. Jeremy had been remarkably efficient as there was a golf cart waiting for us at the entrance.

"We don't have to save the world," Jack said. "I've got a good team of investigators. And if you're not available for autopsies then the bodies can always go to the state lab. They're going to have to get used to you being out for a while after the baby comes. So let's take the trips while we can."

"Don't you think it's weird to pay money to go to a

resort that's twenty minutes from the house?" I asked. "Kind of takes the excitement out of it."

"You're probably right," he said. "It's too easy to think about work when we stay close."

There was a digital map on the dashboard of the golf cart that had been pre-programmed to show us how to get to the golf course.

We drove along the narrow pathway, passing the archery field and another area that was lined with ATVs for off-road adventures. The golf course was on the other side of the property and we wound our way toward the flashing dot on the GPS.

"I'm guessing the flashing dot is Aidan's golf cart?" I asked.

"I hope so," Jack said. "Otherwise we'll probably be introducing ourselves to some very confused golfers."

"I guess a double homicide didn't discourage too many guests from staying on the property," I said.

"I can't imagine it would," Jack said. "It's not like this is a seedy motel on the edge of town. This is high profile and sensationalized. I'm sure anyone who checked out early was immediately replaced by another guest. At their very core, people are just nosy. We've probably got a dozen eyes on us right now."

I snickered and watched as we drew closer to a bright red golf cart with a scalloped awning. It was longer than the regular carts to transport guests, and it had shelves down the side like a metal tool chest and drinks sitting in a cavern of ice in the back.

"That must be him," I said, noticing the young man in pressed khakis and a white shirt with blue trim that the food service workers wore. "Good-looking kid. Doesn't look like he's ever been in trouble a day in his life."

"He reminds me of Eddie Haskell," Jack said. "Why don't we see what he has to say?"

The kid noticed us immediately and stood next to his cart, nodding politely to resort guests as they passed by. He was tall and broad shouldered, and I could see how he'd be an asset to the rowing team. His hair was a dark auburn and there was a smattering of freckles across his tanned face. He was a handsome kid who looked like he belonged in a 1950s soda shop.

"Aidan Chisolm?" Jack asked, showing his badge discreetly.

"That's me," he said. "Dorinda said you stopped by to talk to her. She figured you might do the same for me."

I saw a crack in his exterior when he looked at each of us nervously, and neither Jack nor I said anything. People weren't always comfortable with silence, and usually felt the need to fill it with something.

"I guess I know what you're here to talk to me about," Aidan said, looking around to see if there was anyone close by.

"Why don't you tell us," Jack said.

"All of the golf carts are tracked," he said. "I figured you probably noticed I stayed a little longer than I should have at the villa where those people were murdered." His face turned scarlet, making his freckles stand out across the bridge of his nose and cheeks.

"You doing drugs?" Jack asked. "We found a couple of joints that had been tossed off the back deck."

"Oh, no," Aidan said shocked. "Nothing like that. I'd lose my scholarship."

"Dorinda told us you were finishing up about the same time that she left," I said.

"That's true," he said. "I like Dorinda. She treats all the college kids like they're her own. Brings us snacks and keeps up with what we're doing. It's a real family here."

"So if you were almost finished setting the scene on the deck why did it take you another hour and a half to leave?"

Aidan winced and said, "You see, there's this girl. Her name's Andi, and she works in the pro shop over there." He pointed toward the clubhouse by the first green. "I had a break scheduled right after I finished at the honeymoon villa, and she was just getting off shift. So, uhh, she met me out there and we, uhh…"

He scratched at the back of his neck awkwardly. "I'd nicked an extra bottle of champagne and chocolate-covered strawberries and set everything up so it was real romantic. She likes that kind of stuff. And that deck is epic, even at night. They've got those big lounger beds and you can see the stars and hear the waterfalls, and then there's all the lights in the trees."

"We didn't find any other golf carts at the honeymoon villa until Mr. Harris arrived with the victims later that night. How did she meet you there?"

"Oh," he said, understanding. "She rode one of the bicycles. Anyone can use them all over the property."

"Did you notice anyone else around the villa while you were there? Did you hear anyone come inside?"

If possible his face flushed even more. "I, uh, didn't see or hear anything else. But I, uh, wasn't really paying attention."

"Did you notice anything when you left?" I asked.

"No," he said. "We were in a hurry to get everything back in place and get out of there. I'd lost track of time and I was still on shift. I had to tell my manager that I'd gotten sick and had been in the bathroom the whole time. I loaded Andi's bike up on the back of the golf cart and I dropped her off at the staff parking lot so she could get home. My manager told me to go home early after I told him I'd been sick. I feel bad about that."

"Is Andi working today?" Jack asked.

"Yeah, Sundays are busy days on the golf course," he said. "I guess you're going to need to ask her about everything I told you."

"Just checking off boxes to try and find who murdered those people," Jack said, handing him a card. "If you think of anything else give me a call."

We stopped by the pro shop on the way to our next interview and talked to Andi Belding. She was a pretty, athletic-looking girl who blushed prettily when we asked her about Aidan, but she'd confirmed his alibi down to him dropping her at the staff parking lot.

"Who's next on the list?" Jack asked.

"Donna and Edward Kelso," I said. "And look where they're staying? In the Dowager Villa."

"Am I to assume that it's located close to our murder site?" he asked.

"This is why you make the big bucks," I said. "It's the bungalow closest to the honeymoon villa. Turn left here and follow the path. You'll eventually run into it."

When Jack pulled up in front of the Dowager Villa, I noticed it was a smaller version of the honeymoon villa, featuring the same stone and glass design as the main resort. The villa had a wooden deck that wrapped around its entirety, giving it a cozy yet elegant feel. Nestled among the trees, it offered a picturesque view of the eighteenth hole from the front and the serene expanse of the Potomac River from the back.

"You think they're here or out playing lawn darts somewhere?" I asked.

"There's a golf cart pulled around to the side," Jack said. "Maybe we'll get lucky. How far of a walk do you think it is to the honeymoon villa from here?"

"Maybe ten minutes, fifteen at the most," I said. "It's just around that bend in the path."

It turns out we were lucky. The front door opened and an older couple stepped out, obviously heading out for some kind of activity. They certainly didn't look like they were overly upset at the news that the bride and groom from the wedding they'd just attended had been murdered a villa down from them. But different people handled the news of murder in different ways.

"Mr. and Mrs. Kelso?" Jack asked, showing his badge.

"That's us," Mr. Kelso said, studying Jack's badge intently. He was a distinguished, portly man with wavy silver hair and a bushy salt-and-pepper mustache. He was a couple of inches shorter than his wife and dressed in black swim trunks and a red guayabera shirt. His expression was curious, but not necessarily friendly.

"I'm Sheriff Lawson," Jack said. "This is Dr. Graves. She's the coroner for King George County. We need to ask you some questions about Theo and Chloe Vasilios."

"We've got an appointment at the spa," Mrs. Kelso said.

She was a thin, stern-looking woman with the kind of posture that reminded me of a piano teacher I'd had as a child. The woman had scared me to death, and I hadn't taken very many lessons before deciding piano wasn't my future. Mrs. Kelso had probably been very pretty when she'd been younger, but now her skin was tight with Botox, her lips looked like they'd been stung by a swarm of bees, and her cheeks were so sunken in I didn't know how she chewed without biting them.

She was dressed in white linen pants and a flowing top the color of coral, and her blond hair was long and artfully highlighted and belonged on a much younger woman.

"We won't take up much of your time," Jack said, giving her a smile. "I'm sure they'll make accommodations for you if you explain the situation. The staff here are exceptional."

She huffed and pursed her lips. "It doesn't seem like we have any choice in the matter."

"It's important to find out everything we can so we can find out who killed Theo and Chloe. The two of you were at the wedding."

Jack didn't ask it as a question, but let the Kelsos interpret it however they saw fit.

"And what is that supposed to imply?" Mrs. Kelso asked.

"Settle down, dear," Mr. Kelso piped in, settling a meaty hand on her arm. "They're just doing their job. They've got to ask questions."

"All I heard was an accusation," she said coldly.

"Not at all, ma'am," Jack said easily.

We walked up the steps so we were level with them on the deck, and Mr. Kelso took the hint and guided his wife into a chair. She didn't look like she liked being handled, but she sat in one of the four rockers. Jack and I stayed standing.

"How did you know Theo and Chloe?" Jack asked.

"Oh, we were at Theo's first wedding," Mr. Kelso said. "We've been friends of the family for decades."

"Where are you from?" Jack asked. "I can't place your accent."

"Oh, my wife is American through and through.

A New Yorker. I was born in Scotland, went to boarding school in London, and lived a decade in Dubai before I met Donna in New York while on a business trip." He smiled genially. "So I'm sure my accent is quite hybrid by this point."

"And Theo?"

"We've been friends with Nicholas and Cecelia for years," he said. "So of course, we watched Theo grow up. We thought for a while that Theo and our daughter, Catherine, would end up together. I know Donna and Cecelia wanted it that way. But Theo and Cate are just good friends. She was at the wedding as well, but she's already left to go back to London."

"Were you surprised when Theo announced his engagement to Chloe?" Jack asked.

Donna snorted indelicately. "Theo was a fool, but men usually are when it comes to the wrong kind of woman."

"And Chloe was the wrong kind?" Jack asked.

"She was trouble," Donna said. "You know Theo hired the poor girl out of the goodness of his heart. She was down on her luck and needed the work, so he hired her to manage his restaurants. Theo's always had his father's knack for business. It wasn't long until she was dressing well above her pay grade and being integrated with Theo's circle of friends."

Mrs. Kelso lowered her voice and leaned closer. "Chloe didn't belong, and never would have been accepted. Cecelia told me in confidence that she'd seen Chloe with another man when she'd come to surprise Theo for lunch one afternoon. The man walked out the front door of their home just as bold as you please and right past Cecelia, and Chloe was standing there in the doorway with hardly a thing on. Chloe told Cecelia that Theo was out of town. Can you believe the gall? Bringing a strange man into Theo's home like that?"

"Settle down, dear," he said, patting her arm again. "You're speaking of the dead now."

"I can only assume she brought it upon herself," Mrs. Kelso said testily. "Cecelia immediately went to Theo about the incident, of course, but Theo told her it was nothing of importance and to stay out of it. She was so upset. Theo was her pride and joy, and she hated that he would be throwing his life away on a whore. She wanted grandchildren so badly, and Theo wasn't getting any younger."

"What time did the two of you arrive back here on the night of the wedding?" Jack asked.

"Oh, I don't know," Edward said. "I'd say it was before ten o'clock. We're not as young as we used to be, so we left after the dancing started."

"This resort isn't anywhere close to the wedding venue," Jack said. "Why stay so far away?"

"We've been trying to take the time to stay at The Mad King since they opened," Mr. Kelso said. "We had some friends stay here and they said it's on par with resorts all over the world. It's gotten quite the reputation across the globe. When we got the wedding invitation in January I had my assistant call and see if they had any openings. It was our lucky day because someone had made a cancelation."

Mrs. Kelso cleared her throat and said, "Nicholas of course was able to pull some strings so Theo and Chloe could stay here for their wedding night. There are very few people who can say no to Nicholas."

"Is that so?" Jack asked. "Did you see Theo and Chloe while you were here at the resort?"

"No," Mr. Kelso said. "From my understanding they were only staying the one night and were scheduled to leave early the next morning. The Vasilios private plane was going to take Theo and Chloe to Tahiti for their honeymoon, and there's the private airfield that's not far from here."

"The villa where Theo and Chloe were murdered isn't far from here," Jack said. "Did you hear gunshots that night? See anyone unusual lurking about?"

"We went straight to bed as soon as we arrived," Mr. Kelso said. "We slept late the next morning because we flew in from London for the wedding and were still jet lagged. We didn't realize something had gone wrong until management knocked on our door to inform us about the situation. They also mentioned that certain areas of the resort would be off limits while the police investigated."

"We really have to be off for our appointments," Mrs. Kelso said, coming to her feet. "It's tragic what happened to Theo, but this is the kind of thing that happens when you surround yourself with riffraff. We'll of course stay in town for Theo's funeral. A wedding and a funeral in a matter of days."

"Quite tragic," Mr. Kelso repeated.

"Just one more question," Jack said. "Did you know anything about Chloe? Maybe you overheard something about her background or met some of the guests at the wedding that she invited?"

"Not likely," Mrs. Kelso said, rolling her eyes.

I was mesmerized by her face, waiting for the arch of a brow or the slightest crinkle in her forehead. But the only thing that moved on her face were her eyelids.

"Cecelia told me Chloe didn't have any family, and she didn't really have any friends. She told me the only people Chloe insisted receive an invitation were two men. I don't know who they were, but no doubt she was probably sleeping with them. Cecelia also told me that she'd once overheard Theo talking to Chloe about where she'd grown up, and Cecelia said it sounded like some kind of commune." Mrs. Kelso shuddered delicately. "Filthy people."

Jack handed Mr. Kelso a card and said, "If you

think of any information you think might help us find who did this to Theo give me a call."

"I don't want to discourage you, son," Mr. Kelso said. "But you might be out of your league with this one. Might be best to hand it over to higher authorities. Nicholas has excellent contacts with the State Department. I'm sure he'd make sure you received some of the credit."

"We appreciate your time," Jack said, not acknowledging the comment.

CHAPTER ELEVEN

"Interesting group of people we've been talking to," I said once we were back inside the Tahoe. "They certainly have a different way of grieving a loved one. They didn't look like they'd even shed a tear over the loss."

"I'm not sure she'd have been able to cry anyway," Jack said. "Her face didn't move the entire conversation. We need to talk to Cecelia Vasilios once she's not medicated. I want to know about the man she saw Chloe with."

"And I want to know who besides Dickie was on Chloe's guest list," I said.

"Derby left me a message," Jack said, reading his phone. "Let me call him really quick."

Derby answered on the first ring. "Got your info, Sheriff. I ran the check on Max Ortega like you said.

He's a retired Army Ranger and served two tours in Afghanistan. He's got a long list of commendations.

"He went to work for Nicholas Vasilios about fifteen years ago, but it looks like he made the transition to the son about nine months ago. Nothing pops as unusual about him yet, but I can pull his financials and see if that shakes anything loose."

"What about the ex-wife?"

"Vivica Vasilios," Derby said. "She lives in London full-time and had a flight schedule for yesterday afternoon, but it looks like she cancelled it."

"Probably planning to stay in town for Theo's funeral," Jack said. "Where's she staying?"

"She's got a house in Dupont Circle," Derby said.

"Okay," Jack said. "We'll reach out so we can talk to her. Maybe she knows about the tattoo. Thanks, Derby."

Jack disconnected.

"Have you been able to get the information you need on Theo yet?" I asked.

"No," Jack said, and I could see the irritation in his eyes. "Nicholas Vasilios is using every connection he has at the State Department to block me from investigating. Not only can't I get the information I need from them on Theo Vasilios, but I can't even access NCIC because I've been flagged."

"What does that mean?" I asked.

"It means I'm pissed off, and I'm tired of Nicholas Vasilios trying to force me to give over the investigation to someone else. It makes me wonder why he wants it out of my hands so badly. Because if he spent all that time doing research on all of us, then he knows my background and knows we won't stop until we find the truth."

"Maybe that's what he's afraid you'll find," I said.

"They'll eventually have to give over the information," he said. "But they can certainly delay us for a time. Fortunately, we have Doug. And Margot."

"Speaking of Doug," I said. "Wasn't he supposed to track where Max Ortega went after he dropped off the victims?"

Jack's brows rose as he dialed Doug, and he waited while the phone rang. And rang. "No answer."

"Just send him a text," I said. "Maybe he's taking Oscar out."

"Nobody wants to talk on the phone anymore," Jack said, shaking his head.

"Now *you* sound like your mother," I said, laughing.

Jack's phone buzzed a couple of seconds later and he put it on speakerphone when he answered.

"What have you got for me, Doug?" Jack asked.

"Well, Oscar ate my pizza," he said. "Pulled the whole thing off the counter and scarfed it down before I could save any of it. I had to order a whole other one. But then the pizza didn't agree too good with Oscar, so we had a close call. And I put the kitchen rug in the washing machine, so don't worry about that. Oscar did the rest of his business outside, but man, was it gross. Total waste of a good pizza."

Jack had just closed his eyes as he listened to Doug, and I felt my stomach lurch at the thought of what Oscar might have in store for us later. Oscar was the ugliest and cutest dog ever, and though he was smarter than a lot of humans I knew, he was a dumpster diver at heart. When we didn't keep an eye on him he would break into the pantry and help himself. He and Doug together were doing a lot of damage to our grocery bill.

"Sounds like you have everything under control," Jack said.

"I'm a man of action," he said. "Plus I aced my exam. The scores posted this morning. I keep getting job offers from different places. I mean, the money sounds good, but the jobs sound boring. Anyway, I don't mind school so much. It's not very challenging, but every once in a while an assignment will give me a thread for a new concept that needs to be developed. And I still want to be a cop, so I'm not sure what to do with that."

"You'll be an asset wherever you go," Jack said patiently. "Doug, did you find out anything about where the car went after the Vasilios got out at the resort?"

"Oh, yeah," he said. "The car was clear as day on the security footage. Black luxury sedan, Virginia plates 2361 Echo Charlie. Facial recognition confirmed Max Ortega as the driver. I pulled a deep background check on him if you need it. I had to get back into the Pentagon files to get to the good stuff. Did you know they haven't upgraded their security since the first time I broke in? Who's in charge of that place?"

"It's a question many ask," Jack said. "Go ahead and save the file. I'll read it when I get home. Did Ortega leave the grounds?"

"Yes," Doug said. "The car went through the guard gate three minutes after midnight, drove up to the front entrance. Ortega got out of the vehicle and opened the door for Theo, he was sitting behind the driver's side, and the doorman came and opened the back passenger door for Chloe. The trunk was popped and the bellmen grabbed all the luggage. Chloe was carrying her purse, and she stumbled a little coming out of the car."

"Yeah, she was over the legal limit," Jack said.

"She looks it," Doug said. "These are really great quality security cameras. Everything is very clear."

"I'll make sure to let Oliver Harris know you

approve," Jack said dryly. "Did Ortega follow them inside?"

"No," Doug said. "He and Theo spoke a few words to each other, and then Ortega got back into the car and drove away. The vehicle left through the security gate at twelve twenty-two. I checked Ortega's credit card receipts and he paid for a night at the Holiday Inn in King George. Their security cameras are on network so I was able to tap in and see he arrived at the hotel at one thirty."

"Interesting," Jack said. "Why did it take him an hour to go to a hotel that was only twenty minutes away?"

"I'll text you his address and you can ask him in person," Doug said. "Apparently he lives in the carriage house of Theo's Newcastle property."

"Why would he stay in a hotel instead of just driving home?" I asked.

"Maybe because he had to get up early," Doug said. "He arrived back at The Mad King the next morning at seven thirty-five. I checked the flight logs at Passaqua Airport and the Vasilios private plane was scheduled to depart at nine o'clock on the morning of the murder."

"So Ortega arrived as scheduled, but when Theo and Chloe didn't show up he alerted Oliver Harris to ring them up?"

"It would appear so," Doug said. "Ortega went

into the resort and he and Harris are shown leaving on a golf cart together."

"Really?" Jack asked, looking at me with brows raised. "Send me that address. We're heading to talk to him now. You secured this line before you called me, didn't you?"

"What am I, an amateur?" Doug asked. "Of course I did."

"Good. We've been delayed again getting a deep background check on Theo Vasilios."

"Say no more," Doug said. "See you tonight."

"He'll be a really good cop one day," I said.

"I know. It's not a profession I would want any of my kids to go into. Doug is like Ben. There are no gray areas. There's good and evil, and their goal is to eradicate evil by using whatever means necessary. But there's a price to pay for any cop. There are things that can never be unseen and experiences that live in the depths of your soul until you take your last breath. And those experiences bleed onto spouses and kids. You think Ben's kids don't know something is going on right now? That their lives or their dad's life is in danger?"

"You're worried about our kids," I said, touching his shoulder gently.

"I'm worried that I won't be able to protect them from the kinds of things we see on a daily basis. I just want them to have a normal childhood."

"They will," I said.

"How do you know?"

"Because you're worried about it."

Jack grunted and squeezed my hand and we left The Mad King for what I hoped was the last time.

The drive to Newcastle was made in silence except for the occasional rumble in my stomach. We'd had a busy morning, and hadn't had a chance to stop for lunch.

I loved Newcastle. It was fun and trendy and artistic. The mayor had done a great job of revitalizing a place that I hadn't thought would be able to be revitalized. There was a lot of history in Newcastle. It was the birthplace of a couple of presidents, there were several buildings that predated the Revolutionary War, and it looked like a storybook town. Not to mention tourism was booming because they'd hired a twenty-year-old to run their TikTok page and make it look like the best vacation destination ever.

The streets were cobbled and red bricked, and the businesses leaned toward art galleries and boutiques. There was a popular theater for live productions, and the bar across the street mimicked that of a 1920s speakeasy. Newcastle drew a mix of young professionals, well-off retirees, and creatives.

It was set up like a combination of both the Garden District and the French Quarter in New Orleans, and there was a public park in the center square and a wedding cake of a cathedral right in the middle of it.

We passed the park and drove down tree-lined streets of brownstones that had been built in the last decade, but looked like they'd been there for a century. Once you got past the brownstones the lots and the houses got a little larger, though not by much.

Theo Vasilios's house was a split-level white stucco with an orange tile roof that was much more suited to Greece than Newcastle, Virginia. It was on a corner lot and there was a wrought-iron fence with brick columns that surrounded the property. I could see the carriage house at the back corner of the property.

"Nice neighborhood," I said. "What do you think these houses cost?"

"The cheapest is probably a million at minimum," he said. "Property values in Newcastle have skyrocketed over the last five years or so."

Jack parked street side since the driveway was narrow, and we walked along the path that led to the carriage house. There were three bays for vehicles on the bottom level, and circular black stairs led to the upstairs living quarters.

Max Ortega was waiting for us on his balcony, dressed in gray sweats and a white T-shirt. His feet were bare, and I could see the weapon tucked in the side of his sweatpants. He'd known we were coming. Probably had security cameras all over the property.

"Max Ortega?" Jack asked, showing his badge.

"That's me," Max said.

"We need to ask you a few questions about Theo and Chloe Vasilios."

There was a long pause before Max finally said, "Come on up."

I followed Jack up the circular staircase, but I kept my eyes on Max Ortega. He didn't look like anyone you'd want to tangle with. I was guessing he was somewhere in his early fifties. His dark hair was cut close, but there were hints of gray, and his beard was short. It was obvious he kept himself in excellent shape. His eyes were dark and studied us intently as we made our way up.

"I'm surprised you're still on the case," Max said. "I figured they would have brought in the State Department to shut you down by now."

"They're trying," Jack said, shrugging. "This isn't my first rodeo."

Max might have smiled, but I couldn't be sure. He didn't look like the kind of man who smiled all that often.

"I've seen your file," Max said. At Jack's long stare

Max shrugged. "I was curious if you'd be able to handle it. I've got connections of my own."

"And?" Jack asked.

"You can handle it," Max said. "They're not going to like that. Come on inside. You want water?"

"I'll take some," I said before Jack could answer for me.

"This is Dr. Graves," Jack said. "She's the coroner for King George County."

"Nice to meet you," Max said, nodding in my direction.

We stepped into the kitchen, and Max opened a cabinet that I saw was a built-in pantry and took out two bottles of water. The kitchen was small, but neat with white cabinets and shiny stainless-steel appliances. There was an island with three barstools that divided it from the living room. There were two arched doorways that must have led to a bedroom and bathroom.

"Have a seat," Max said, gesturing to a white couch with bright blue pillows.

Other than the couch, a matching chair, and a patterned rug that matched the pillows, the only other décor in the room was a large-screen TV on the wall. No pictures, no personal items, nothing that would give away anything about the man who lived here.

"We talked to Nicholas Vasilios," Jack said. "He mentioned that you used to be his head of security."

"Still am technically," Max said. "Nicholas loaned me out to Theo, and hired a temp to take my place. He told me Theo needed someone to watch out for him."

"Was Theo in danger?" Jack asked.

"I don't know if Theo was in danger, but he didn't always make the best life choices. I was assigned to him after he met Chloe."

"Chloe was one of those bad life choices?" I asked.

"According to Nicholas she was," Max said. "I liked her. She was a sweet kid who was in way over her head. And I say kid because that's what she was. I've got a daughter about her age, and if she decided to marry someone old enough to be her father you wouldn't find all the pieces of him."

"She didn't have anyone to look out for her," I said.

Max sighed. "No, she didn't."

"What do you know about her background, where she came from?" Jack asked.

"Nothing much," Max said. "I know someone tried to run her off the road and it scared her. She started jumping at shadows and looking over her shoulder. I figured it had to be someone from her past."

"Max," Jack said easily, leaning back in his chair. I recognized that look in Jack's eyes. It was like a lion just before he was about to pounce on his prey. "You're the third person who's lied to me about not knowing anything about Chloe's background. It's starting to piss me off. And before you say anything, if you read my file then you know I will find out."

Max stared at Jack, his arms crossed over his chest. Finally he let out a sigh and said, "This whole thing is a mess. All I can tell you is that there's a reason Theo took Chloe in under his wing, and it wasn't because they were romantically interested in each other. Theo had once been in the same predicament that Chloe was in, trying to escape his past and get his life back. But not everyone has Nicholas Vasilios to come to the rescue with his checkbook like Theo did. Theo was lucky."

"So Theo felt sorry for her and offered to marry her?" Jack asked. "Why didn't he just pay off whoever was trying to get to her?"

"I think he tried," Max said. "I don't know the details. All I know is that Theo left town to make a deal for Chloe and some guy shows up at the house while he's gone. Theo left me here to keep watch, and this guy walks up to the front door and rings the bell. I saw him on the cameras. So I get my weapon and let myself in the back door of the house. Chloe had just gotten out of the shower and was in her robe. She didn't let him in the house, but whatever he said spooked her."

"You didn't hear what he said?" Jack asked.

"No," he said. "She was pale and shaking, and of course Theo's mother comes marching up seconds after the guy says his piece and leaves. But I didn't recognize the guy and she wouldn't tell me what he said or if he threatened her."

"What'd he look like?" Jack asked.

"Mid to late twenties. Clean cut. Mixed race. Jeans and a T-shirt. I couldn't see a car, so I don't know what he was driving. He took off on foot toward the park and disappeared."

"You ever see this guy around?" Jack asked, holding out his phone so Max could see the picture on it.

"Sure," Max said. "Dickie Harlowe. I ran a background on him early on. Chloe was pretty stuck on him."

"Yet she married Theo," Jack said.

"Because he could protect her," Max said. "That Dickie guy cared a lot about Chloe, and I think Chloe really loved him, but he's kind of a mess. Drinks too much. I think she knew at the end of the day he wouldn't be reliable. Chloe and Theo had an arrangement. She stayed in a separate suite in the house. She had her own space. Theirs wasn't exactly a love match."

"What about sex?" Jack asked.

Max shrugged. "Maybe. I don't know. Everyone's got needs, and they were going to be husband and wife. But I never saw them touch or flirt with each other. They were friends."

"Did Theo know about Dickie?"

"Sure," Max said. "It didn't bother him. He wasn't in love with her. And he always had companionship whenever he wanted it, so he wasn't hurting. I don't think he ever really got over his ex-wife. Blamed himself ever since the divorce."

"We were told Chloe only invited two people to the wedding," I said. "Dickie was one of them. Do you know who the other was?"

Max hesitated a moment, and then said, "Yeah, I know him. Nice kid, about her age. Name's Emmett Parker. Started coming around about a month before the wedding. Chloe seemed pretty happy to see him—obviously someone she'd known for a while."

"Where'd he come from?" Jack asked.

"No idea," Max said. "I only met him a couple of times. Clean-cut kid, very polite. Quiet type. He and Chloe spent a lot of time talking when he'd visit. He made her laugh, and there was far too little laughter in her life. Theo didn't seem to mind him being around. I got the impression Emmett was like a little brother to her. I figured maybe they'd worked together back when she was waiting tables. He mentioned once that he was a student."

"Got a contact for him?" Jack asked.

Max picked up his phone from the counter, scrolled through it, then wrote down a number on a pad of paper. "This is the number I have for him. I don't know where he lives."

"What was your gut feeling on this Emmett kid?" Jack asked.

Max shrugged. "He seemed all right. No red flags that I could see. Wasn't in love with her like Harlowe was, so he wasn't desperate to impress or get her attention. Just seemed like they had a connection."

Jack nodded, making a note of the information. "We pulled the security footage from The Mad King. You dropped Theo and Chloe off right after midnight, but you didn't check into the Holiday Inn until one thirty. That's a long time delay for a twenty-minute drive."

Max's expression didn't change, but something flickered behind his eyes. "I stopped at Briggs's Bar on the way. Figured I'd try to get lucky since I had a few hours before I had to be back. Had a couple of drinks, struck up a conversation with a redhead who looked promising, but she'd had too much to drink and nothing came of it. So I left and checked into the Holiday Inn."

"How'd you know Theo and Chloe were dead?" I asked.

Max's jaw tightened. "I went back to pick them up for the airport the next morning. Arrived at seven thirty, checked in at the front desk. They tried to call the villa, but no answer. The manager—Harris—got concerned after a few tries and suggested we go check on them. I didn't like it. Theo's always punctual. We took one of those golf carts out to the villa."

He paused, and I saw something haunted cross his face. "Harris used his master key. We found Theo first, in the master bedroom. Single shot to the head. Blood everywhere. Called out for Chloe, but somehow...I already knew. Found her in the second bedroom."

He cleared his throat. "I've seen combat. I've seen men blown apart by IEDs. What they did to her... that wasn't just killing. That was sending a message."

"Do you know what the message was?" Jack pressed.

Max's eyes hardened. "If I did, I'd be hunting them myself instead of sitting here talking to you."

"Theo and Chloe both had a tattoo on the bottom of their foot," I said. "Know anything about that?"

"There's a lot I don't know about either of them," Max said, but his careful non-answer told me he knew exactly what the tattoo meant.

"I was sent by Nicholas to protect them. And now

they're both dead. I told Theo I needed to stay that night. It doesn't do any good to have a bodyguard when you send him away."

"Is that what the two of you talked about when you dropped them off?" Jack asked.

"Yeah," Max said. "I was trying to get him to change his mind. Their villa had two bedrooms. But he said they would be fine for one night, and that I'd see them a few hours later when it was time to go to the airport. There wasn't much I could do but leave. I checked into a hotel so I could stay close by. But it wasn't close enough to save them."

His hands tightened around his water bottle. "You know what gets me? I'm good at what I do. Been keeping people alive for thirty years. And the one time I'm not there—the one time I follow orders instead of my gut—this happens."

"You could save me time and help me find the killers faster if you didn't hold out on me," Jack said. "You know more than you're saying."

"I was a Ranger," Max said, his dark eyes intent on Jack's. "My career has always been about knowing more than I say. If you're as good as your file claims, then you don't need me. Others might think differently, but sometimes self-preservation is more important than trying to stop a machine that can never be dismantled."

"The truth is always more important than our personal wants," Jack told him.

"There we disagree," Max said. "I learned that the hard way. I'll show you out."

He stood, and we followed him out onto his narrow balcony, the afternoon sun glinting against the orange tile roof of Theo's house. The spiral staircase loomed ahead, a descent into shadows. Jack turned to hand him a card when a deafening crack split the air.

Time seemed to slow. I caught a flash of movement, the impact of the bullet striking Max's skull, the spray of blood and brain matter hitting my face like warm rain. Max crumpled to the ground in front of us, his body going instantly lifeless. I stood frozen, blood dripping down my cheek, my mind struggling to process what had just happened.

"Down, down!" Jack shouted, grabbing me and pulling me toward the door.

Another shot rang out, the bullet embedding itself in the doorframe inches from my head. Wood splinters stung my cheek as Jack dragged me inside, throwing me behind the kitchen island as he drew his weapon.

"Stay down," he ordered, his voice deadly calm despite the chaos. He was already on his phone, calling for backup, giving our location with precision.

I looked past him to the balcony where Max Ortega lay facedown, a pool of crimson spreading beneath him. His water bottle had rolled to the edge of the balcony, teetering there, before finally falling over the side.

My hands trembled as I wiped blood from my face. The metallic smell filled my nostrils, making my stomach turn. In the distance, I could hear sirens already wailing.

"Jack," I whispered, my eyes fixed on Max's body. "Look at his foot."

The impact of the bullet had knocked Max's body in such a way that one of his bare feet was visible, sole facing up. And there, clear as day on the bottom of his foot, was the same pattern of dots we'd found on Theo and Chloe.

"We're dealing with something bigger than a jealous lover or a professional hit," I said, my voice steadier than I felt. "This is systematic. They're eliminating everyone with that tattoo."

"And everyone who might know what it means," Jack added grimly, his eyes scanning the surrounding buildings for the shooter.

I realized with chilling clarity that Max had known exactly what the pattern meant. And he'd died rather than tell us.

CHAPTER TWELVE

I couldn't stop shaking.

The taste of copper filled my mouth, and I realized I'd bitten my tongue when Jack had thrown me to the floor. I sat with my back against the kitchen island, my knees drawn to my chest, trying to steady my breathing. My hands were coated in Max's blood, dark crimson already starting to dry and crack in the creases of my palms. I could feel it on my face too, splattered across my cheeks and forehead like some macabre war paint.

One second. That's all it had taken. One second between Max Ortega being alive—his lips forming words, eyes narrowed in careful calculation as he measured what to tell us—and the next, his skull exploding in a spray of bone and brain matter. If Jack had moved a half step to the right, if I had leaned forward to hear Max better, that bullet could have found either of us instead.

The roar of the gunshot still echoed in my ears, a phantom sound that wouldn't fade. Beside me, Jack crouched in tense vigilance, his weapon drawn, dividing his attention between the balcony door and the windows that faced the street. His face was a rigid mask, but I could see the barely contained fury in his eyes.

My own rage was building beneath the shock, clearing the fog of disbelief. Someone had tried to kill us—or at the very least, hadn't cared if we were collateral damage. Outside, I could hear the approaching sirens, their wail cutting through the quiet afternoon. Voices shouted in the street below as officers secured the perimeter.

The baby.

My hand instinctively moved to my stomach, still flat but no longer empty. I'd been so caught up in the immediate danger that I hadn't even thought about the tiny life growing inside me. For a dizzy moment, a surge of nausea threatened to overwhelm me—not morning sickness this time, but pure, primal fear.

Jack must have sensed my spiraling thoughts. His blood-spattered hand found mine, squeezing gently.

"We're okay," he said, his voice steady. "We're okay."

But we weren't okay. Max Ortega was dead. His

body lay just feet away from us, cooling in the after-noon breeze that drifted through the shattered glass of the balcony door. And whoever had killed him was still out there, methodically eliminating anyone who might know what those tattoos meant.

They were cleaning house. And judging from the precision of that shot, they were professionals.

"Sheriff!" I heard a familiar voice call out from downstairs.

"We're in here, Cole," Jack said, his voice unnatu-rally calm despite the carnage surrounding us. "Anyone see the shooter?"

Heavy footsteps thundered up the spiral stair-case, and Cole appeared in the doorway, weapon drawn. His eyes widened as he took in the scene—Max's body sprawled on the balcony, the blood-spat-tered walls, and Jack and me huddled behind the kitchen island. He holstered his weapon and stepped carefully into the apartment.

"Not that we've found," Cole said, coming into the kitchen and getting a good look at both of us. His professional demeanor couldn't quite mask his shock at our blood-soaked appearance. "We've got check-points set up in a three-block radius, but nothing has popped so far. The only place he could have made that shot from was the bell tower of the cathedral."

Jack stood and held out a hand to help me to my feet. My legs felt weaker than I wanted to admit, and

I leaned into his strength more than I intended. The dizziness was returning, and I focused on my breathing to keep from passing out. In, out. Simple. Mechanical. One step at a time.

"Are you two okay?" Cole asked, concern etching deep lines around his eyes. "You're not hit?"

"No," I said, taking assessment of my body now that I was standing. My medical training kicked in, pushing aside the personal horror to make room for professional detachment.

"Anything on us belonged to the victim. I need an evidence bag."

I'd left my medical bag in the car, but I wanted to make sure we collected all the pieces of Max Ortega's skull and brains in case there were bullet fragments inside. Every bit of evidence mattered now. I refused to let whoever did this get away because we missed something in the chaos.

"From the damage done to his skull it was a high-caliber rifle," Cole said, his eyes traveling to the balcony where Max lay in an expanding pool of crimson.

I could tell I was in shock, and I was trying to ground myself and focus on the work ahead. I could fall apart later. Later, when we were safe. Later, when Jack and I were alone. Later, when the weight of how close we'd come to dying could be processed in private. Right now, there was work to do.

We stepped back out onto the balcony and stood over the body. The afternoon sun illuminated the scene with an inappropriate cheerfulness, glinting off the wet blood that had splattered across the white railing. The coppery scent hung thick in the air, mingling with the faint smell of gunpowder. A pair of mockingbirds chirped in a nearby tree, oblivious to the human tragedy below them.

"Kill shot through the skull and into the wall of the carriage house," Jack said, pointing to the cracked stucco where the bullet had entered the wall. His hand was steady, his voice clinical, but I could see the tension in every line of his body. "Downward trajectory supports that he most likely made the shot from the bell tower. It's the only location in Newcastle that's high enough to give him a clear shot. That would be about a two-hundred-yard shot. Not a big deal for someone with the right training."

I couldn't help but picture it—a shadow figure in the church bell tower, setting up a rifle with practiced hands, watching through a scope as Max stepped onto his balcony with us. Waiting for the perfect moment. The casual brutality of it made my stomach turn.

"You get any useful information out of him?" Cole asked, keeping a professional distance from the body. His eyes kept darting between us and the corpse, as if trying to reconcile how differently this scene could have played out.

"It was more about what he didn't say than what he did say," Jack answered, his jaw tightening. "Let's get this scene wrapped. I want you and Martinez at my home office in three hours. I'm going to go pay another visit to Ambassador Vasilios."

"Hopefully not looking like that," Cole said, mouth twitching as he gestured to our blood-soaked clothing.

Jack looked down at his clothes and said, "It's tempting." The grim humor barely masked the dangerous edge in his voice. I'd heard that tone before—when Jack was past diplomacy and moving into retribution territory.

"You want backup?" Cole asked, obviously reading the same warning signs in Jack's demeanor.

"Yes. Have two officers in uniform follow me out," Jack said. "My patience has run thin with whatever game is being played. I can put two and two together, and if the State Department thinks they can protect Nicholas Vasilios from what's coming down on his family then they're all deceived."

Jack stopped and looked at me, his expression softening slightly. "Anything you need to do here?"

"No," I said, my professional mask firmly in place despite the chaos of emotions churning beneath the surface. "I need to reach out to Lily."

"She's already on the way," Cole said. "She said she was swinging by to pick up Sheldon on the way. He heard the callout on the police scanner."

"Okay, good," I said. "We can put him on ice for now. I'll deal with him tomorrow."

The crime-scene team came up shortly after dressed in their white jumpsuits and gloves, and one of them stood in front of Jack and meticulously tweezed the brain matter and bits of skull into a bag. The methodical, detached nature of their work was strangely comforting—a reminder that no matter how personal this felt, it was still a crime scene that needed processing like any other.

I stood watching in dazed bemusement until another tech came up and started to do the same to me. I closed my eyes, preferring not to think about what I might be covered in. The sensation of someone plucking bits of a dead man from my hair and skin was surreal, dissociative. Part of me wanted to laugh at the absurdity of it all, a sure sign that shock was still working its way through my system.

"The shower in my office at the sheriff's office is closest," Jack said once we'd been picked clean and were back in the Tahoe. The smell of blood still clung to us despite the team's efforts, and my clothes felt stiff and heavy with Max's dried bodily fluids.

"I don't have any clean clothes at your office," I said, staring out the window as Jack drove away from the crime scene. The quaint streets of Newcastle scrolled by, their charm now tainted by what we'd experienced. I'd never look at the church bell tower the same way again.

"We'll go home then," he said. "We can shower and then I can go pay a visit to Ambassador Vasilios."

"You want to go alone?" I asked, turning to study his profile. His jaw was set in that stubborn way I knew too well.

"I think it'll be better if you're not there," he said, his knuckles white on the steering wheel. "I'll have deputies there for backup. Maybe we can come to a gentleman's agreement as far as this case is concerned. I'm hoping that he's causing interference to protect his son's reputation."

"And if you're wrong?" I asked, the unspoken danger hanging between us. If Nicholas Vasilios was behind this, Jack was walking straight into the lion's den.

"Then he might very well be behind it all," he said, his voice hard as granite. "There's no gray area here. He either thinks he's protecting his family or he's intentionally trying to let someone get away with murder."

I leaned back against the headrest, the adrenaline finally beginning to ebb, leaving exhaustion in its wake. The image of Max's foot—with that same pattern of dots that had been on Theo and Chloe—

kept flashing in my mind. Whatever that symbol meant, people were dying to keep it secret.

And now Jack was heading straight for the man who might be orchestrating it all.

By the time we made it back home, the adrenaline and shock had started to fade, leaving me hollow and vulnerable. My body betrayed me with violent tremors that I couldn't control, waves of delayed terror rolling through me like aftershocks from an earthquake. I'd seen death before—I made my living among the dead—but I'd never been so close to becoming one of them. Never felt someone else's life explode across my skin in warm, wet fragments. Never watched the light disappear from a person's eyes one second before it could have been mine.

I stared at my trembling hands, disgusted at my weakness. I knew this was par for the course—I'd been there before when cases had gone sideways— but it always made me feel like a weakling, like I was somehow failing at the strength Jack seemed to possess in endless supply.

"Dickie's car is gone," Jack said, breaking the silence as we sat in the driveway, both of us reluctant to leave the safety of the Tahoe and face what had happened.

"Thank God for small favors," I said, my voice sounding strange in my own ears. "According to Max, it sounds like maybe Chloe did care about Dickie. I feel sorry for him."

I found myself thinking about how quickly life could end. How Chloe had been planning to run away with Dickie only to end up dead on her wedding night. How Max had been alive and talking to us one moment, then gone the next. How fragile everything was. How close we'd come.

Jack sighed, his eyes focused on something distant. "Dickie's a product of his upbringing who has refused to grow up and take responsibility for the things he can change. I feel sorry for the boy he was. But how he is as a man is sorely lacking. The best thing for Dickie would be to check in to rehab and get away from his father for a while. Maybe forever. He's done nothing but look for a woman to love him since we were fifteen years old. He's had good women, and none of them are ever enough, because he doesn't think that *he's* enough."

My lips twitched despite the rawness inside me. "Your psychology is showing."

"That doesn't make me wrong," he said, a flicker of the usual Jack shining through the battle-ready sheriff who'd gotten us through the past few hours.

Jack came around and helped me get out of the Tahoe, his hand steadying me when my knees threatened to buckle. He rubbed my arms when he felt my shivers, and I leaned into his warmth, needing the solid reality of him. Alive. We were both alive when we so easily might not have been.

"Come on," he said, his voice gentler than I'd heard it all day. "Let's get you in a hot shower."

Oscar came running to meet us at the door like he usually did, but he skidded to a halt when he saw us, nose twitching at the metallic scent of death that clung to our clothes. He turned and ran back upstairs to Doug's room, nails clicking against the hardwood in his hasty retreat.

"I guess we look worse than I thought," I said, teeth chattering so hard I worried they might crack. The shock was hitting me in earnest now, my body temperature plummeting despite the warm spring day.

Jack ushered us both upstairs to the third floor where our bedroom was located. I caught a glimpse of us in the mirror—blood-spattered ghouls with haunted eyes—before he guided me into the bathroom and turned on the shower. Steam began to fill the room, but even that warmth couldn't touch the ice forming in my core. My arms and legs were leaden and uncooperative, and I fumbled helplessly with my sweater, unable to coordinate my movements.

"That was a cashmere sweater," I said as Jack

gently but efficiently stripped my ruined clothes off. The strange, disjointed thought floated to the surface of my mind, a trivial concern amidst the horror of the day. "I liked it."

"I'll buy you more," he said, his voice rough with emotion as he peeled away the blood-stiffened fabric. His hands lingered on my skin, reassuring himself I was whole and unharmed before he guided me into the shower. "I'm going to use the shower in the guest bath. I don't even want to think about what's in my hair right now. Take your time. I'll be back."

I grunted and moved under the hot spray, a sob escaping as my muscles cramped from the excessive shivering. My body was processing what my mind couldn't yet face—how narrowly we'd escaped. The image of Max's face as the bullet struck him replayed in vivid detail, and I wondered if he'd known in that final millisecond what was happening. If he'd felt fear, or pain, or if it had been too quick for him to register anything at all.

I watched in morbid fascination as pink-tinged water swirled around my feet and disappeared down the drain. Someone's life—their hopes and fears and memories—reduced to a bloody residue circling a shower drain. I pressed my forehead against the cool tile as tears finally came, mingling with the water streaming down my face.

I cried for Max, for the daughter he'd mentioned who would never see her father again. I cried for the life growing inside me that had almost lost both parents before ever taking a breath. I cried from the sheer relief of still being alive when death had brushed so close I could taste it.

I don't know how long I stood there letting the water sluice away my tears, but I eventually found the energy to scrub my head with shampoo and wash my body, reclaiming my skin from the horror that had marked it.

"You okay?" I heard Jack ask, and I turned to see him come in through the clear glass shower wall, his face etched with concern.

"Yeah," I said, though we both knew it wasn't entirely true. "Much better now. A little hungry. We haven't eaten anything since this morning." The mundane observation felt like reaching for normalcy in a world turned upside down.

"I texted Doug and told him to order pizza," Jack said.

He wore a towel wrapped low around his waist, his body still damp from his own shower. Droplets of water traced paths down his chest as he grabbed a clean towel for me and spread it over the warming bar. I watched the steady movements of his hands, grateful for his strength when mine had deserted me.

"Good thinking," I said, letting the hot water beat

down on my neck, not yet ready to leave its comforting embrace.

I heard the shower door open and sighed, but instead of urging me out, Jack stepped in behind me, wrapping his arms around my waist. I felt him press against me, solid and alive. He turned me in his arms and dropped his forehead so it rested against mine, our breaths mingling in the steam.

"That was a close one today," he said, his voice breaking as he tightened his grip on me. "Just a slight shift in any direction and it could have been either of us. I keep seeing it happen, over and over. I keep seeing it being you instead of Max."

"Yeah," I whispered, looking up to meet his eyes. I put my hand to the side of his face, feeling the barely contained emotion trembling beneath his skin. The invincible Sheriff Lawson was gone, replaced by just Jack—my husband—terrified of losing me, of losing everything we'd built together.

And then he kissed me with a desperate intensity that took my breath away. I felt the raw energy pouring off of him, the need to affirm life in the face of death, and I met it with equal fervor. His hands clutched at me like I might slip away if he loosened his grip, and I pressed myself against him, needing the solid reality of his body against mine.

"I don't want to be rough," he rasped, coming up for air and somehow pulling me closer.

I kissed him again, pouring everything I had into it—all the fear, the relief, the desperate joy of still being alive—and said, "I won't break."

I needed this as much as he did. Needed to feel his heart pounding against mine, to know with absolute certainty that we had survived. That whatever darkness was closing in around us, we still had this—each other, our love, and the life we'd created together.

CHAPTER THIRTEEN

An hour later, Doug and I were set up in the office sharing a pizza and poring over the data that Margot had accessed by not necessarily legal means on Theo Vasilios.

"Let's start with financials," I said. "It's been mentioned more than once that the Vasilios men like to throw money around. Let's see where Theo was throwing it. I want to get through this stuff before Cole and Martinez show up."

"Maybe Jack will get lucky and we'll be able to do this aboveboard by the time they get here."

"Here's hoping," I said, eyeing the last piece of pepperoni.

"You might as well take it," Doug said. "We can always get more later."

"Thanks," I said, taking the pizza.

"Whoa, looks like Theo was the sole beneficiary of his grandfather's estate. His name was also Theodore Vasilios, and it looks like he was part of the Greek royal family up until 1974 when the Greek government did away with all royal titles and positions. Having no title didn't stop him from building wealth though. He was a very successful businessman internationally. He died when Theo was only twenty-three years old and all of his assets went to Theo to be held in a trust until he reached the age of thirty-five."

"That's a long time to wait when you're twenty-three," I said.

"Looks like he received the full amount when he turned thirty-five, plus all real estate holdings and business ventures," Doug said. "He's partnered with several businesses himself in the last ten years, but it looks like Theo doesn't have the golden touch like his grandfather did. Most of the businesses have failed or are fledgling. If he'd been good at it he'd be pushing billionaire status."

"Who inherits if Theo dies?" I asked.

"That information isn't available," Doug said. "At least not electronically. Theo's attorney is in Greece, but it looks like he got on a flight and is scheduled to land at Reagan International about ten o'clock tonight."

"Other than business has Theo had any unusual spending?" I asked.

"He paid too much for that house in Newcastle, and he purchased a couple of other homes—one in Santa Monica and another in London. He was paying Chloe ten grand a month to manage his businesses. He spent a ridiculous amount of money on shoes and suits, and also a lot on transatlantic flights to London. It looks like he went regularly about every six weeks and would stay for a week."

"Even after he met Chloe?" I asked.

"Yes," Doug said.

"Did Chloe ever travel with him?"

"Once," Doug said, pulling up flight logs and credit card receipts. "Looks like she stayed at the Shangri-La."

"I thought Theo had his own place in London?"

"He does," Doug said, shrugging. "Chloe checked into the hotel under her name and identification. I don't know if Theo stayed there with her or not. His signature isn't on any of the restaurant bills or the spa."

"Interesting," I said, trying to bring something to the surface of my memory, but I wasn't sure what it was. And then it came to me. "The ex-wife. Nicholas said something about Theo's ex-wife. Apparently they've maintained a good relationship since their divorce, but he mentioned that she'd flown in from London for the wedding."

"Margot flagged her on the list," Doug said. "Vivica Anders Vasilios." Doug whistled when her picture came on the screen. "Holy cow. She's a former Miss Universe. Originally from Denmark. It looks like she met Theo at the University of St Andrews in Scotland while they were students there. They married a year later in a very lavish ceremony in Greece. The same year Theo's grandfather died. They were married for eight years. No children."

"Did she ever remarry?" I asked.

"No, but no reason to," Doug said. "She made out like a bandit in the divorce, and not because the court ordered it. Theo made sure she was set for life."

"Maybe a guilt offering for his sins," I said. "Apparently she's got a house on Dupont Circle. Jack reached out to let her know we need to speak with her. I'm guessing it's on the to-do list for tomorrow."

"Sign me up for that trip," Doug said. "She's someone who deserves to be seen in person."

I smacked him lightly on the back of the head. "Stop thinking with your hormones for a second."

"I'm sixteen," he said, grinning. "I don't know what else I'm supposed to think with."

I laughed and said, "Nicholas told us that Theo had lost his way for a time and that Vivica had been very patient with him."

"Lost his way how?"

"That's the big question. Could be drugs or alcohol. Or something that would cause a grown man to get a tattoo on the bottom of his foot."

"Like the Illuminati," Doug said.

"Does that mean you found the tattoo in the SMT database?" I asked.

"Nope," he said. "There's nothing anything even remotely like it that I can find."

The doorbell rang and I looked at the time. "Shoot," I said. "Put everything on Theo Vasilios away for now. That's going to be Cole and Martinez."

"They won't care if we're digging deep into the victim," Doug said.

"Yeah, but sometimes it's better to not put people in the position of lying for you if they're ever subpoenaed to testify. Don't worry. Jack will get the State Department to release those records."

I'd opened the door expecting Cole and Martinez, but I was surprised to see Dickie on our doorstep again.

"Hey," I said. "What's wrong? Are you sick?"

He laughed but there was no humor in it. "No," he said. "I just decided to pick today for whatever reason to quit drinking."

"That's great," I said. "I was just about to make some coffee."

"God, no," he said. "You make terrible coffee. At least let me do it." And he led the way into the kitchen, making himself right at home.

"Jack had to run down a lead on a case," I said carefully, not mentioning Chloe's name. "He should be back soon."

"I didn't come here to see Jack," he said. "I came to talk to you."

My brows rose in surprise at that bit of information. "Me?" I asked, watching as Dickie moved around our kitchen with practiced ease. His expensive clothes were wrinkled, and his normally perfect hair was disheveled. His hands were steady though, methodically measuring coffee grounds. I studied his profile, trying to see the boy I'd known hidden in the man he'd become.

"You've always told me the truth," he said quietly. "Even when I didn't want to hear it. I need that right now."

I leaned against the counter and crossed my arms. "Okay."

Dickie turned to face me, his eyes red rimmed and haunted. "How messed up am I? On a scale of one to ten?"

"Is this some weird intervention in reverse?" I asked.

The coffee maker started to burble and hiss behind him, filling the kitchen with the rich aroma of the good beans Jack kept in the freezer.

"I sat in my car for three hours before I drove here," Dickie said, his voice barely above a whisper. "I had a bottle of Macallan 25 on the passenger seat. I kept picking it up and putting it back down. It would have been so easy to just..." He rubbed his face, and for a moment he looked impossibly old.

"Dickie—"

"Do you know what my father said to me when my divorce was finalized?" he asked. "He didn't even look up from his newspaper. He just said, 'Harlowes make terrible husbands. Sign a prenup for your next one.'"

I winced. I'd met Dickie's father enough times to know the ruthless banker behind the polished façade.

"My grandfather drank himself to death," Dickie continued. "My father is working on it. And here I am, following the same path like it's the only one I know how to walk."

I moved to the cabinet and pulled down two mugs. "Did you ever talk to anyone after your divorce?"

"What, like a shrink?" He laughed that hollow laugh again. "Harlowes don't do therapy. We buy bigger houses, faster cars, and younger women."

"How's that working out for you?" I asked, pouring the coffee.

"About as well as you'd expect," he said, accepting the mug I handed him. "I thought Chloe was different. I thought I was different with her." His voice cracked. "Now she's gone and it was all a lie, and I'm just...here. Still the same screwed-up rich kid who can't figure out how to be a man."

I guided him to the kitchen table, and we sat. The fading sun made shadows dance across the wood floor.

"You know what hurts the most?" he asked. "I keep thinking if I'd been better—more like Jack, maybe—she might have trusted me enough to really tell me what was going on. I might have been able to protect her."

"You don't know that," I said gently.

"I do know that," he insisted. "She didn't trust me because I'm not trustworthy. I've spent my whole life proving that to everyone. I'm unreliable. I drink too much. I sleep around. I use my money to paper over all my problems." He stared into his coffee. "And the worst part is, I like being that guy. It's easy. Comfortable. There are no expectations."

"Dickie," I said, reaching across the table to touch his hand. "You came here today. You left the bottle in the car. That counts for something."

He looked up, his eyes shining with unshed tears.

"Does it? Because from where I'm sitting, it feels like too little, too late."

"It's never too late to change," I said. "Trust me, I know something about family legacies."

He nodded slightly. We both knew what I meant —the shadow my parents had cast over my life, the darkness I'd fought to escape.

"How did you do it?" he asked. "How did you become...you, instead of them?"

I considered my answer carefully. "I stopped waiting for permission to be better. I decided that their sins weren't mine to carry. But mostly, I let people help me. Jack, his parents, you guys—"

"I've never let anyone help me," Dickie admitted. "Not really. I've let people bail me out, clean up my messes, but actually help me? That would mean admitting I needed it."

"And now?"

"Now I'm sitting in your kitchen at—" he checked his watch, "—five o'clock on a Sunday afternoon, stone-cold sober for the first time in...I don't even know how long. And I'm terrified."

"Of what?"

"Of finding out who I really am without all the... artifice. What if there's nothing there?"

I reached out and took his hand. "Richmond Dexter Harlowe, I've known you for most of your life. Before the fancy cars and the designer suits. Before you learned how to charm your way into any woman's bed. You were kind. You were funny. You were the one who helped me pass Ms. Tompkins's computer science class when I was failing miserably."

"That was a lifetime ago," he said, but I could see a flicker of something in his eyes—recognition, maybe.

"That person is still in there," I insisted. "And I think you came here today because you want to find him again."

Dickie's eyes filled with tears. "I don't know how."

"You start by asking for help," I said. "Real help. Professional help."

He tensed. "My father—"

"Isn't the one who has to live your life," I cut in. "What do you want, Dickie? Not what your father wants, not what the Harlowe legacy demands. What do *you* want?"

He was quiet for so long I thought he might not answer. When he did, his voice was small, almost childlike. "I want to not hate the man I see in the mirror. I want to be someone who could have deserved Chloe. I want to be the man she could have loved. I want to stop drinking just to make it through the day." His shoulders slumped. "I'm so tired, Jaye."

I squeezed his hand. "I know a place. It's discreet.

Private. The kind of place where even a Harlowe could go without making the society pages."

"You think they can fix me?" he asked, a hint of his old self-mockery in his voice.

"I think they can help you fix yourself," I said. "But you'd have to be all in. No half measures."

He took a deep, unsteady breath. "What about the investigation? Jack told me to stay in town."

"Did you make a formal statement?" I asked.

"This morning," he said. "With my attorney like Jack said."

"Good, that'll make it easier. I'll talk to Jack. He loves you and will want the best thing for you. And this is the best thing."

Dickie stared down at our joined hands, then back up at me. For a moment, I caught a glimpse of the boy I'd known—earnest, uncertain, but with a good heart beneath all the bravado.

"How do I start?" he asked.

"I'll make some calls," I said. "And then you'll need to pack a bag."

The misery in his eyes broke my heart. Along with the self-loathing was a grief so deep it was palpable. A grief over the woman he'd never get a chance to love.

"Dickie," I said. "I believe Chloe did love you." I held up a hand before he could argue. "No, wait. Listen. We've uncovered some things in this investigation I can't really go into, but we believe Chloe felt she had no choice but to marry Theo. There are witnesses who say they knew of your relationship with her, that Theo knew about it too and he didn't care. Because he wasn't in love with her. But she did believe that he could help keep her safe.

"The last time the two of you were together, I don't believe it was her being cruel. I believe it was her loving you as best she could and saying goodbye. Maybe you and Chloe had more in common than you realized, both of you trapped by the pain of your past and unsure how to break free."

Tears had been trailing slowly down his cheeks, dripping onto the table.

"It's easier thinking she might have loved me, despite being me," he said. "So thank you for that."

"I promise to be here, every step of the way," I said. "The rest is up to you."

I felt something shift between us—not just friendship, but a deeper understanding. We'd both faced our demons. Maybe now, finally, Dickie was ready to face his too.

CHAPTER FOURTEEN

I'D MADE A LOT OF HELPFUL CONNECTIONS DURING MY short stint at Augusta General—when I'd still been working with the living instead of the dead. So it hadn't taken long for me to make a few phone calls and get Dickie set up for next steps. The center in California specialized in addiction treatment for high-profile clients. They had discreet intake procedures, no press access, and a success rate that justified their astronomical fees. Dickie wouldn't bat an eye at the cost, but the real price would be confronting the demons he'd spent a lifetime avoiding.

Martinez and Cole still hadn't arrived—neither had Jack for that matter—and I was starting to wonder if something had come up. I was used to cop hours and cop life, so I didn't give it too much thought. I'd told Doug I'd be back in about an hour, and then I'd driven Dickie back to his place, helped him pack a bag, and then taken him to the airport in Richmond so he could catch the last flight of the day to LA. My friend Louise was going to pick him up at the airport. The choices Dickie made after that were his to decide, but at least he had a starting place.

By the time I got back to the house, the driveway was full of cars, so I pulled around to the side and parked over by the garage that held all of Jack's man toys. His Tahoe was parked in its usual spot, so he was back from his trip to see Ambassador Vasilios. The fading light of evening cast long shadows across the yard, and I felt the weight of the day settle into my bones. I was exhausted, but I knew we were far from done.

I walked into the comforting chaos of home. Oscar barked excitedly at so many people coming to visit, and the smell of food wafted from the kitchen. I'd lost track of the time somewhere along the way and realized it was almost seven.

"Hey," Jack said, coming from the back of the house. The lines around his eyes had deepened since this morning, and there was a tension in his shoulders that hadn't been there before. Whatever happened with Nicholas Vasilios hadn't gone well. "Where have you been? Doug said Dickie stopped by."

"Yeah," I said. "Long story. I'm really hoping he's not a viable suspect at this point because I just took him to rehab."

Jack looked at me surprised. "Of his own free will? Or did you have to tie him up and kidnap him?"

"He said it's what he wants. I called a friend and got everything set up for him. He's got a chance, Jack. A real one."

"Well," Jack said, rubbing a hand over his face in exhaustion. "At least I know where to find him if he needs to be questioned again." He softened slightly. "And I hope it works out for him. I'd like to see him break the cycle."

"What happened with the ambassador?" I asked. "Why are there so many cars out front? Who's even here?"

"Also a long story," Jack said. "I just walked in the door myself, so I'm guessing Doug is hosting something that revolves around food in our kitchen. I did see that Cole and Martinez are here, so maybe we can get some work done. I need aspirin."

I put my hand on his shoulder, feeling the knots of tension there. "Are you okay?"

"Yeah, it's been an interesting day. It'll be easier to tell everyone at one time what's happened." He covered my hand with his for a moment, drawing strength from the contact. In that brief touch, I felt what he wasn't saying—the strain of watching bodies pile up, of racing the clock against a killer who seemed to be one step ahead.

I followed Jack into the kitchen and noticed the pizza delivery guy had made another trip. There were pizza boxes stacked on the island, and half a dozen people stood around the granite slab, eating and talking. The easy camaraderie of law enforcement—making jokes over food while discussing death. It was how we all coped. I was glad to see there weren't as many people as it had sounded like when I'd first walked in.

Cole and Martinez and Derby were there, all in comfortable off-duty clothes, though Cole had switched out his Stetson for a baseball cap. I hadn't seen Martinez in a week, not since we'd closed our last case. He'd taken some personal time off, and I had to say I couldn't blame him.

Our last case had involved a child who'd been sold as part of a trafficking network. There were some cases that weighed heavier than others, and there were some victims that would stay imprinted in your mind forever. That had been one of those cases.

But Martinez seemed to be in good spirits tonight, and he was in jeans and a black T-shirt, which was very unlike Martinez to wear something so casual. His black hair had been freshly cut, and he wore a gold chain around his neck, so he wasn't a complete slouch like the rest of us. The week off had done him good.

I understood why the cops were here. I was a little hazy on Lily and Sheldon.

"We got invited for the food," Lily said, reading my mind. "Hope you don't mind. But after we picked up the body in Newcastle and dropped him off, Cole said Doug invited everyone for pizza and Sheldon was hungry."

"My mom made tuna casserole," Sheldon said with a shudder. "It doesn't agree with me, so pizza is the more preferable option. Did you know casseroles are the official food of funerals across the country? Why don't we serve casseroles at viewings instead of cookies?"

"Because it's easier to clean out cookie crumbs from a casket than limp noodles," I said, helping myself to another slice of pizza. The baby was demanding sustenance, and I was happy to oblige. The scent of pepperoni and cheese was irresistible after the day we'd had.

I sometimes wondered if the pizza delivery man thought weird things were going on at our house with the number of orders Doug sometimes called in a day, but between morning sickness and an intense afternoon hunger, I was grateful for the easy access.

"So what happened with the ambassador?" I

asked Jack. "Do you have access to everything you need to proceed in the investigation?"

The room quieted, everyone sensing that Jack was about to deliver significant news. He'd always had that effect on people—the ability to command attention without raising his voice. It was what made him an exceptional sheriff.

"Yeah," Jack said, his voice carefully neutral. "I'm waiting for the judge to sign the warrant for full access. But it's not because the ambassador and I came to an agreement. It's because he's dead."

My eyes widened in shock. "Wait, what? What do you mean dead?"

"Local law enforcement was already on scene when I arrived," Jack said. "He allegedly put a gun in his mouth and pulled the trigger."

"Allegedly," I said, recognizing the skepticism in Jack's voice. "Who discovered the body?"

"There were several 911 calls from the golf course with reports of a gunshot," Jack said. "Local law enforcement responded, and they had to break down the door when no one answered. Cecelia Vasilios was so medicated she slept through the whole thing. The cops found her in an upstairs bedroom. Nicholas was in the library where we'd met with him this morning."

"Where were Tweedledee and Tweedledum?" I

asked. "Isn't that the whole point of having intimidating-looking security?"

"That's the million-dollar question," Jack said. "I want to find out who those two are and track them down. I want deep background checks. Something doesn't add up."

The energy in the room shifted as everyone began to process the implications. Another body. Another connection to the mysterious tattoo. Another thread to unravel.

We all moved into the office where Doug had already set up Margot and the whiteboards. The space was prepared for a proper investigation briefing—multiple screens displaying data, photos pinned to a corkboard, timelines drawn on whiteboards. Doug had been busy in my absence.

"As you can see, we're set up for action," Doug said, winking. "Isn't that right, Margot?"

"Oh, have you all come back from your little kitchen party?" she asked sweetly. "You could have invited me, but you left me here alone. Was it so you could have Lily to yourself?"

Cole coughed and Doug turned an unusual shade of pink. "No way," Doug said. "You know you're my best girl. We've talked about this before. I can't take you everywhere I go. It's not possible."

"It is possible," she said. "It's why you won't download me on your phone. You just don't want me with you all the time. Well, maybe I don't want to be around you all the time either."

"Maybe we could discuss this later, Margot," Doug said. "We're kind of in the middle of a case here."

"Sure, just put me off until later," she said, the anger in her voice making me wince.

"You've got the whole team here. Why would you need me?" She didn't give time for an answer. "Well, it just so happens I've got better things to do."

With that declaration, there was a flash on the screen that I could only assume was the equivalent of a slamming door and Margot was gone.

"Margot?" Doug asked, typing on the keyboard in a frenzy. But there was no answer.

"Oh, great," Cole said. "You've lost control of your robot. That should end well."

"She'll come back around," Doug said. "She always does. I'll just have to do everything manually for now."

Everyone took a seat at the table, some more hesitant than others since they weren't used to Margot. Laptops and file folders were strewn across the top as we all settled in to dig through piles of information that had been collected over the last twenty-four hours about this case.

Jack remained standing, positioning himself at the head of the table. This was Jack in his element—

commanding, focused, a force of nature who could organize chaos into clarity. Despite the exhaustion evident in the shadows under his eyes, he seemed to draw energy from the challenge before him. I'd always admired his ability to remain steady in the midst of a storm.

"Let's put everything we know on the table," Jack said. "We've got five bodies in two days, and I want to understand why."

He moved to a large whiteboard and began creating a murder board, writing names and drawing connections between them. In the center, he placed photos of Theo and Chloe Vasilios—our original victims. Then Max Ortega and Nicholas Vasilios. Four deaths, all connected somehow.

"What ties these people together?" Jack asked, looking around the room. "The obvious connection is family—Nicholas is Theo's father. Max worked for both Vasilios men at different times. And Chloe married into the family."

"And the tattoos," I added. "We've confirmed that Theo, Chloe, and Max all had identical dot pattern tattoos on the bottom of their feet. Can you find out from the medical examiner in Arlington if Nicholas has the same?"

"I've requested that information from the ME handling Nicholas's case," Jack said. "We should know soon."

"What about the security guards you mentioned?" Martinez asked.

"Jaye and I got the privilege of meeting them earlier," Jack said, drawing our attention back to the board. "They looked like hired muscle to keep anyone away from the ambassador. One was American—he looked like former military. The other was foreign. Looked like a thug. See what you can pull up on them. I want to know why they conveniently disappeared."

"Got it," Doug said as photographs and information began to post on the whiteboard wall. "You're right about the American military. Derek Rogan. Twenty years Army, honorable discharge, worked private security ever since. Been with Vasilios for at least seven years according to employment records. Divorced twice. Not the sharpest tool in the shed looking at his aptitude tests, but he's loyal."

"He would have worked with Max," I said.

"We know what happens to loyal employees in this case," Cole muttered. "They end up dead."

"And the other one?" Martinez asked, leaning forward.

"That's where it gets interesting," Doug said, twisting back and forth in the ergonomic chair. "His credentials say Joe Winsome. You'd think he was the boy next door he's so American on paper. I'm running him through facial recognition now."

"No way he's American. His accent was Slavic," Jack said. "Eastern European at a minimum. Ortega mentioned to me when we interviewed him that this Winsome guy was a recent addition—a fill-in after Max was assigned to Theo full-time."

Doug's fingers flew across the keyboard and there was a crease in his forehead as he muttered under his breath. "Come on, baby. Cough up the goods. That's good. That's a good start."

"I always feel like we should leave the room whenever he starts talking to the computer like that," Martinez said.

"You're a laugh a minute, Martinez," Doug said. "But I've got the goods. Turns out Joe Winsome's Social Security number belongs to a guy who died in 2008."

"Anything else?" Jack asked, adding to his notes on the board.

"I've found mention of our mystery Slavic friend in some less than reputable mercenary forums," Doug said. "Still working on a real name, but he's connected to at least three political assassinations in the last decade. Whoever he is, he doesn't come cheap."

"I wonder how he got connected with the ambassador," I said, trying to piece together the timeline in my head.

"Guys like that get a reputation," Jack said. "Mercenaries for hire."

"A couple million per job," Doug chimed in. "Payable in cryptocurrency, of course. Very difficult to trace, but not impossible for someone of my capabilities."

Derby was working on his own laptop. I always wondered if he was threatened by Doug's ability to ferret out information, but Derby was a pretty affable guy.

"I pulled everything I could find on Rogan," Derby said. 'Since he went private he's kept a minimal digital footprint. He hasn't updated his Facebook in three years, no Instagram, no dating profiles."

"Not everyone broadcasts their breakfast choices to the world," Martinez said dryly.

"Everyone leaves some kind of digital footprint behind," Derby said. "Normal people leave breadcrumbs whether they mean to or not."

"I'm guessing Rogan isn't normal people," I said.

Cole nodded. "Ambassador's security detail? These guys are trained to stay under the radar. Being ambassador is a presidential appointment. These guys would have to work with secret service from time to time. They'd know protocols."

"Still doesn't explain where they both disappeared to when Nicholas allegedly decided to eat his gun," Jack said, circling Winsome's and Rogan's names on the board.

Sheldon, who had been uncharacteristically quiet, raised his hand like he was in a classroom. "Umm, I have a question. If Mr. Vasilios killed himself—"

"Allegedly," Jack, Cole, and I said in unison.

"Right, allegedly," Sheldon continued. "The probability of both security guards leaving the property and giving the ambassador the opportunity to kill himself is very low. The percentage of people who kill themselves while a loved one is in the house is less than one percent."

"Maybe he fired the help first," I said. "If Nicholas was involved with the death of his son and Chloe then maybe he was overwhelmed with guilt and decided to take the easy way out."

"Or maybe he didn't kill himself at all," Jack said, the unspoken implication hanging in the air. "See if you can find addresses for these guys," he added to Doug. "I want to send deputies to pick them up. They were either negligent, complicit, or something happened to them too. Did we ever get a match from the fingerprint found at the scene?"

"I can confirm that the print found on the 9mm that was left behind as well as the print on Chloe Vasilios are a match," Doug said. "I ran it through the system and didn't get a match initially. But then I ran it through this other program that I created that, uh, has a more encompassing reach—"

"I didn't hear that," Derby said.

"—and I found a match in the juvenile system."

Derby groaned and dropped his head in his hand. "I'm still not hearing this since."

"Probably best," Doug said. "I was able to find a name. The print matched to a kid named Cory Maybury. He'd been picked up a few times for shoplifting, then he moved to grand theft auto. He ended up in the system."

"Where is he now?" Jack asked.

"Dead," Doug said. "At least that's what the federal government says. He ended up in a boys' home and ended up getting stabbed for stealing some kid's cigarettes."

"Except he's not dead if his fingerprints are on our murder weapon," Jack said.

"Exactly," Doug said. "I'll find the thread. There's always a trail. People don't just create new lives without adding a bump to the system.

I studied the board, the victims' faces staring back at me. What connected them beyond the obvious? What were we missing?

"We should talk to Emmett Parker," I added. "Put him on the board. Max Ortega mentioned him as the other person Chloe invited to her wedding besides Dickie. If he was close enough to Chloe to be one of only two guests she invited, he might know something about her past."

"Good point," Jack said, writing the name on the board. "Doug, see if you can get a phone number for Emmett Parker. Cole, see if you can make arrangements for both him and Vivica Vasilios to meet us at the station in the morning."

"Sure thing," Cole said, making a note.

"I've got something," Doug announced suddenly, his fingers flying across the keyboard. "I cross-referenced the Slavic guy's height, build, and the scar on his left ear with international intelligence databases—"

"Technically off limits to civilians," Derby muttered.

"—and got a hit," Doug continued, ignoring the interruption. "His name is Josef Visek. Former Czech Special Forces, went mercenary around fifteen years ago. Known aliases include Miklos Petrov, Anton Dragovic, and Joe Winsome. And here's the money trail. A series of payments from a Cayman Islands account to another account in Liechtenstein, then transferred to a cryptocurrency wallet. The initial account traces back to a shell corporation with ties to—would you like to guess?—our dearly departed Ambassador Vasilios."

"How much?" Jack asked.

"Two hundred and fifty thousand dollars," Doug said. "Transferred three days ago."

"Right before the wedding," I said. "So Nicholas hired this Visek guy for something, and I'm guessing it wasn't just to stand around looking menacing."

Martinez leaned forward. "Could he be our shooter? For Theo and Chloe?"

"Or for Max Ortega," Lily said. "That was a professional hit if I've ever seen one. That shot from the bell tower required serious skill."

"It still doesn't explain the tattoos," I said. "Or why Nicholas would want his own son dead."

"Yeah, the money doesn't make sense," Jack said. "Two hundred and fifty thousand dollars is nothing. Most highly trained personal security easily make that, and that figure is on the low end. It's not enough money for a professional kill for one of our victims, much less all three of them. It smells of a setup to me."

Jack added Visek's name to the board, drawing a line to connect him to Nicholas and adding a question mark next to the line connecting him to each murder.

"Ding, ding, dong," Doug said. "You win the prize, Jack. The payments from Nicholas Vasilios to Josef Visek are staged. When I trace it backward, it's bouncing from accounts all over the world and different names and shell corporations. Someone wants us to believe Nicholas hired Visek."

Jack stepped back, studying the murder board with narrowed eyes. "So we've got four dead bodies, all connected to the Vasilios family. We've got mysterious tattoos. We've got a professional mercenary who may have been hired to commit these murders. And we've got a web of financial transactions designed to confuse investigators."

He turned to face the team. "We're missing something fundamental here. What's the motive? Why kill Theo and Chloe on their wedding night? Why eliminate Max Ortega, who was just doing his job? Why make Nicholas's death look like a suicide?"

"And where does Chloe fit into all this?" I asked. "We know she was hiding from something in her past, trying to establish a new identity. What was she running from?"

Jack's phone buzzed on the counter. He glanced at it and his shoulders tensed. "Finally," he said. "Judge Monroe just signed the warrant. We've got full access to all the information Nicholas was trying to hide from us—both his personal records and Theo's State Department file. Dead men don't get the luxury of covering their tracks from the grave."

"That was fast," Cole said.

"Monroe owes me," Jack replied without elaborating. "Doug, can you—"

"Already on it," Doug said, typing furiously. "State Department servers, here we come."

I almost rolled my eyes at Doug's dramatics. It wasn't like he didn't have the file already opened somewhere on his laptop.

The atmosphere in the office was electric as we leaned in, waiting for the next piece of the puzzle. Even Oscar seemed to sense the tension, sitting alert at Jack's feet.

"Initial access granted," Doug announced. "Downloading files now. Extensive encryption... Working through it... My, my, someone really didn't want some of these files seen. Margot's going to be pretty upset she missed all this."

"Time frame?" Jack asked.

"Half an hour or so," Doug said. "They've got a halfway decent coder at the State Department, but he's not as good as me. As ambassador, Nicholas would've been able to request that certain files were classified due to his position, but it wasn't a matter of national security or it would've been buried deeper."

"While that's processing," Jack said, turning back to the board, "let's go over what we still need to do.

I watched Jack as he outlined our next steps, his energy infusing the room despite the exhaustion I knew he felt. This was what made him exceptional—his ability to see the big picture while keeping track of every detail, to lead without dominating, to push without breaking his team. In moments like this, I could see why Doug idolized him, why Cole and Martinez followed him without question, why an entire county had entrusted their safety to him.

Jack's phone rang again and he frowned at the screen.

"Lawson," he said. "Hold on, Riley. Let me put you on speaker."

"We've got a situation out on James Madison Parkway, about two miles east of the Potomac Mills exit. Black Mercedes sedan parked on the shoulder. Officer Jimenez stopped to offer assistance and discovered a body in the back seat. Male, mid-fifties, hands bound, gunshot to the back of the head."

Jack's eyes met mine across the room, and I saw the same thought reflected there—another connection, another body, another piece of the puzzle.

"Any ID on the victim?" he asked, though I think we all knew what was coming.

"Driver's license identifies him as Derek Rogan, sir."

"Damn," Cole said softly.

"Secure the scene," Jack said. "Dr. Graves and I are on our way." He disconnected.

"Everyone else keep digging into those files. I want to know everything about Josef Visek. Cole and Martinez, let's find Emmett Parker and Vivica Vasilios fast. If they know anything they could be next on the hit list. Offer to send police protection until we can talk to them.

"Derby, keep working on that financial trail. There's got to be something there that tells us who's really pulling the strings."

Everyone nodded, tasks assigned, purpose clear.

Jack looked at me. "Ready for another body?"

"Just another day at the office," I said, "Five dead bodies in two days? Perfectly normal."

"Doug, see if you can sweet-talk Margot into coming back and keep digging into the State Department files to see what the cover-up is."

Doug sighed. "Yeah, yeah," he said. "I might need to step out of the room for that conversation."

"Whatever you've got to do," Jack said. "And one more thing. You guys be aware of your surroundings. You're all uncovering things tonight people have died for. We have no idea who might be next on the hit list, and I don't want any of you taking any chances."

As I followed Jack out to the Tahoe, I couldn't shake the feeling that we were racing toward something much bigger than what we'd originally thought was a double homicide—it all pointed to something organized and dangerous.

<hr>

CHAPTER FIFTEEN

<hr>

The spring night had become chilly as we drove toward the crime scene in my Suburban. We'd chosen it over Jack's Tahoe so we could transport the body. There was no need to get Lily and Sheldon out of the house to follow behind us when we could do it ourselves.

Flashing blue and red lights illuminated the darkness ahead, reflecting off the black water of the Potomac in the distance. Jack's face was grim in the dashboard glow, his jaw set in that way that told me he was putting pieces together in his head.

"This is becoming a pattern," I said, breaking the silence.

"Someone's cleaning house," Jack agreed. "And they're not being subtle about it."

I regretted not grabbing a jacket on our way out

to wear over my coveralls, and I wrapped my arms tight around myself. Jack turned up the heater.

Each new body brought us closer to understanding what connected them all—and also potentially closer to whoever was responsible. The thought sent an involuntary shiver down my spine that had nothing to do with the temperature.

We pulled in behind three patrol cars and an unmarked sedan I recognized as Riley's. The Mercedes was parked at an odd angle on the gravel shoulder, its hazard lights still blinking uselessly into the night like a distress signal that had come too late.

Riley met us at the perimeter tape. He was tall and lanky, and he always looked a little uncomfortable in his starched uniform. He was a country boy at heart, and knew the woods and rivers like the back of his hand. He had sandy hair and plain brown eyes, and he was married to a nice woman named Becky I'd met a time or two.

"Sheriff," he said. "Doc. Not your normal Sunday night."

"Show me," Jack said.

Riley lifted the tape for us, and I ducked under after Jack. As we approached the Mercedes, I could see the rear driver's side window had been shattered. Glass glittered on the ground like malevolent diamonds in the flashlight beams. The sight of the black sedan stirred something in my memory.

"The vic is in the back seat," Riley said. "Hands bound behind him with zip ties. Single gunshot wound to the back of the head. Execution style."

Jack circled the car slowly, his trained eyes missing nothing. "Who found him?"

"Jimenez. He was running radar when he spotted the car. Thought it might be a breakdown. When he pulled up, he saw the broken window and realized something was wrong."

"Any witnesses?" Jack asked, peering inside the vehicle.

"Not a one," Riley said. "This stretch of road is pretty quiet after dark. Only traffic is the occasional truck headed to or from the industrial park."

I pulled on gloves and opened my medical bag. "CSI on the way?"

"They're here," he said. "Waiting on you to give them the go-ahead."

I nodded and circled to the driver's side rear door where the window had been shot out. The interior dome light cast an eerie glow over the scene, turning everything surreal.

Derek Rogan sat slumped against the door, his head tilted at an awkward angle. Blood and brain matter had sprayed across the beige leather upholstery in a surprisingly neat starburst pattern. His hands were zip-tied behind his back, the plastic cutting deep into his wrists where he'd struggled against his restraints.

"Single penetrating gunshot wound to the occipital region," I said, noting the neat hole at the base of his skull. "No exit wound. Bullet's still inside."

Jack bent down beside me, shining his flashlight along the floor of the car. "Look at this," he said, pointing to a small shell casing that had rolled under the front passenger seat. "9mm. Professional. Clean."

"He's still warm," I said, touching the area beneath his neck. I pulled out my thermometer. "There are signs of early onset rigor in the smaller muscles of his face and neck. I'd estimate TOD at approximately two hours ago. Maybe less. This was recent."

Jack straightened up and scanned the surrounding area. "Killer couldn't have gotten far. Not on foot."

"There would have been a second vehicle," Riley said. "This is too isolated for public transportation, and it's a five-mile walk to the nearest gas station."

"So at least two people," Jack said. "One to drive Rogan here in his car, another to follow in a second vehicle for the getaway."

"Just like Theo and Chloe," I said quietly. "Two shooters."

I leaned in closer, examining the bullet wound with my penlight. "Clean shot, close range—probably pressed right against his skull. No stippling or powder burns on the skin around the entry wound, but there's some on his hair. Shooter was careful."

"Something's off," Jack said, circling the car again. "He's experienced, former military. How'd they get the drop on him?"

I checked Rogan's mouth and nostrils. "No signs of drug use or sedation. His pupils aren't dilated."

"Check his neck," Jack suggested.

I gently turned Rogan's head and spotted a small puncture mark just below his left ear. "Possible injection site. Could be a tranquilizer or paralytic."

"That explains why a man with his training didn't put up more of a fight," Jack said.

I continued my examination, noting defensive marks on his knuckles. "He did try to fight, though. His right hand has bruising consistent with landing a punch. His suit's expensive but rumpled like he's been wearing it awhile. And there's a stain on his cuff that looks like coffee."

Jack circled the car again, his flashlight beam cutting through the darkness. "Why kill him? He's just a bodyguard doing his job."

"Wrong place, wrong time?" I suggested. "Or maybe he saw something he shouldn't have."

"Likely the latter," Jack said. "A professional like Rogan would have noticed if his employer was being targeted. He might have tried to intervene if someone was trying to take Nicholas out. Or force him to commit suicide."

"It's a shame the ambassador died in Arlington County," I said. "I'd like to examine those autopsy results and see if there's a possibility it's a staged suicide."

I completed my examination, documenting everything with methodical precision. Riley approached with a black body bag, and I said, "We can move him now. I'll add him to the autopsy list for tomorrow. It won't take me long for either him or Max. We already know cause of death, so there's no need for the full treatment."

Jack helped me maneuver Rogan's body into the bag while the CSI techs continued processing the vehicle. The weight of him reminded me how substantial a human life is—and how quickly it can be taken away.

"You think the same person who killed Max Ortega got to this guy?" Riley asked as we zipped the bag closed.

"I don't know," Jack said. "Different weapon, same precision. Josef Visek was former Special Forces, so he fits the bill. Even for the calculated placement of the gunshot wounds on Chloe Vasilios. For now, he's our primary suspect. Professional hit man for hire."

We loaded Rogan's body into the back of my

Suburban. The gurney wheels clacked against the metal floor, an oddly final sound in the quiet night. Jack closed the rear door and turned to Riley.

"I want roadblocks on all major highways out of the county," he said. "And a full description of Josef Visek to every deputy. He'll be riding with someone. Expect both to be armed and extremely dangerous."

"What about the vehicle he might be driving?" Riley asked.

"Unknown," Jack said. "But he had to have a second car here to get away after killing Rogan. Check traffic cams for anything leaving this area in the last hour."

"On it, Sheriff."

As Riley walked away, Jack's phone buzzed. He looked at it and his jaw tightened.

"Doug?" I asked and he nodded.

Jack helped me into the Suburban and then went around to the driver's side and got in, and then he put the phone on speaker.

"What's up, Doug?"

"So something popped I figured you'd want to know about," Doug said. "Two years before Theo and Vivica Vasilios divorced, Theo disappeared."

"Disappeared how?" I asked as Jack pulled out onto the highway. The headlights carved a tunnel through the darkness, and I had the unsettling feeling that we were being watched from beyond that circle of light.

"He dropped off the grid entirely. No credit card usage, no phone records, no travel documents. He was just...gone. For more than a year. That's when his ex-wife filed for divorce on grounds of abandonment."

"How does someone just disappear for that long?" Jack asked. "Was a missing person report filed?"

"Yes," Doug said, "But then it was withdrawn by Vivica. I guess Theo reached out and let her know where she could send the divorce papers. It was uncontested, and that's when Theo gave her a very generous settlement."

"So it was a guilt offering," I said.

"And then some," Doug said. "I found property records that were in both Vivica's and Theo's names that were donated to something called New Dawn Fellowship. She'd filed an initial complaint with the divorce proceedings that Theo forged her signature and gave the properties away. She withdrew the filing, but everything electronic leaves a trail, and I had to dig to find it but it was there."

"Good job, Doug," I said, feeling a surge of excitement. A new lead—something concrete to pursue.

"What the hell is New Dawn Fellowship?" Jack asked, his voice tight with controlled urgency.

"I'm still working on that," Doug said. "You want to talk about safeguards, boy do they have it. Their digital security is no joke. Multiple layers of encryption, servers bouncing all over the globe. They don't want to be found."

"So Theo paid off the ex-wife for giving away marital assets," Jack said. "Then what did he do?"

"The time he spent off the grid is a mystery," Doug said. "All of this happened a few years before his thirty-fifth birthday when he was set to come into his inheritance from his grandfather."

"What do you want to bet New Dawn Fellowship knew all about the inheritance?" Jack asked.

"That's a sucker's bet," Doug said. "But get this, I ran Nicholas Vasilios's financials for the same three-year period, and the last year that Theo was gone, Nicholas made four separate payments totaling right at twelve million dollars."

"To New Dawn Fellowship?" I asked, sitting up straighter.

"I don't know yet," Doug said. "Nicholas was ambassador at the time, so he used the State Department to set up dummy accounts and move money through a couple dozen different accounts. I'm peeling back all those layers to see who was the recipient of all that money."

"So when did Theo decide to rejoin society?" I asked, my mind racing to connect the dots.

"Theo leaves a digital footprint again about a week after the fourth payment was made by Nicholas. And then he's back in the tabloids and living the high life as if nothing had happened."

I processed this as we drove through the darkness. "So Nicholas paid someone off to get his son back from this New Dawn Fellowship."

"Or paid to keep something quiet," Jack suggested. "People don't usually shell out twelve million dollars unless they're desperate."

"And the tattoos?" I asked. "How do they connect?"

"I'm still working on that," Doug said. "But get this—I just found a reference to a ceremonial branding for new members in an archived news article about a cult investigation. The reporter mentioned matching tattoos on initiates' bodies as a symbol of their new family. The article was about a different group, but the description matches."

"So Theo joined this group, something happened that made Theo want to leave, and Nicholas paid a fortune to extract his son," I said. "And now someone's on a killing spree, and three of our victims have the same tattoo on the bottom of their foot."

"You gotta brand your members, right?" Jack asked. "Not a lot different than the Hells Angels."

"That makes the most sense," I said. "Cults often

mark their followers—it creates belonging and makes it harder to leave."

"Doug," Jack said. "The car Rogan was found in—it's a black Mercedes sedan. The car that ran Chloe off the road a few months back was also a black sedan. Let's run vehicles of those on our lists and see if anything pops."

"On it," Doug said.

"What if Rogan wasn't just working security for Nicholas? What if he was also tracking Chloe? Or trying to scare her? Maybe Nicholas knew exactly where she'd come from and didn't want his son to be dragged back into it. So he's the one who plans to eliminate her. Maybe things just went wrong the night Theo and Chloe were killed, and Theo was murdered too."

Jack grunted at the theory, and I heard a rumble of voices in the background on the phone.

"I'm putting you on speaker," Cole said. "We got in touch with Emmett Parker and Vivica Vasilios."

Jack and I exchanged a quick glance, both of us surprised at how quickly Cole had managed to track them down.

"What did you find?" Jack asked, his eyes returning to the dark road ahead.

"Parker was easier than we expected," Cole said. "He's a student at Ridgemont Community College in Richmond. Lives about a block from campus in one of those cheap student apartment complexes. Kid answered on the first ring."

"Did he know about Chloe's death?" I asked, still trying to piece together how this young man fit into Chloe's mysterious past.

"Yeah, he'd seen it on the news. He seemed real upset," Cole continued. "He agreed to come to the sheriff's office tomorrow morning before his first class. Said he could be there by eight."

"Good work," Jack said. "What about Vivica Vasilios?"

"That's where it gets interesting," Martinez's voice came through the speaker. "She wants to meet tonight. Said she doesn't care how late it is."

"Tonight?" I asked, glancing at the clock. It was just after nine.

"Her exact words were that she feels her life might be in danger," Martinez said. "She was pretty insistent about talking to you specifically, Sheriff. Said it has to be tonight."

Jack's grip tightened on the steering wheel. "Where is she?"

"She's staying at The Tides in King George," Cole answered. "Said she'd meet you in the hotel bar. It's open until midnight."

The Tides was a boutique hotel that had opened about a year ago, catering to the wealthier visitors to our area. It was sleek, modern, and expensive—the kind of place that served tiny portions on enormous plates and called it cuisine.

"She's flying out on the Vasilios private plane back to London first thing in the morning," Martinez added. "Sounds like she's in a hurry to put distance between herself and whatever's happening here."

"Or someone," Jack muttered.

"We'll drop Rogan's body at the lab and then head straight to The Tides," I said.

Jack nodded. "Cole, arrange police protection for Vivica immediately. Send someone you trust who won't be easily intimidated."

"Already done," Cole said. "You want us to keep digging?"

"Yes," Jack said. "Focus on New Dawn Fellowship. That name keeps coming up, and I want to know what we're dealing with. And see if Doug or Margot can pull anything from Theo's State Department files —there has to be something there that ties all this together."

Jack disconnected.

We drove in silence for a few minutes, both of us processing the latest developments. The body of Derek Rogan lay in the back of my Suburban, another victim in a rapidly expanding case that seemed to grow more complex with each passing hour.

"What do you think Vivica knows?" I finally asked.

Jack's face was half illuminated by the dashboard lights, casting deep shadows across his features. "Enough that she's afraid for her life. Enough that she's willing to risk talking to us before fleeing the country."

"You think she knows about New Dawn Fellowship?"

"She was married to Theo when he disappeared," Jack said. "She filed for divorce because of it, then withdrew the complaint when he resurfaced. Yeah, I think she knows a hell of a lot more than she's ever told anyone."

"Let's get this body dropped off quickly," I said. "I've got a feeling time is running out for anyone who knows what those tattoos really mean."

Jack nodded grimly as he turned into the driveway of Graves Funeral Home. "And I've got a feeling that before this night is over, we're going to wish we didn't know either."

THE TIDES HOTEL GLEAMED LIKE A PHOSPHORESCENT jewel against the night sky. Ultramodern and sleek, its glass façade reflected the moonlight in rippling patterns that mimicked the nearby Potomac. The architecture was all clean lines and sharp angles, a stark contrast to the Colonial and Victorian buildings that dominated most of King George County.

The front entrance was flanked by tall sculptural water features, creating a gentle rushing sound that greeted us as we walked in. The lobby soared three stories high with a ceiling made entirely of glass, allowing guests to stargaze from plush seating areas. A massive chandelier made of what looked like thousands of crystal teardrops hung from the center, catching the light and scattering it like rain.

"This place screams charge it to your expense

account," I said to Jack as we crossed the marble floor.

Despite the late hour, the lobby was immaculate, with not a cushion out of place.

Jack nodded toward a plainclothes deputy seated in a wingback chair near the entrance, pretending to read a newspaper. The man gave Jack an almost imperceptible nod in return.

"They didn't waste any time," I said quietly.

"Cole's one of the few people I know who works as fast as I do," Jack replied, guiding me toward the bar with a light touch at the small of my back.

The bar was called The Undertow, a nod to the hotel's nautical theme. The space was dimly lit with blue accent lighting that created the illusion of being underwater. The back wall was a massive aquarium filled with exotic fish that drifted lazily behind the bartender. A live pianist played soft jazz in the corner, the music just loud enough to ensure private conversations remained private.

Despite being close to ten o'clock on a Sunday night, there were still a handful of patrons. A couple in casual ware sat closely at the bar, leaning into each other's space. Two businessmen in expensive suits nursed whiskeys while discussing figures in low voices. A well-dressed woman sat alone at a high-top table near the window, staring into a glass of red wine.

And then there was Vivica Vasilios.

She sat in a round corner booth with her back to the wall, giving her a clear view of both the entrance and the windows overlooking the street. Even from a distance, it was evident why she'd once been crowned Miss Universe. Her beauty was timeless, the kind would turn heads in any room. Her platinum-blond hair was pulled back in a sleek chignon, accentuating high cheekbones and a jawline that could cut glass. She wore a simple black top and slacks and diamond studs in her ears.

I noticed a man at the bar stealing glances over his gin and tonic, but Vivica seemed oblivious, her attention focused on the door and the street beyond the windows. Her fingers drummed nervously on the table, and she kept checking her watch. A nearly untouched martini sat in front of her.

She spotted us almost immediately, her posture straightening as we approached. I could see relief flash across her face before it settled back into carefully composed neutrality.

"Sheriff Lawson," she said, her Danish accent giving the words a musical lilt. "Thank you for coming so quickly."

"Ms. Vasilios," Jack said, sliding into the booth across from her. I took the seat beside him. "This is Dr. Graves, our county coroner."

"Yes, of course," Vivica said, her ice-blue eyes

meeting mine with surprising intensity. "You would have examined—" She hesitated. "Theo."

Up close, I could see the fine lines of strain around her eyes and mouth. Her perfect complexion couldn't quite hide the shadows of exhaustion beneath expertly applied makeup. Despite her beauty, there was a brittleness to her, like fine crystal on the verge of shattering.

"Your security detail arrived promptly," she said, nodding toward the plainclothes deputy at the end of the bar. "There's another one across the street. I saw him when I arrived." Her eyes darted to the window. "I appreciate the precaution, though I'm not sure it will matter in the end."

A server approached, and Jack ordered coffee for both of us. I noticed Vivica's hands trembling slightly as she lifted her martini, taking the smallest of sips before setting it back down.

"You said you feel your life is in danger," Jack said once the server had gone. "Why?"

Vivica's gaze swept the room before returning to us. "Because I knew this would all catch up with Theo one day," she said, her voice barely above a whisper. "And now that he's gone, there aren't many people left who know the truth."

"About New Dawn Fellowship?" I asked.

Her eyes widened fractionally. "You've been thorough in your investigation."

"We've found the name, but not much else," Jack said. "What can you tell us about them?"

Vivica's shoulders tensed, and she glanced nervously at the window again. "Not here. We're too exposed."

"The men watching your back are good at their jobs," Jack assured her.

She gave a brittle laugh. "You don't understand what you're dealing with, Sheriff." She leaned forward, lowering her voice further. "New Dawn isn't just some cult in the woods. They have resources, connections. People in positions you wouldn't believe."

"Start at the beginning," Jack said, his voice calm but insistent. "Tell us about your marriage to Theo."

Vivica sat back slightly, considering his request. After a moment, she seemed to make a decision.

"We were young," she began. "Well, I was young. Twenty-two when we married. Theo was a little older, but emotionally—" She made a dismissive gesture with her hand. "He was charming, handsome, wealthy. The son of an ambassador. It was like a fairy tale for a girl who'd grown up in modest circumstances in Copenhagen."

Our coffee arrived, and Jack thanked the server before turning his attention back to Vivica.

"The first two years were good," she continued. "We split our time between London and Greece. I was modeling, and Theo was supposedly learning the family business, though he mostly partied and spent money. He was immature, restless. Drank too much. Did drugs occasionally. He was always looking for something more exciting, more meaningful than diplomatic functions and society events."

She traced the rim of her martini glass with one perfectly manicured finger. "The next couple of years of marriage weren't as good. He partied hard, and the drugs bothered me. And then there was another woman. It was quite public in the tabloids. I told him I wouldn't compete, and that he could either get help or we were finished.

"He was apologetic and said he had a business trip, and when he was back we would discuss options. He flew to the United States, and he simply didn't come home."

"Where was he going?" Jack asked.

"Florida supposedly," she said. "To look at a home he wanted to buy, and he was checking on a hotel his grandfather had left him to oversee. He was supposed to meet with his attorney and board members to discuss investment opportunities. He was supposed to be gone two weeks." Her eyes took on a faraway look. "I got a call from his father, Nicholas, and he told me not to worry. That Theo had called him and said he'd checked into rehab in Palm Beach. I was hurt, of course, that Theo didn't call me directly. But at the same time I was relieved he was getting help. I wanted to be patient and supportive."

"But something changed your mind," Jack prompted.

"About a month after he disappeared, I started noticing strange things," she said. "My personal items moved around in the London flat. My mail opened and then resealed. Cars following me when I went out. I thought I was being paranoid at first."

She took another tiny sip of her martini, her hand steadier now as she launched into her story. "Then I started receiving phone calls. No one would speak when I answered, but I could hear breathing on the other end. I was terrified. I wanted to talk to Theo, to tell him what was happening."

"So you contacted the rehab center," I said.

Vivica nodded. "He'd been gone for months by this point, and I'd seen Nicholas and Cecelia at a family gathering. I casually mentioned how proud I was of Theo to Cecelia and led her to believe I knew what facility he was staying at. She let the name of the center slip—Serenity Valley in Palm Beach. I called them, thinking I could at least leave a message for Theo." Her expression hardened. "They had never heard of Theodore Vasilios. He had never been a patient there."

"That's when you filed the missing person report?" Jack asked.

"Yes. The London police took the report, but they weren't overly concerned. A wealthy man decides to leave his wife—not exactly uncommon in their experience." Her mouth twisted in a bitter smile. "A week after I filed the report, I received a letter from Theo. He said he was fine, that he just needed space. That he'd made a mistake when marrying me. He hadn't been ready and had other interests he wanted to pursue."

"Did you believe it was from him?" I asked.

"It was his handwriting," she said. "But something about it felt...off. Still, what could I do? He was an adult who had chosen to leave. So I filed for divorce."

"And that's when you discovered the properties he'd given away," Jack said.

Vivica's eyes narrowed. "You really have been thorough, Sheriff." She nodded. "Yes. During the asset disclosure process, my attorney discovered that Theo had donated several valuable properties to an organization called New Dawn Fellowship. He had forged my signature on the transfer documents."

"How did you respond?" I asked.

"My attorney filed a dispute, of course. These were jointly owned properties worth millions." Her fingers began drumming on the table again. "Three days later, I received a visit from a law firm I'd never heard of, representing Theo. They offered me a settlement that was extremely generous. More than generous, actually. All of Theo's liquid assets, plus family jewelry that had been left to him through his grandfather. In exchange, I would withdraw the dispute and sign a nondisclosure agreement."

"That seems excessive for a routine divorce," Jack observed.

"It was," Vivica agreed. "Especially since he had no grounds since he was the one to abandon the marriage. I wanted to refuse—not because of the money, but because something felt wrong about the whole situation." She swallowed hard. "Then my attorney's office was broken into. His files were ransacked, but nothing was stolen except my case documents. The next day, he called to tell me he could no longer represent me. He sounded terrified."

I exchanged a look with Jack. "What did you do?" I asked.

"What could I do? I took the deal." Shame flickered across her face. "I was scared. I had no idea what I was dealing with, but I knew it was dangerous. The divorce was finalized quickly after that, and for a while, I thought it was over."

Jack leaned forward. "When did you see Theo again?"

"Almost a year later," she said. "He showed up at

my apartment in London, unannounced. He looked...different. Thinner. More serious. He apologized for everything—for leaving, for the properties, for frightening me. He said he'd made a mistake getting involved with some people who had taken advantage of him, but that his father had helped him get out."

"Did he mention New Dawn Fellowship?" Jack asked.

Vivica nodded, her eyes darting around the room again. "Not at first. It took years before he told me the full story. We...reconnected that night. He was different—more mature, more present. We began seeing each other again, secretly at first."

"You became lovers again," I said, neither a question nor a judgment.

"Yes," she admitted. "For the past fifteen years. I never stopped loving him, despite everything. But I never trusted him enough to marry him again, either." She gave a sad smile. "He understood. We had an arrangement that worked for both of us. I had my life in London, my career, my freedom. And Theo...well, Theo had his demons to manage."

"Which brings us to Chloe Matthews," Jack said. "What can you tell us about her?"

Vivica's expression darkened. "That poor girl. I only met her a few times. Theo told me how they met—how she reminded him of himself in some ways." She shook her head. "He was trying to help her."

"Help her how?" I asked.

"She had escaped from New Dawn," Vivica said, lowering her voice even further. "But she hadn't paid the price to leave like Theo had."

"Nicholas's twelve million dollars," Jack said.

Vivica's eyebrows rose in surprise. "You know about that too? Yes. The price for leaving New Dawn is steep—financially and otherwise. Theo hadn't turned thirty-five yet, so he hadn't fully received his inheritance from his grandfather, so Nicholas paid for Theo's freedom. But Chloe just ran. And they don't let people leave, not without consequences."

"What can you tell us about New Dawn Fellowship?" Jack asked. "What are they, exactly?"

Vivica glanced over her shoulder before answering. "On the surface, they're a spiritual retreat center and self-improvement organization. They own property throughout Virginia and several other states. They recruit wealthy, influential people—or people with potential to be wealthy and influential. They promise enlightenment, purpose, truth."

"And beneath the surface?" I asked.

"A criminal enterprise," she said flatly. "Money laundering, blackmail, extortion. They isolate you from your family and friends, take control of your assets, make you dependent on them for everything.

And once you're in, the only way out is to pay—with money, with silence, sometimes with your life."

"And the tattoos?" Jack asked.

Vivica unconsciously rubbed her foot against her ankle. "A mark of membership. The pattern represents their belief system—the points of enlightenment, they call it. Everyone who joins receives the mark. It's supposed to be a reminder that you belong to them, body, soul and spirit."

"Who leads this organization?" Jack asked.

"A man named Paul Prather," Vivica said, a visible shudder running through her. "He makes David Koresh and Jim Jones look like Billy Graham. Charismatic, brilliant, utterly ruthless. He founded New Dawn thirty years ago after leaving another cult where he was second-in-command. Decided to start his own, more profitable version."

"He's operating here in the United States?" Jack asked.

"He was," Vivica said. "Nicholas's involvement alerted the State Department to the group, along with your FBI. Paul got wind that there was going to be an FBI raid on the compound, so he picked up and moved. He's got several hundred followers. They all just left."

"Where'd they go?" I asked.

"He bought an island," Vivica said. "It's not a US territory, and he moved the entire operation there."

"And now they're cleaning up loose ends," I said. "Theo, Chloe, Max Ortega, Nicholas, Derek Rogan..."

"And I'm next," Vivica said, her voice cracking slightly. "They're eliminating anyone who knows too much, anyone who could expose them. I should never have come to the wedding. I should have stayed in London. But he asked me to be there. Needed my support. They were being married in name only, but marriage was the only way Chloe would have the protection of his family name."

"You were okay with that?" I asked.

"My name is still Vasilios," she said pridefully. "Our arrangement would have continued as it always had. She was just a child. He would never have pursued her sexually."

"How did you know that Max and Nicholas were dead?" Jack asked, studying her carefully. "Those deaths haven't been widely reported yet."

Vivica's eyes locked with his. "Because I still have the Vasilios name, and I have access to things most people don't. And I noticed that I've been followed since yesterday afternoon, just like before."

"Let me guess," Jack said. "A black sedan?"

"Yes," she said, curiously. "I hired a private security firm and they got me out of the city and I checked in here. Nicholas told me that I could use the family jet to take me home. He said they'd be staying for the funeral so wouldn't need it right away."

"You trusted Nicholas to make sure you made it home alive?"

"I trust the company I hired," she said.

She nodded to the couple that I'd noticed before who only seemed to have eyes for each other. But I saw the woman glance at us out of her periphery.

"Though I do appreciate you sending extra protection," she said. "I'm well covered. But I'm leaving first thing in the morning. That's why I insisted on meeting tonight."

"These contacts that you have available because of your name," Jack said. "Can they help us identify who's killing?"

"You'll never pin Prather down," she said.

"I don't care about Prather," Jack said. "If the FBI have a bead on him, he's their problem. I care about who's coming into my county and killing people."

She sighed and looked down at the table. "They didn't tell me specifics. They just confirmed what I already knew—that I was a target. But they mentioned Prather had sent soldiers after me to clean up loose ends."

"Soldiers?" I asked.

"That's what they call their enforcers," Vivica explained. "Devoted members who handle the organization's dirty work. They're paired with apprentices —newer members who show potential for violence. It's how they groom the next generation of soldiers. Prather says it's for protection, because the world is jealous of the utopia he's created. But it's really just an excuse to enforce his will."

A chill ran down my spine as I thought of the evidence pointing to the two shooters at each scene. The soldier and his apprentice.

"Do you know any names?" Jack asked. "Anyone specific who might be targeting former members?"

Vivica shook her head. "There's nothing more I can tell you. Almost all the information I have is because Theo shared with me. I need to go and get packed. I'm leaving at dawn."

"We could put you in a safe house," Jack said. "Keep you out of sight until they're caught."

"I'll feel better once I put an ocean between us. No one is safe from New Dawn once they've decided you're a liability," Vivica said, gathering her small clutch purse. "Not even you, Sheriff. Especially not now that I've told you all this."

"Indulge me," he said. "Let my deputies escort you back to your room. And stay there until morning. Don't open the door for anyone but us."

Vivica hesitated, then nodded. "All right. But I'm still leaving on that plane tomorrow."

"That's fine," Jack agreed. "I'll feel a lot better if it's my guys who see you onto the plane. You might trust the firm you hired, but I don't."

"I appreciate that," she said, letting out a shaky sigh.

Jack signaled to the deputy at the bar, who discreetly rose and positioned himself near the exit. And then we watched her walk away, spine stiff and shoulders straight, daring anyone to take her down.

"You think she's hiding something?" I asked.

"I think she's terrified," he replied. "And people who are terrified rarely tell the whole truth. They keep pieces back—leverage, escape routes, contingency plans."

"Emmett Parker," I said. "If everything she said is true then he could be in imminent danger. Chloe could have confided in him."

"We've got men on him," Jack said, but he picked up his phone. "But I'll get a deputy to knock on his door. Maybe they can talk him into going to a safe house."

"I'd feel a lot better if he did," I said, watching Jack's face as he was transferred by dispatch to the officers watching Emmett Parker's apartment building.

The longer Jack listened, the more his expression darkened. I saw the minute clenching of his jaw and the tightening around his eyes that told me something was very wrong.

"What is it?" I asked when he finally lowered the phone. "What happened?"

Jack's eyes met mine, and I saw a flicker of cold fury there. "Emmett is gone. They were just about to call me when dispatch connected us. One of the deputies found his apartment door open. There were signs of a struggle—overturned furniture, broken glass. Emmett was nowhere to be found."

"How'd he get out?" I asked, my stomach dropping. "I thought you had people watching the building."

"Plank was one of the first responding deputies set up around the perimeter. He and Chen had the front and back door of Emmett's ground floor apartment covered," Jack explained, his voice tight with controlled anger. "Plank said they had phone communication with Emmett when they first arrived, so they didn't physically check to see if he was inside the apartment. He thinks Emmett must have taken that last call under duress, that someone had already taken him."

"He could be dead already," I said softly, the image of Max Ortega's exploding skull flashing unbidden through my mind.

I saw the anger in Jack's eyes deepen, his fist

clenched so tight his knuckles were white. The muscle in his jaw jumped with tension.

"I know," he said, his voice deadly calm—the kind of calm that preceded a storm. "But we're not going to give up on him yet."

CHAPTER SEVENTEEN

Morning light streamed through our bedroom windows, turning dust motes into floating diamonds and illuminating the trees that were clustered around our property in a way that should have been beautiful. Instead, the brightness stabbed through my eyelids like tiny daggers, intensifying the nausea that had woken me twenty minutes earlier.

I sat on the edge of our bed, nibbling a piece of dry toast and sipping lukewarm peppermint tea, trying to breathe through the wave of sickness that had become my daily ritual. The floor-to-ceiling windows offered spectacular views of the dense trees and the distant ribbon of the Potomac.

On any other morning, I might have appreciated the way the rising sun painted everything in gold.

Today, it was just another assault on my queasy stomach.

Jack emerged from the bathroom, already dressed for the day in black BDUs and a black polo shirt with the KGSO logo over the breast—he was dressed for justice. The scent of his soap and shampoo wafted across the room, but even that familiar, usually comforting smell made my stomach roll.

"Coffee's ready downstairs," he said, buckling his duty belt.

I closed my eyes and swallowed hard. "God, please don't mention coffee."

Jack paused, studying me. "That bad today?"

I nodded, taking another small bite of toast. "The weird thing is, the thought of coffee is absolutely repulsive. The smell is—" I cut myself off, breathing slowly through my nose. "Yesterday I would have killed for a cup. Today, the smell alone might kill me."

"Pregnancy is very strange," Jack said, sitting beside me on the bed, careful not to jostle the mattress. "My mom said she couldn't stand the smell of garlic when she was pregnant with me. Dad couldn't even eat it in the house. Then the day after I was born, she demanded Italian food with extra garlic bread."

I smiled weakly. "Maybe don't talk about food

right now. Let's hope my coffee aversion is temporary. I can't imagine facing the dead every day without caffeine."

Jack put his hand on my stomach, his fingers spread wide as if he were protecting us both. I was only a few weeks along, and wouldn't be showing for weeks yet. But the simple gesture grounded me, a reminder that the misery would pass and something miraculous waited for us on the other side.

Jack's face softened as he looked at my still-flat stomach, his usual sharp focus giving way to something gentler, more vulnerable. Sometimes I forgot how much he'd always wanted children, how ready he was for this next chapter of our lives.

"What's the plan for today?" I asked, setting my mug aside.

Jack's expression shifted into a hard line. "The search for Emmett Parker is still ongoing. I've got teams working in shifts—uniformed officers doing door-to-door in the neighborhood around his apartment, plainclothes checking transit hubs, hotels, the works. Derby's monitoring cell towers and credit card activity."

"Any leads?" I asked, my heart sinking at the grim set of his jaw.

"Nothing solid yet. At least we haven't found another body by the side of the road." He ran a hand over his hair. "I'm heading out to join the search team in Richmond. Richmond PD is letting us drive this operation even though it's on their turf."

I nodded, worry gnawing at me. "Be careful, Jack. If New Dawn Fellowship is as dangerous as Vivica says—"

"I know," he said, cutting me off gently. "I'll have Cole and Martinez with me. We'll be fine."

But I could see the tension in his shoulders, the careful way he was choosing his words to avoid alarming me. Jack never downplayed danger unless he was truly concerned. This was the part about being a cop's wife I hated, knowing when he walked out the door it might be the last time I saw him.

"What about Vivica?" I asked. "Did she make it to the airport?"

"The plane just took off," he said. "My deputies said there were no issues. It was a smooth transport."

I nodded, relieved that at least one potential victim was out of harm's way.

"Emmett was the weak link," I said. "He's just a kid. No private security."

Jack grimaced and I knew it weighed on him. "You heading to the funeral home?"

"I want to get started on those autopsies. Max Ortega and Derek Rogan should be pretty straightforward, given the obvious cause of death, but there might be details we missed."

Jack leaned over and pressed a kiss to my forehead. "Call me if you find anything. And Jaye—" his eyes met mine, serious and intent, "—be careful. We still don't know who's involved in all this."

"I'm going to be locked in my lab with two dead bodies," I said, attempting humor. "I think they're past doing me harm."

Jack didn't smile. "Promise me you'll keep your phone on you. And lock the doors."

"I promise," I said. "Now go find Emmett."

He kissed me again, lingering a moment longer than usual, his hand cupping my cheek. When he pulled away, his eyes were dark with an emotion I couldn't quite name.

"I love you," he said simply.

"I love you too," I replied, watching as he headed for the door. "Both of us do."

That earned me a smile before he disappeared, his footsteps echoing down the hall.

I sat in the quiet of our bedroom for a few more minutes, listening to the sounds of Jack moving around downstairs—keys jingling, the distant murmur of his voice as he called dispatch, and finally the soft thud of the front door closing. The Tahoe's engine rumbled to life outside, and then faded as he drove away.

The house felt emptier without him, larger somehow, even though I knew Doug was asleep a floor below me. He wouldn't be up for a while—Doug and mornings didn't exactly go together. I rubbed my arms against a chill that wasn't entirely physical and forced myself to stand. The nausea had subsided to a manageable level, and I had work to do.

The funeral home parking lot was empty when I pulled in just after seven, my Suburban the only vehicle apart from the other Suburban parked under the portico, ready for Victor Mobley's funeral later that morning. I made sure to park where Sheldon could still get the body loaded and lead the procession to the grave site.

The funeral home loomed against the brightening sky, its red-brick façade and white columns picture perfect. I waved to the Hendersons, an elderly couple who faithfully sat on their front porch across the street every morning, rain or shine, watching the town wake up. Mrs. Henderson lifted her coffee mug in greeting, and Mr. Henderson tipped his hat. Their presence was comforting, a reminder of the normal, everyday world that continued to exist alongside murder and cults and mysterious tattoos. How strange it must be to live in that ordinary world.

I unlocked the side door and walked into the

mudroom, leaving my bag hanging on the hook. I stuck my phone in the zipper pocket on my sweats because I promised Jack I'd keep it on me. But the reality was I never checked my phone when I was in the middle of an autopsy, and I could go hours without taking a call or a text. I decided the best compromise was to wear my smartwatch so Jack didn't worry, but even then I was a little apprehensive. I never wore jewelry during an autopsy. Sometimes things fell into open cavities and you had to fish them out. Ask me how I know.

The chill of early spring still lingered in the air, and the building's old bones creaked and settled around me as I stepped inside, locking the door behind me.

The silence was absolute, broken only by the soft ticking of the grandfather clock in the hallway. I'd spent countless hours alone in this building, and yet this morning, the emptiness felt different—heavier, more watchful.

I shook off the feeling and went into the kitchen, my footsteps echoing on the tile floors. I filled the electric kettle for more tea, the metal spoon clinking against ceramic as I measured out loose leaves. While I waited for the water to boil, I pulled up the blinds to let light into the room. The morning sun glinted across the island and the glass cake plate that had held fresh muffins the day before. Emmy Lu wouldn't be in until nine, but she always brought sweet treats with her.

The kettle clicked off, and I poured steaming water over the tea leaves, inhaling the delicate scent of chamomile and mint. With the warm mug cradled in my hands, I began my usual morning routine—checking the day's schedule, reviewing paperwork, making a mental list of everything that needed to be done before opening at ten.

Victor Mobley's funeral was the only service scheduled for today, a small graveside ceremony at eleven. The Hells Angels had cleared out yesterday, leaving behind a surprising lack of damage and an even more surprising thank-you note for our hospitality. Sheldon had been inordinately proud of how well he'd handled the outlaw bikers, though I suspected they'd simply been amused by his nervous enthusiasm.

I made my way to the viewing room where Mobley's casket sat, its polished mahogany gleaming in the soft light. The viewing room was peaceful, with cream-colored walls and tasteful floral arrangements flanking the casket. I checked that everything was in order—the photos displayed properly, the guest book placed on the antique table by the door, the funeral programs stacked neatly beside it.

The lid of the casket was closed for transport, but I opened it to ensure everything remained perfect after the somewhat rowdy visitation yesterday. Victor looked peaceful, his leather vest and rings in place as his family had requested. I adjusted his collar slightly, brushing away a stray bit of lint from his shoulder.

"Looks like you're all set for your final ride, Mr. Mobley," I murmured, closing the lid with a soft click.

As I turned to leave the viewing room, a floorboard creaked somewhere upstairs. I paused, head tilted, listening. It was an old house, random noises were common—the settling of wood, the expansion and contraction of pipes, the whisper of air through vents. But something about this noise felt different. Deliberate.

"Hello?" I called out, my voice sounding unnaturally loud in the quiet space. "Sheldon? Emmy Lu? Is someone there?"

No answer came, only the continuing silence and the steady ticktock of the grandfather clock in the hallway. I shook my head at my own jumpiness. Between the murders, the cult, and Jack's warnings, I was letting my imagination run wild.

I pulled my phone from my pocket, checking the time. Still early. I sent a quick text to Lily, confirming when she'd be in to assist with the autopsies, then tucked the phone back in my pocket.

The paperwork for the cemetery was in my office,

and I needed to make sure it was ready for the record keeper at the cemetery. I made my way down the long hallway, past the arrangement room and the casket showroom, toward Emmy Lu's office at the front.

The hallway seemed longer this morning, the shadows deeper in the corners despite the sunlight streaming through the windows. I felt a prickle at the back of my neck, the unmistakable sensation of being watched. I turned around, scanning the empty corridor behind me, but saw nothing out of place.

"Get it together, Jaye," I muttered to myself. "You've got pregnancy brain."

Emmy Lu's office door was ajar. I pushed it open slowly, eyes sweeping the room. Everything looked normal. Her desk was stacked neatly with files, my chair pushed back at the angle I'd left it. The blinds were closed, casting the room in shadow.

I flipped on the light and moved to the desk, rifling through the stacks of paper until I found the cemetery paperwork. I slipped it into a folder and placed it right on top so it was easy to find, then headed back into the hallway, pulling the door firmly shut behind me.

The sound of movement came again, this time from the direction of the arrangement room. A soft shuffling, like feet on carpet.

"Hello?" I called again, my heart rate picking up. "Is someone here?"

I stood perfectly still, straining to hear over the suddenly loud pounding of my heart. The building fell silent once more, but the prickle of unease had become a cold weight in my stomach. I wasn't alone.

"Sheldon, is that you? This isn't funny."

I began walking quickly back toward the kitchen and my lab. I'd be safe in my lab. I could lock myself inside, and no one could get in. My hand reached for my phone, ready to call Jack, when another sound stopped me in my tracks.

A door closing, followed by footsteps—not bothering to be quiet anymore.

I spun around, adrenaline surging through my body. The hallway behind me was empty, but the footsteps continued, getting closer. My eyes darted to the nearest exit, calculating whether I could reach it before whoever was approaching turned the corner.

I never got the chance to find out.

The blow came from behind, a sudden, explosive pain at the base of my skull that sent white-hot sparks shooting across my vision. I was falling before I registered what had happened.

My last coherent thought before darkness claimed me was of the baby, a desperate prayer that it would be safe even as consciousness slipped away like water through my fingers.

Then, there was nothing but blackness.

CHAPTER EIGHTEEN

Consciousness came in waves, each one bringing me closer to a reality I wasn't sure I wanted to face. The first thing I registered was the smell—musty carpet, hot metal, and the faint copper tang of my own blood. The second was darkness, absolute and suffocating. The third was movement—a nauseating, lurching motion that told me I was in a vehicle.

I was in a trunk.

Terror seized me, my heart hammering so violently I thought it might crack my ribs. My wrists were bound behind my back, plastic cutting into my flesh when I tried to move. My ankles were similarly restrained with zip ties, cinched tight enough to numb my feet.

Just like Derek Rogan.

The thought sent ice through my veins. I'd seen

his body, the neat hole in the back of his skull, the calculated execution. I was being taken to die the same way.

The vehicle hit a pothole, and my head slammed against something hard. Pain exploded behind my eyes, and I tasted bile. I tried to orient myself, to think past the panic, but the car swerved sharply, and my stomach revolted. I retched, unable to turn away as vomit splashed back onto my face and neck. The acid burned my nostrils, blending with the coppery smell of blood and intensifying my nausea.

The baby.

A new level of fear gripped me. I wasn't just fighting for my life anymore. I pressed my cheek against the rough carpeting, trying to steady my breathing. In. Out. Stay calm. Stay alive. For the tiny life depending on me.

The car took another sharp turn, then began to bounce over what felt like gravel. We were leaving paved roads behind. My body slid across the trunk, slamming against the wheel well. Something in the darkness jabbed into my ribs—a tire iron, maybe. I twisted, trying to position it between my bound hands, but another violent swerve sent it sliding away from me.

My head throbbed where I'd been struck. Warm blood trickled down my neck, seeping into the collar of my shirt. I tried to focus on the sounds outside—

the crunch of gravel, the whine of the engine, anything that might tell me where we were headed. But the effort sent another spike of pain through my skull, and darkness swallowed me again.

The next time I opened my eyes, I was no longer moving.

Cold metal pressed against my back, and harsh fluorescent lights buzzed overhead, searing my retinas. I blinked slowly, my vision swimming into focus. I was in a chair—a metal folding chair—and my wrists were still bound behind me, now secured to the back of the seat. My ankles were zip-tied to the chair legs, the plastic cutting deeper as I instinctively tried to move.

A warehouse. Industrial ceilings soared above me, crisscrossed with metal beams and exposed ductwork. Concrete floors stretched in all directions, stained with oil and marked with tire tracks. The vast space was empty except for a few wooden pallets and the chair I was bound to. Tall windows near the ceiling let in angled beams of morning light, illuminating dust motes that danced in the stagnant air.

I recognized the layout—we were in the industrial park off James Madison Parkway, the same area

Riley had mentioned when we'd found Rogan's body. The symmetry wasn't lost on me.

The place felt abandoned, a hollow shell where no one would hear me scream. I tested my restraints and found no give. Whoever had secured me knew what they were doing.

Think, Jaye. Think.

My head throbbed with each heartbeat, and I could feel dried blood crusted on my neck. My tongue felt swollen, my mouth parched. How long had I been unconscious? Minutes? Hours? Jack would have noticed I was missing by now. He would be looking for me. All I had to do was stay alive until he found me.

A door screeched open somewhere behind me, the sound of metal against concrete setting my teeth on edge. Slow, deliberate footsteps approached, circling until they stopped directly in front of me.

Emmett Parker.

He looked younger in person than in the photos Doug had pulled up—barely nineteen, with a boyish face that still carried traces of adolescent softness. His hair was sandy blond, cut close on the sides but longer on top, falling across his forehead in a way that might have seemed innocent in any other context. He wore jeans and a plain gray T-shirt, so ordinary it was jarring.

But his eyes...God, his eyes. They were pale blue,

almost colorless, and utterly void of emotion. They assessed me with clinical detachment, like I was a specimen under glass. When he smiled, the expression never reached those eyes.

"Dr. Graves," he said, his voice surprisingly deep for someone with such a youthful appearance. "I'm glad you're awake. Josef said you might not make it. Guess your skull's thicker than it looks."

He crouched in front of me, bringing his face level with mine. His breath smelled of mint gum and something metallic, like pennies.

"Where is he?" I asked, my voice a rasp.

"Josef?" Emmett shrugged one shoulder. "Setting up a little distraction across town. Fire department and police will be very busy in about twenty minutes." His lips curved in that empty smile again. "He told me to wait until he gets back before I kill you. A good soldier follows orders."

The casual way he said it—like he was discussing the weather—made my skin crawl. I swallowed hard, trying to ignore the way my heart was slamming against my ribs.

"You're the apprentice," I said. Not a question.

His eyebrows lifted slightly, the first genuine expression I'd seen on his face. "You've been doing your homework. I'm impressed." He stood and walked a slow circle around me, his fingertips trailing across my shoulders. "But then, you've been very thorough in your investigation. Too thorough.'

I had to keep him talking. As long as he was talking, I was breathing.

"How did you get involved with New Dawn?" I asked, working to keep my voice steady. "With Paul Prather?"

Emmett paused behind me, and I felt his hands rest on my shoulders. His thumbs pressed into the tender spot where my neck met my skull, not quite hard enough to hurt, but a clear reminder of how vulnerable I was.

"My, my," he whispered. "Someone knows more than they should. I guess it's a good thing you're going to die."

His thumb pressed into my flesh hard enough to make me whimper, and then he pulled away.

"Paul saved my life," he said simply, moving back into my field of vision. "I was fourteen, living on the streets after running away from my third foster home. Got caught stealing from the wrong people. They stabbed me and left me for dead in an alley."

He pulled up his shirt, revealing a jagged scar across his abdomen. The puckered tissue formed a crooked line from his navel to his ribs.

"They didn't do a very good job," he continued, dropping his shirt. "Paul found me. He has a gift for finding broken things with potential. He took me to New Dawn, had me patched up, made sure the authorities thought I was dead. The old me ceased to exist, and I became someone new." His eyes took on a fervent gleam. "Someone better."

"New Dawn," I echoed. "The cult."

His expression hardened. "It's not a cult. It's a family. A community. Paul protects us, teaches us. Some of us he trains to protect the others."

"Like you."

"Like me," he agreed, looking pleased that I understood. "I was special. Paul saw it right away. I had the right...temperament. Not everyone's suited to be a soldier."

"Is that where you met Chloe?" I asked.

His face softened slightly at the mention of her name. "We were in the same education group. New Dawn is very progressive—we had schools, medical facilities, everything we needed. Chloe was smart. Too smart for her own good." The momentary softness vanished. "She escaped right after graduation. Hid on a supply ferry. I'd just been selected as an apprentice then."

"And they sent you after her."

He grinned. "Not right away. I had to study, train. Learn to shoot, to fight, to blend in. Paul always keeps track of his children, even the ones who try to leave. When I was ready, he told me a secret—he knew exactly where Chloe was."

Emmett began to pace, his movements fluid and controlled. "She was a traitor, and she hadn't paid the price to leave. There are laws for traitors."

"So he sent you to kill her," I said. "You and Josef."

"Josef was already in place. Paul had helped Max get a position with Ambassador Vasilios years ago, after Theo had paid the price and freed himself. Chloe meeting Theo—" he laughed, "—that was just good luck. That idiot she was sleeping with connected them."

"Dickie," I said, closing my eyes.

"Once Chloe and Theo were together, Paul arranged it so Max went to Theo, and he sent Josef into Nicholas's security detail. Chloe was good at staying off the grid. But once she hooked up with Theo, it was game over." He stopped pacing, his expression animated now. "She never questioned how I found her. I made it seem like Theo had helped me just like he'd done with her. Poor kid escaped from a cult trying to make something of himself." His voice took on a mocking tone. "I made sure I got an invitation to the wedding, pretending to be her friend."

"And then what?" I prompted when he fell silent, staring into the middle distance.

He snapped back to the present. "Then Josef and I drove to The Mad King and checked in as father and son. Room 314. We were already there when the happy couple arrived. Max was driving them. He knew exactly what time to arrive.

"It wasn't hard to take a golf cart out where people were playing glow disc golf and leave it there," Emmett continued. "We'd planted bikes behind some trees earlier in the day. Then we rode to the honeymoon villa and waited for them. The rest is history. We were back playing disc golf within half an hour."

The clinical way he described the double murder sent chills down my spine.

"Why'd you kill Max if he was one of you?" I asked.

"Because he was getting soft," he said. "He didn't care about killing the girl, but he was pretty pissed when he found out Theo was dead."

"You killed Theo's dad. And Derek Rogan."

"All soldiers who fell in battle," he said, with an odd formality. "Josef handled Max and Nicholas. They were too well trained for an apprentice like me. Nicholas knew too much, of course. He'd been through all this before when he'd paid for Theo's freedom. It had been my job to drug the wife while Josef made Nicholas eat his gun. I heard she still hasn't woken up. Maybe I gave her too much."

A flash of pride crossed his face. "But I did pull the trigger on Rogan. He would've tried to stop us from killing Nicholas if we hadn't tranqued him and tied him up."

"You shot him in his car. Execution style."

"Clean. Efficient." He mimed a gun with his fingers, pointing at my forehead. "Just like you'll be."

"You made mistakes," I said, desperate to keep him talking. "You left your gun behind at the honeymoon murder scene. Your fingerprints were all over it." And then I don't know why I said what I did, but I opened my mouth anyway. "Cory Maybury. Isn't that your name?"

The change was instantaneous. His face contorted with rage, and he backhanded me so hard my head snapped to the side. Stars exploded across my vision, and I tasted blood.

"Don't call me that!" he screamed, looming over me. "That name is dead! I am Emmett Parker! I am a soldier of New Dawn!"

I spat blood onto the concrete floor. "That name is in the system now. Your juvenile record. The FBI knows who you are."

His hands closed around my throat, fingers digging into my windpipe. "You don't know anything about me!"

"I know Paul Prather is using you," I choked out,

vision darkening at the edges. "You're just a tool to him. Expendable."

He released my throat, and I gasped for air, lungs burning.

"You're lying," he said, but uncertainty flickered behind his eyes. "Paul chose me. He saw my potential."

"He saw a vulnerable kid he could manipulate," I said, each word scraping my raw throat. "Do you think you're the first soldier he's sent to die for him?"

"Shut up!" he roared, drawing a pistol from the back of his waistband. He pressed the barrel against my forehead, the metal cold against my skin. "You don't know what you're talking about."

I was scared spitless. But I had nothing to lose. I could see death in his eyes. "I know the New Dawn compound has moved," I pressed on, feeling the gun tremble against my skull. "I know Paul left the country after the FBI started closing in. He abandoned his followers, Emmett. He abandoned you."

Fury blazed in his eyes. "You're lying!"

"He's on his island somewhere, safe and comfortable, while you're here doing his dirty work. When was the last time you actually spoke to him? Not to Josef, not to some intermediary. To Paul himself?"

Doubt crept across his face, just for an instant. Then it hardened into resolve.

"It doesn't matter," he said, his voice flat again. "Orders are orders."

The gun pressed harder against my forehead, and I closed my eyes, thinking of Jack, of our baby, of all the things I would never see.

And then the gates of hell opened up and all I could do was pray for mercy.

"Drop the weapon! Police!"

The shouts echoed through the warehouse, followed by the crash of doors being breached. Red laser sights danced across Emmett's chest as officers swarmed in from multiple entrances, weapons drawn.

"Drop it now! Hands in the air!"

For a terrible moment, I thought he might pull the trigger anyway. His finger twitched on the guard. Then, with mechanical precision, he set the gun on the floor and raised his hands above his head.

"On your knees! Hands behind your head!"

Emmett complied, his face a blank mask as officers tackled him to the ground, securing his wrists with handcuffs. More police flooded into the warehouse, checking corners, clearing the space.

And then Jack was there, rushing to my side, his face a storm of relief and anguish.

"Jaye," he breathed, kneeling in front of me. His hands trembled as he cut through the zip ties. "Are you hurt? Oh, God. Look at you."

"I think I'm okay," I whispered, falling forward into his arms as my restraints gave way. "How did you find me?"

"Your watch," he said, holding me like he'd never let go. "Doug tracked your heart rate spike and location. They'd left your phone at the funeral home, but didn't see your watch. We already had Josef in custody—caught him trying to set a fire at the community center. We had your approximate location, but we wouldn't have made it in time if we'd had to search all these warehouses. Josef gave up Emmett's location in exchange for consideration."

Relief washed over me in a dizzying wave. It was over. We were safe.

Over Jack's shoulder, I watched as officers led Emmett away. He walked with his head high, that empty smile playing at his lips. As he reached the door, he turned to look at me one last time.

"He'll find you," he called, his voice ringing with certainty. "Paul never forgets his children."

Jack's arms tightened around me. "We've got them both now. The FBI is taking over the New Dawn case. They'll find Prather. And those two killers are off the streets."

The adrenaline that had kept me going suddenly drained away, leaving me hollow and trembling. The room began to spin, darkness creeping in from the edges of my vision.

"Jack," I mumbled, my voice sounding far away even to my own ears. "I don't feel…"

The last thing I heard was Jack calling my name, his voice tight with fear as I slipped into darkness once more.

EPILOGUE

THE RHYTHMIC BEEPING OF MONITORS PULLED ME FROM the darkness, each electronic pulse drawing me closer to consciousness. White ceiling tiles swam into focus, and the antiseptic smell of hospital disinfectant filled my nostrils. My body felt weighted, limbs heavy against crisp sheets.

I turned my head and found Jack exactly where I knew he'd be—in the chair beside my bed, leaning forward with his elbows on his knees, his head bowed. His fingers were loosely entwined as if he'd been praying. Maybe he had been.

"We have to stop meeting like this," I said, my voice hoarse and unfamiliar to my own ears.

Jack's head snapped up, his eyes bloodshot from exhaustion but suddenly bright with relief. A smile broke across his face like sunrise, though it trembled at the edges.

"There she is," he said softly, reaching for my hand. His warm fingers wrapped around mine, gentle yet desperate, as if he could anchor me to this world through touch alone.

"The baby?" I asked immediately, my free hand moving to my stomach.

"Fine," Jack assured me, his voice catching. "The baby's fine. You've got a hard head, and apparently the little one inherited it."

A laugh escaped me, but it quickly transformed into a weak cough. Jack helped me take a sip of water from a cup on the bedside table, his hand steady on mine.

"Well, well, well," I heard a familiar voice say from somewhere in the room.

It was only then that I noticed Lily sitting in a chair in the corner, her legs tucked beneath her, an open medical textbook balanced on her knees. She closed it with a soft thump, her face lighting up as she moved to the other side of my bed.

"I knew you were being weird," she said, grinning triumphantly as she checked the monitors. "Morning sickness. Food aversions. Emotional outbursts."

"I wasn't having emotional outbursts," I protested weakly.

"I saw you tear up as soon as 'Son of a Preacher

Man' started to play," Lily countered, her eyes dancing with amusement.

"It made me sad," I said, smiling as much as my battered face would allow.

Lily's expression softened as she reached for my wrist, taking my pulse even though the monitor was doing the same job. It was a gesture of connection more than medical necessity.

"Your secret's safe with me," she promised, glancing between Jack and me. "Though I should warn you, I'm not sure how long it'll stay that way. You haven't exactly been subtle about it. Emmy Lu is bound to catch on before too long."

"How long have I been out?" I asked, noticing the dimming light through the window.

"About ten hours," Jack said. "They gave you something for the pain, and your body took what it needed."

"Concussion?" I asked.

"Mild," Lily confirmed. "CAT scan was clear. No internal bleeding, no skull fracture. You'll have a headache for a few days, but nothing permanent."

I nodded, wincing as the movement sent a dull throb through my temples. "And the case?"

Jack and Lily exchanged a look.

"They've both been charged," Jack said, his jaw tightening. "Emmett's staying loyal to Prather. Won't say a word except to spout cult propaganda. The prosecutor says he's got the emotional maturity of a teenager with the moral compass of a shark."

"And Josef?" I asked.

"Older and wiser," Jack said, a note of disgust in his voice. "He cut a deal before his lawyer even finished his coffee. He's pinning everything on Emmett, claiming he was just there to supervise the apprentice, teach him the ropes. Says he never pulled the trigger."

"That's crap," I said, anger flaring through the fog of medication. "The shots on Chloe were too precise. And the sniper shot that took out Max—"

"We know," Jack assured me. "Special forces records confirm Josef was a trained sniper. Too much of a coincidence. But the prosecutor is willing to play along to get information on New Dawn. Josef's offering up everything—locations, bank accounts, names of other members."

"He's scared," Lily observed. "And he should be. From what I've heard, this Prather guy doesn't tolerate failure."

She checked the IV in my arm, adjusting the flow slightly. "I should go update your chart and let Cole know you're awake. He's been calling every twenty minutes since they brought you in." She squeezed my hand. "Don't overdo it, okay?"

Lily slipped out, closing the door softly behind her. In the sudden quiet, Jack's composure seemed to crumble. He brought my hand to his lips, pressing a kiss against my knuckles.

"I thought I was going to lose you," he said, his voice rough with emotion. "When we burst into that warehouse and I saw him with the gun to your head..." He trailed off, swallowing hard.

"But you didn't," I reminded him, squeezing his hand. "I'm right here."

"The look in that kid's eyes," Jack continued, as if he needed to say it aloud to exorcise the memory. "He was going to pull the trigger. Even after we told him to freeze, I thought he was still going to do it."

A shadow crossed his face, something dark and primal that I rarely saw in him.

"My finger was on the trigger, Jaye. I was ready to take the shot." His eyes met mine, haunted. "It took more willpower not to pull it than I thought possible. If he'd even twitched in your direction..."

"But he didn't," I said softly, understanding the weight he carried. "And you didn't."

Jack nodded, but the shadow lingered. I reached up to touch his face, tracing the line of his jaw with my fingertips.

"You found me," I said. "That's all that matters."

He turned his face into my palm, pressing a kiss there before looking back at me with sudden intensity.

"I've been thinking," he said, "About the house."

"What about it?" I asked, momentarily confused by the change of subject.

"It needs a nursery," Jack said, a new lightness entering his voice. "And maybe a fence around that part of the yard near the creek."

I laughed, feeling some of the tension drain from my body.

"Oscar's going to have a new human to boss around soon enough. He'll love it." Jack sobered slightly. "I can't wait to build this life with you, Jaye. A real one, with 3 a.m. feedings and first steps and Christmas mornings."

I thought of all we'd faced—murders and cults and personal demons—and all we'd survived. There would be more cases, more darkness to navigate. New Dawn was still out there, Paul Prather hiding on his island enclave. Dickie was battling his own demons in rehab. The world was still chaotic and dangerous and unpredictable.

But in this moment, with Jack's hand in mine and our child growing safely inside me, I felt something I hadn't expected to find in the aftermath of so much death.

Hope.

"We're a good team," I said, drawing him closer. "The best."

Jack leaned in, his lips brushing mine in a kiss that tasted of coffee and relief and promises. Outside the window, the setting sun painted the room in gold, casting long shadows that would soon give way to night.

But for now, there was light. And for now, that was enough.

Dirty Valentine

September 30, 2025

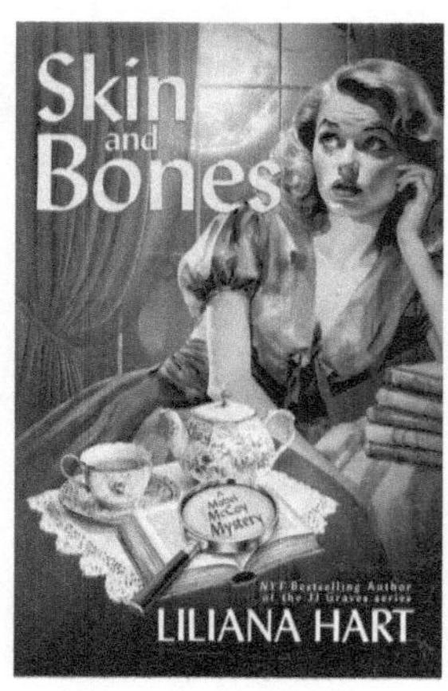

Dear Readers,

I'm so excited to introduce you to a brand new mystery series, coming summer 2025! I've had the character of Mabel McCoy rattling around in my head for almost a decade, but I couldn't figure out where she belonged or what her story should be. Needless to say, Mabel McCoy's story came to me one day in a rush, and I couldn't wait to start writing. I hope you enjoy this series as much as I have writing it.

You can Pre-Order Skin and Bones, book one in

the Mabel McCoy Series anywhere books are sold. Here's the back cover blurb!

Mabel McCoy, a young and widowed tea shop owner in the quaint coastal town of Grimm Island, South Carolina, finds her life as calm as a perfectly steeped cup of tea. The highlight of her month is hosting the Silver Sleuths Murder Society at her charming shop—a group of spirited seniors with a penchant for mysteries. She loves the tranquility and wouldn't have it any other way.

But when a dashing new sheriff arrives in town with a backlog of baffling cold cases, Mabel's peaceful existence is upended. She's reluctantly drawn into a tangled web of lies, deceit, and murder that goes far deeper than she ever imagined. With the Silver Sleuths eager to put their fictional detective skills to the test, Mabel must navigate the treacherous waters of real-life mystery-solving. Secrets emerge, old wounds resurface, and Mabel must uncover the truth before it's too late.

Will the Silver Sleuths unravel the town's darkest secrets, or will this be a mystery too perilous for even their sharp minds?

THE LIES WE TELL

By her calculations, Grace Meredith had exactly five and a half seconds to take out six targets before an alarm sounded. She had a round in the chamber and five in the magazine of her M40A5. Piece of cake.

She ignored the mosquitoes the size of hummingbirds searching for exposed flesh, and she disregarded the sweat that dripped steadily down her spine as she looked through the scope of her rifle. The temperature was in the mid-nineties, but the canopy of trees that blanketed the area held the heat in like an oven and slowly baked anyone who didn't have shelter with a running AC. Her body and mind were disciplined, so the discomforts barely registered.

Colombia wasn't known for its gentle climate. Or

gentle anything for that matter. Gemino Vasquez was Colombia's baddest arms dealer, and lately his biggest client had been North Korea. But Vasquez had something Grace wanted very badly. Something that would bring in a big, fat paycheck from the South Korean government.

She shifted slightly, and the bark of the large tree branch she'd lain on for the last four hours ground against her stomach. But her focus was absolute. Not even the hundred-and-fifty-foot drop to the ground could distract her.

The orange sun blazed just over the tops of the trees, but it would disappear completely in another twenty minutes. By the time it was gone, she'd have the flash drive in hand and already be across the border to Venezuela.

Grace did one final check of all her equipment and took a deep, steadying breath, slowing her heartbeat so her pulse would be in time with-b each shot. She'd hit the sentry at the top of the Vasquez compound first and then take the rest in order from left to right. She pushed her feet against the tree for balance. The clock ticked in the background of her mind as she put the slightest amount of pressure on the trigger.

"One," she whispered. She didn't wait to watch him fall but moved to the next target. Five seconds until the report from her rifle reached their ears. Five seconds for five more kills.

Two...

Three...

Four...

Five...

Six...

Grace didn't stop to check the accuracy of her shots. She never missed a target. She hung her rifle on a tree branch, already missing the feel of it in her hands. Time was of the essence now, and she couldn't afford to be burdened with too much equipment—she'd have to leave it behind. The new guards would be driving up soon for the shift change, and she had to be long gone by then.

She unzipped her supply pack, pulling out a lightweight pipe no longer than her forearm. It looked completely worthless at first glance. In reality, it was a military prototype she'd borrowed from her former life. She hit the button on each end of the pipe and it expanded in length until it was almost as tall as she was, and then she hit the button in the center and waited as wings made out of a synthetic material unfurled to complete the hang glider.

"No time like the present," she said, swallowing as she perched on the edge of the tree and looked out across the jungle. She had a straight shot into the compound, but any shift in wind would have her hurtling into trees. Falling to her death wouldn't bring her the money she needed, so she had no choice but to take a leap of faith. Literally.

Fifteen minutes until all hell breaks loose.

Grace grasped the bar and jumped. The bottom dropped out of her stomach as she free-fell for just a brief moment, and then the air caught beneath the wings and she soared through the treetops like a phantom. It took all her strength and concentration to keep the glider on a straight path to the compound roof, and when her feet touched the ground her muscles were fatigued and her skin coated with perspiration.

She hit another button on the long metal tube and the glider folded itself back up until it was small enough to fit back in her pack.

The body of the first sentry she'd shot lay face down in the greenish-blue water of the swimming pool. A hazy cloud of blood ballooned from under him, and his arms and legs floated like waving ribbons.

Her eyes and ears were alert, but all that greeted her was growing darkness and silence. Even the animals and birds in the jungle knew something bad was about to go down.

Grace unhooked the harness and pulled her SIG from a thigh holster. She stood silently next to the gray door that led from the roof down a set of stairs to the main floors of the house. Two heartbeats passed before she opened the door and slipped inside. It was quiet, but that wasn't unusual at this time of the day according to her intel—six sentries on duty surrounding the compound, only two guarding Vasquez's private suite of rooms.

Vasquez's stupidity only made her job easier.

Grace walked silently down the thickly carpeted hallway as if she weren't about to steal the schematics for a new superweapon—a weapon that used state-of-the-art laser technology—and sell it to another country. But the closer she got to Vasquez, the more her spine tingled in awareness that something was wrong. That tingle had saved her life more than once, and she never ignored it. The hallway opened up into a landing just as she reached Vasquez's private rooms. Weak light filtered through the windows and cast rainbows as it pierced the glass chandelier that hung overhead.

She saw firsthand exactly why her spine was tingling.

Both sentries were slumped against each other— a dead man's embrace—one with a broken neck and the other with a hunting knife in his carotid. Efficient work considering the size of the sentries.

She pushed the bodies out of her way with her foot and eased the door open, her trigger finger at the ready on her SIG. All that mattered was the flash drive. If she didn't produce it, then she didn't get paid.

She crept into the room. The smells of new death were thick and cloying in the heat, and she could taste the fresh blood in the back of her throat with every breath she took. Dust motes danced in the air, and long shadows were cast in the fading sunlight.

Grace waited for her eyes to adjust and listened for sounds of footsteps, but all she heard was the gentle whir of the wicker fans that rotated slowly on the ceiling. She moved silently, staying close to the wall as she checked his suite.

Vasquez's bedroom was bigger than her whole apartment—the furniture oversized and ornate, the colors garishly red. He was set up for sex. The interesting kind of sex by the looks of things. Restraints and various whips and other tools lined one whole wall, and torn condom packages littered the floor. It looked like Vasquez had a busy day. Too bad his afternoon hadn't turned out so hot.

Gemino Vasquez's body lay spread-eagle on his bed. He was naked, and his eyes were open and unseeing. Two shots to the center of the forehead screamed of a professional hit. He hadn't been dead long. She couldn't stop the bitter disappointment when she saw the flash drive was gone from the chain on his right wrist.

"Hell," she whispered and moved to check the covers of his bed, just to make sure it hadn't come off in the struggle. But she knew in her heart it was long gone. Professionals didn't leave loose ends behind. And this was definitely professional. What ticked her off even more was that whoever did it managed to sneak in right under her nose. He had to have known she was watching through her scope and snuck in through the one blind spot she had at the back of the compound.

The stir of air behind her was the only warning she had before an arm locked around her throat.

"Looking for this?" a deep voice whispered in her ear. He held the flash drive in front of her face.

He pressed close against her back and squeezed his arm tighter around her throat so she had to breathe shallowly through her nose. Grace winced as he pressed his fingers against the pressure points of her wrist, and her pistol fell uselessly to the floor with a dull thunk.

Fear never had a chance to take hold. It was anger that drove Grace. Anger that had kept her alive the last couple of years. And she knew how to wield it. She threw her head back and aimed her heel at his knee simultaneously. He dodged her blows as if he'd been expecting them, but the distraction was enough for him to loosen his grip. She swept her leg and brought him to his knees, reaching down for the knife in her boot. The blade gleamed once in the fading sunlight just before it was knocked out of her hand and across the room.

He outweighed her by close to eighty pounds, and he had a good eight inches on her in height. They grappled and rolled, each one blocking the other's strikes with only seconds to spare. It was a well-choreographed dance.

A familiar dance.

The surprise of recognition took her off guard, and she looked up into laughing blue eyes framed by thick, dark lashes she'd always been jealous of. She had time to register that he'd let his hair grow—a shaggy mane of ink black that curled just over his ears and collar,and a face that was covered in a short, stubbled beard—just before her legs went out from under her. She hit the carpet with a thud. A hard body pressed her into the floor, and he held her wrists captive above her head.

"Hello, darling." His breath whispered against her skin. "You've been practicing. Who's your new sparring partner?"

"Gabe," she said. "What do you want?" She bucked beneath him, annoyed at the familiarity of his weight on her.

"I want you, of course." His lips glanced across her cheek to the corner of her mouth, and she sucked in a breath that brought her body even closer to his. After everything he'd done, he was still the only man who could make her feel less than whole when their bodies weren't fused together. She hated him for it. She hated herself for it.

"Go to hell." She struggled against him, but he shifted his weight to hold her down.

"I've been there, thanks." He cupped his hand against her cheek—gently—softly. "You still feel good against me. Stop wiggling and we'll talk. Don't you want to at least hear my offer? Especially since I did your dirty work for you."

She stilled her body and relaxed, hoping he'd get distracted long enough for her to make a move, and she spoke through gritted teeth. "I don't want anything you have to offer. Just give me the flash drive."

"I figure we have exactly four minutes to get out of this place before the new guards show up for the shift change and Armageddon begins. All I'm asking is that you come back with me and hear me out. If you decide to turn me down, then I'll give you the flash drive with no hard feelings, and you can claim your bounty."

Grace stared at him and tried to decide if he was bluffing. "You know I don't trust you."

"Yes, I believe you've told me that before," he said, his gaze hard. "But what I'm offering will pay more than double any of the jobs you've recently taken. Hear me out."

"Fine." She knew her options were limited. "What are we waiting for?"

"Our rendezvous point is on the other side of the border," he said, rolling off of her. She ignored the hand he reached out to help her up. "We've got twenty minutes to get there or we miss our ride."

Grace had no choice but to follow him out of one hell and into another.

***

The woman hadn't changed a bit in all the years he'd known her. She still kept her deep auburn hair braided tightly down her back while she was working. But he knew what it looked like spread across his pillow, and he knew what it felt like as it slithered like silk across his chest—glorious—a bright flame that was cool to the touch.

He looked at her critically, trying to decipher exactly why he was still attracted to her after the two years they'd spent apart. There wasn't just one thing about her that stood out, but the entire package. Her face was thinner now—her cheekbones more pronounced—but it was still the face of a sea goddess. Eyes the color of emeralds, slightly tilted at the corners, and full lips that haunted his dreams.

She was every desire he'd ever had wrapped in one tiny package.

He let his gaze drift down her body. She was thinner all over. The lush curves he remembered were gone, replaced by a compact body of pure muscle and athleticism. She glanced back at him and raised a brow at where his gaze had landed.

Gabe smiled, but it didn't reach his eyes. He'd been wrong. She'd changed a lot. There was a hardness about her now that hadn't been there before. When she'd first started with the CIA, there had been hope and an ideal of the greater good. Now there was just emptiness—a cold, green stare that didn't believe in anything—and it scared the hell out of him. Because it was no one's fault but his own.

"We've just crossed the border into Venezuela by my calculations," she said, slowing to a jog. "How much farther is your rendezvous point?"

"About another mile. Keep the sound of water to your immediate left." He put his hand on her arm before she could take off again. "Wait."

She stopped dead in her tracks, and Gabe could tell she was trying to hear what he had. They were silent for a few more seconds before the sound came again.

She blew out an annoyed breath. "It's the new guards. You always did have ears like a bat."

"What do you have on you?" he asked.

"My SIG and a hunting knife. How many do you think there are?"

"No more than a dozen. They're noisy bastards. And not too fast." He pulled his own pistol from the small of his back and checked the magazine. "I'll give you a boost." He replaced his weapon in his pants and laced his fingers together. He arched a brow as she looked back at him with irritation.

"I'm really tired of climbing trees." She exhaled and put her foot into his hands. He launched her up so she could reach the lowest branch, and she swung herself up with ease.

"Do you have good visibility?" Gabe asked.

"Yeah, I see them," she said. "You'll have to draw them close enough so I'm within range."

"Try not to hit me by mistake."

Her grin was sharp as she looked down at him. "Oh, it wouldn't be a mistake."

"That's what I'm afraid of." Gabe left her there to go meet trouble head-on.

He found cover behind a tree trunk the size of a small car and waited patiently. Heavy footsteps crunched over twigs, and he stuck out his foot as two of them passed by. One of the guards tripped and went sprawling to the ground, and Gabe struck out at the other with a palm to the chest, stopping his heart instantly. He broke the neck of the one who was

already down before the man could rise off his knees.

Gabe ignored the steady stream of fire that came from behind him—despite her wanting to kill him, he trusted Grace to fight at his side during battle. It was after the battle that worried him.

He went searching for his next victim.

Only a few minutes passed before he stood in the middle of a ring of twelve guards—all of them dead. None of them had fired a shot. She was even better than he remembered.

Grace was waiting for him when he caught up to where he'd left her.

"Time's ticking," he said, looking at his watch.

They picked up the pace and ran the last mile in silence and slowed as they came to a winding dirt road with deeply rutted tire tracks, making footing tricky.

"Did we miss the pickup?" Grace asked.

A forest-green Humvee coated with a thick layer of dust came out of the trees behind them and pulled to a stop. Grace had her weapon out and her finger on the trigger.

"He's mine," Gabe said, opening the back door.

Grace slid across the hot leather seat.

The driver turned and looked at Gabe. Logan Grey had worked with him on other missions. He was a quiet man, tall and sinewy with muscle. He wore his dark-blond hair long, not as a fashion statement, but to help cover the terrible scars on the back of his neck. Logan was former MI6, but an almost fatal accident had gained him retirement before he was ready. Gabe hadn't hesitated at snatching Logan up to join the team. No one knew explosives better than Logan Grey.

"You cut it close, boss," Logan said. "In thirty seconds I wouldn't be here."

"Let's roll," Gabe said. "Be on the lookout for company."

Logan glanced once at Grace and then nodded, putting his submachine gun in his lap.

Gabe closed the window that divided the front and back seat so he and Grace had complete privacy.

"Who's your friend?" Grace asked.

"Logan Grey. Don't worry. He's heard all about you and still agreed to help me find you."

"I'm sure he's a real stand-up guy."

"He'll grow on you," Gabe said, keeping his gaze on the terrain around them, looking for threats. "So what do you think? It's just like old times. We always made a great team."

"Tell me what you want, and then let me go," she said. "I've got a tight schedule to keep."

"You don't have another job lined up once you deliver the flash drive to the South Koreans. Looks like you're a free agent." Gabe watched for a reaction, but she showed no surprise that he'd been keeping up with her movements. She waited him out with her silence and a hard look, and he decided to give in to the unspoken standoff...just this once.

"I've left the CIA," he told her.

"I heard. Congratulations. Let me go."

Gabe smiled and stretched out across the seat, crowding her with the length of his legs, but she didn't budge an inch. "Did you hear I'd joined the private sector and opened my own agency?"

She laughed, low and sexy, and the smoky sound swirled around him until he was dizzy with desire. "So, good boy Gabriel Brennan has decided to become a bad boy and go rogue. I assume the agency is displeased by your decision?"

"Not at all," he said, shrugging. "They know when something is out of their control. My agency is privately funded and our reputation is above reproach. Even the CIA recognizes the benefits unknown money can buy. Governments are still hampered by rules, for the most part. Sometimes there are jobs where the rules need to be broken. That's when they call me."

"Well, bully for you," she said. "You always did manage to get what you wanted. Everything Gabe Brennan touches turns to gold."

"Nothing could be further from the truth, and you know it," he said quietly. Gabe waited patiently for her to make eye contact. It didn't take her long. She'd never been a coward.

She tilted her chin defiantly. "I don't know anything about you. I never did. Our life together was a lie. I'm not even sure you know the real you."

He kept his face impassive, even though her words pierced his heart. "How long are you going to pretend she's not sitting here between us?"

"Don't mention her!" The quiver in her voice was quickly controlled. "I'll get out of this car and disappear off the face of the planet. If you want me to stay, then the past stays in the past. It's nonnegotiable."

"Fine," Gabe said. "Whatever you say."

The SUV slowed to a stop, and Gabe pushed the door open, not waiting to see if she'd follow. It was a stupid idea to think he could fix things—to heal the wounds that had been bleeding for the last two years.

Gabe's Gulfstream sat ready for takeoff on the hard-packed dirt the small Venezuelan city called an airport. He went up the stairs and then turned to face Grace, sure she'd still be in the car. But she stood at the bottom of the steps, her face carefully blank.

"You can either come with me or you can leave. The choice is yours," Gabe said without emotion, tossing her the flash drive.

She caught it one-handed and stared at him, studying him, trying to read every angle of the situation as she'd been trained to do at the agency. She finally nodded and started up the steps. "I'll come. A deal is a deal. And my word means something."

Gabe flinched before he could control it and let the pain roll through him. He had a feeling that before this job was over, she'd have one more reason to hate him.

AVAILABLE AT ALL RETAILERS

ACKNOWLEDGMENTS

Getting a book to publication takes an amazing team of people. I'm fortunate to have had these people in my corner for years.

To my editor—Imogen Howson for always making me better.

To my cover designer—Dar Albert for always blowing me away with your talent.

To my children—You're all so special. You have gifts and abilities beyond measure, and I'm excited to see what God has in store for each of you.

To Scott—thank you for answering a ridiculous amount of law enforcement questions and acting out weird scenarios with me. Any mistakes are mine alone.

Liliana Hart is a *New York Times*, *USA Today*, and Publisher's Weekly bestselling author of more than eighty titles. After starting her first novel her freshman year of college, she immediately became addicted to writing and knew she'd found what she was meant to do with her life. She has no idea why she majored in music.

Since publishing in June 2011, Liliana has sold more than ten-million books. All three of her series have made multiple appearances on the *New York Times* list.

Liliana can almost always be found at her computer writing, hauling five kids to various activities, or spending time with her husband. She calls Texas home.

If you enjoyed reading this, I would appreciate it if you would help others enjoy this book, too.

Recommend it. Please help other readers find this book by recommending it to friends, readers' groups and discussion boards.

Review it. Please tell other readers why you liked this book by reviewing.

Connect with me online:
www.lilianahart.com

facebook.com/LilianaHart

instagram.com/LilianaHart

bookbub.com/authors/liliana-hart

ALSO BY LILIANA HART

JJ Graves Mystery Series

Dirty Little Secrets

A Dirty Shame

Dirty Rotten Scoundrel

Down and Dirty

Dirty Deeds

Dirty Laundry

Dirty Money

A Dirty Job

Dirty Devil

Playing Dirty

Dirty Martini

Dirty Dozen

Dirty Minds

Dirty Weekend

Dirty Looks

Dirty Liars

Dirty Valentine

Addison Holmes Mystery Series

Whiskey Rebellion

Whiskey Sour

Whiskey For Breakfast

Whiskey, You're The Devil

Whiskey on the Rocks

Whiskey Tango Foxtrot

Whiskey and Gunpowder

Whiskey Lullaby

The Scarlet Chronicles

Bouncing Betty

Hand Grenade Helen

Front Line Francis

The Harley and Davidson Mystery Series

The Farmer's Slaughter

A Tisket a Casket

I Saw Mommy Killing Santa Claus

Get Your Murder Running

Deceased and Desist

Malice in Wonderland

Tequila Mockingbird

Gone With the Sin

Grime and Punishment

Blazing Rattles

A Salt and Battery

Curl Up and Dye

First Comes Death Then Comes Marriage

Box Set 1

Box Set 2

Box Set 3

The Gravediggers

The Darkest Corner

Gone to Dust

Say No More

Laurel Valley

Tribulation Pass

Redemption Road

Midnight Clear

Forgiveness River

Atonement Trail